A World I Never Made

"I picked up *A World I Never Made* and was riveted from start to finish. An adventure to places both exotic and intimate, told with great sensitivity, inventive plotting, and propulsive suspense. Jim LePore is a great discovery."
— William Landay, author of
The Strangler

"*A World I Never Made* is an outstanding first novel, and a wonderful thriller. The story moves very quickly, almost to the point that the reader feels as if they'll miss something if they put the book down even for a moment . . . I'm looking forward to James LePore's next work; this one was a gripping read that I would recommend to anyone."
— Blogcritics

"A compelling page-turner—one of those wonderful books with characters as strong as the story and a story worth reading. Don't miss it."
— M.J. Rose, author of
The Memorist

"I highly recommend this compelling suspense story filled with vivid characters and haunting storylines.
A story that will stay with the reader long after the final page."
— Bella Online

"Nothing could have torn my attention away from this story. *A World I Never Made* by James LePore is a must read for thriller fans!"
— Cheryl's Book Nook

"The plot of this intriguing, suspenseful novel is taut, moves rather rapidly, and mesmerizes the reader with each new complex, mysterious detail. James LePore knows how to spin an international thriller tale that slowly reveals an inner, fascinating depth to each character and to the developing connections between each and all. Well, well-done, James LePore!"
— Crystal Reviews

"Author James LePore has created a remarkable, gripping tale of suspense in his debut novel. *A World I Never Made* is filled with strong, vividly described international characters to whom the reader will quickly form an attachment, all the while being transported through wonderfully described exotic lands. The combination creates an atmosphere of breathless suspense affording readers a desire to continue reading up until the thrilling, yet tender, conclusion."

— Feathered Quill Book Reviews

"The suspense will keep you white-knuckled as the plot unfolds with plenty of depth and intelligence. In fact, *A World I Never Made* kept me so enthralled that I simply didn't want it to end. So if you're looking for a new author who can knock you breathless with a clever thriller, James LePore is the one to pick."

— Nights and Weekends

"The key to this exciting thriller is the cast, especially the Nolan father and daughter . . . fans will enjoy this one sitting suspense thriller."

— The Mystery Gazette

"James LePore writes in an exciting and most readable style. He is an artist at building the suspense as the story progresses to its ultimate conclusion. There is just enough doubt about the possible outcomes to keep the reader wondering and turning pages. *A World I Never Made* is a fine tale filled with love, adventure, mystery and suspense."

— Mainly Mysteries

"A carefully crafted, well written book with a rich cast of characters and a plot as complicated and convoluted as the characters themselves."

— Reader Views

"An unputdownable novel."

— Everything Distills into Reading

BLOOD OF MY BROTHER

JAMES LePORE

To Kay and Jim LePore.
May they rest in peace.

This is a work of fiction. Names, characters, places, and incidents either are the product of the author's imagination or are used fictitiously. Any resemblance to actual events, locales, organizations, or persons living or dead, is entirely coincidental and beyond the intent of either the author or the publisher.

The Story Plant
The Aronica-Miller Publishing Project, LLC
P.O. Box 4331
Stamford, CT 06907

Copyright © 2010 by James LePore

Jacket and interior design by Barbara Aronica-Buck

ISBN-13: 978-0-9819568-8-6

Visit our website at www.thestoryplant.com

All rights reserved, which includes the right to reproduce this book or portions thereof in any form whatsoever except as provided by US Copyright Law. For information, address The Story Plant.

First Story Plant Printing: December 2010

Printed in The United States of America

Acknowledgments

The final version of this novel is much different and, hopefully, much better than its first and many interim iterations. For reading those in-progress manuscripts, and offering their often helpful and always sincere comments, I am grateful to the following people: Jay Breslin; Steve Carroll; Bill Evans; Dave and Meryl Ironson; Bob, Pat, Joe, and Jerry LePore; Erica, Adrienne, and Jamie LePore; and Greg and Joy Ziemak. I hope they enjoy the final version, much of which will be new to them. I am also very grateful to my friend and editor, Lou Aronica, for his high level of professionalism and his passion for excellence. Working with him, with each new book I learn more of the craft and I get to go deeper into the land of imagination.

For teaching me how to land a small aircraft in an emergency (while sitting at my desk), I thank Frank Hippel, pilot and friend.

I save my most important acknowledgement for last. I thank my wife, Karen, for her love and encouragement, and for the example she sets for me in all things.

The voice of thy brother's blood crieth unto me from the ground.

                — *Genesis 4:10*

Prologue
10:00 AM, July 12, 1967, Newark

In July of 1967, Jay Cassio, who would be turning five in September, started a prekindergarten program at St. Lucy's School on Sheffield Street in Newark, New Jersey's oldest, largest, and about to be most turbulent city. At the time, St. Lucy's church and grammar school were at the spiritual and cultural center of the city's First Ward, an enclave of Southern Italians that for sixty years had stubbornly clung to the customs and values of Italy's Campagnia region from whence they and their parents had come in the great migration of the late nineteenth and early twentieth centuries.

The school, housed in a nondescript but sturdy brick building next to the beautiful gothic church, started teaching grades K through six to the children of the first wave of Italian immigrants in 1906. Now it drew equal numbers of black and Hispanic boys and girls, their parents looking to the Sisters of Charity as sources of discipline and respect in the ghetto that, as a direct consequence of the mindless placement of a massive public housing project in its midst, the First Ward was fast becoming. An only child, with no cousins, Jay was slow to socialize. Taller than the other boys, he had not been picked on, or challenged; but shy, an involuntary air of isolation about him, neither had he been approached in friendship.

Jay lived a half block from the school, on Seventh Avenue, on the fourth floor of a four-story tenement, with his parents, A.J. and Carmela. The first floor was taken up by his father's bakery, Cassio's, founded by his great-grandfather in 1903. He was not lonely or afraid at school, but if he needed comfort ever, he had only to look down the short half-block of Sheffield Street to where it formed a T with Seventh Avenue. There, directly in sight at all times, were Cassio's large, old-fashioned plate glass windows, through which, if he stared long enough, he could spot his father at work. Sometimes, A.J., in his white baker's apron, his thick, black hair dusty with flour, would catch his eye, smile, and wave. On either side of the Cassios' tenement were similar four- and five-story buildings with stores below and apartments above. If he was unable to see his father, the familiar faces of the women and small children who spent so much of their lives on the stoops and sidewalks in front of these tenements were always a delight to Jay, who, handsome, his large, gray eyes set perfectly below a clear brow and long, silky lashes, was a favorite in the neighborhood.

In the summer of 1967, when weeklong spasms of destruction called *race riots* swept the country's major ghettos, Newark's eruption was arguably the worst. A second tier city with virtually no national identity, its angry blacks were fueled to even more furious and mindless violence by their seeming invisibility compared to the attention given to Harlem and Watts. There was no Park Avenue or Rodeo Drive in Newark, no story of fabulous wealth threatened by mobs; only a series of bleak and poor neighborhoods made exponentially bleaker and poorer by six days of mayhem and death.

On the day the Newark riots started, Jay went at the morning recess with a group of children to the ice cream truck on the corner of Seventh Avenue and Sheffield Street. The day was warm and balmy, not oppressively hot. Sirens could be heard blaring along Broad Street, about ten blocks away, the main artery leading from the First Ward to Newark's slowly dying downtown. These were a common enough sound in the neighborhood. A hearse and three limousines, black and gleaming in the midmorning sun, were parked in front of St. Lucy's. On the opposite side of Sheffield Street, directly across from the church, were Buildings D and E of the Columbus Homes, eight, featureless twelve-story "apartment" buildings erected by the federal government in 1955.

The First Ward was poor now, and bleak, but the *projects*, as they were universally called, were poorer and bleaker, a no-man's-land teeming with drug addicts and the forerunners of today's gangbangers. This gaunt "housing project," surrounded by an aura of despair and menace, marked off a boundary keenly observed by the remnants—like the Cassios—of the old Italian-American community who were clinging to a last hope that the neighborhood would survive. There were no trees on Seventh Avenue or on Sheffield Street, nothing to block Jay's view of his small piece of the world, or to soften its hard and grimy edges.

Jay paid for his Eskimo Pie, peeled off its silver wrapper, and drifted over to the cyclone fence that surrounded the schoolyard. There, as he did every day, he would eat it while watching the doings of his classmates, absorbed in these creatures called other children, like him and not like him. When he reached the fence he heard a loud pop coming from the direction of the projects. He gazed that way, and then his attention was drawn to the front of the church, about fifty feet away, to his right, where a man in a black suit was kneeling, holding his arm, and where a bronze coffin had fallen with a loud clang to the sidewalk. Immediately there were two more pops, and a motorcycle policeman, who was one of two that were about to lead the funeral procession to the cemetery, was toppling from his seat, and the mourners, dressed in black, were pointing up to the roof of Building E and scrambling for cover along the sides of the hearse and the limos.

Jay watched, amazed, his ice cream forgotten, as the second cop dragged his fallen comrade to the sidewalk side of the hearse, and then pulled his two-way radio from his belt and began shouting into it. The two nuns who had brought the children out to the street, one an old crone straight from Italy's Potenza Province, hated and feared by the entire class, the other a young Irish beauty with a mesmerizing, lilting accent, swung swiftly and forcefully into action, herding the group through the gate in the cyclone fence and harrying them like border collies toward the school. Jay, out of sight of the nuns, was about to join his classmates when a boy whom he knew to be named Danny—a brash, stockily built boy, with big eyes wide apart and a shock of black hair—grabbed his arm and said, "We won't see anything from in there. Follow me!"

Jay did. He dropped his ice cream and followed Danny as he ran down Sheffield Street, darting past the mourners and policemen huddled behind the limousines, up the wide imported stone steps of the church, whose massive wooden doors stood open to the summer day. Then, once inside, up more steps at the side of the vestibule to the bell tower, where large open-air arches gave a perfect panoramic view of the scene below, as well as across the street to the roof of Building E.

"Look!" said Danny, pointing up.

Kneeling at the parapet was a black man of indeterminate age, shirtless, his muscles rippling, a rifle cradled in his arms. In silhouette, the sun behind him, there was a stillness, an ease, to this figure, as if he had been manning this rooftop, waiting to shoot white people, for years. Directly below, the coffin squatted on the sidewalk, forlorn, while the pallbearers and other family and friends of the deceased tried their best to attend to the two injured men in the shelter of the limos. The cop was bleeding from a chest wound, a deep maroon stain spreading across his pale blue shirt. Sirens were screaming close by.

Looking toward Seventh Avenue, the boys saw an ambulance and four police cars round the corner and hurtle toward the church. The man on the roof took careful aim at the lead car. When it stopped and the policemen in it jumped out, he fired off three shots—*pop, pop, pop*—then he ducked and was seen no more. The boys ducked, too. When they looked up a second later, there were cops running toward the entrance of Building E, and others were lined up behind their cars, firing rifles up at the parapet. The ambulance attendants, one black, one white, jumped out and began working on the cop with the chest wound. The firing stopped and all was still and quiet except for a harsh static from the radio of the lead patrol car. There were no other injured cops on the ground.

"I know that cop," said Jay.

"Which one?"

"The one bleeding."

"Who is he?"

"He comes in the bakery."

"What bakery?"

"My dad's. Cassio's."

Jay pointed to the bakery, and was astonished, as he did, to see his father running out of the front door, unwrapping his apron as he went, heading for the entrance to the school. He wove through a gathering crowd of people, white from Seventh Avenue, black from the projects, but was stopped at the foot of Sheffield Street by two cops who were manning a hastily thrown up roadblock. A.J. Cassio, bulky and muscled from years of making bread by hand, and not past his prime at thirty-three, went chest to chest with one of the cops, shouting something and pointing toward the school. The second cop took hold of A.J.'s arm and quieted him down, then turned and headed into the schoolyard.

"That's my dad," said Jay.

"He's looking for you."

Jay said nothing, his gaze fixed on his father, who was staring intensely toward the school entrance. The first cop, who had kept his composure throughout, was now carefully steering A.J. away from the roadblock. The wounded cop directly below was now on a stretcher and being lifted into the ambulance, while cops in flak jackets were leading the mourners back into the church.

"Does he hit you?" Danny asked.

"No."

"That's good, but remember, we came to the church to say a prayer."

Jay turned and looked Dan fully in the face for the first time. On that face was a combination of beguiling innocence and sly defiance—the dark brown eyes laughing at some inner joke—that Jay was to encounter in joy and exasperation times without number in the years to come.

1.
7:00 PM, September 1, 2004, Newark

The phone was ringing as Jay Cassio walked into his office in the old Fidelity Bank building near the Essex County Courthouse in Newark. He picked it up, swinging the cord wide as he settled himself into the leather covered, padded swivel chair behind his desk.

"Hello, law office," he said.

"Jay? Al Garland. How are you?"

"I'm fine, Al," Jay replied. "What's up?"

"Do you represent a woman named Kate Powers?"

"Yes, I do," Jay said. "Why?"

"What's Kate's story?"

Jay did not answer. He leaned back in his chair and ran the fingers of his free hand through his thick, wavy, dark brown hair, hair that fell below his ears and down the nape of his neck, and that was just beginning to go white at the temples. He had known Al Garland, the Essex County Prosecutor, for ten years, and never once had he called, out of the blue, to ask a question like this. A question he could not answer without violating Kate Powers's attorney-client privilege.

"You're kidding, right, Al," he said, finally.

"The Newark police just found her head in the Passaic

River. They're on the way to her house right now. Don't count on getting paid for a while."

"Jesus. Are they sure it's her?"

"The head was in a garbage bag. Her wallet was in it, too."

"Jesus . . ."

"I need your file, Jay," Garland said abruptly. "They're doing a subpoena."

"Slow down, Al," Jay said, trying at the same time to both fend off and to absorb the image of Kate Powers's severed head floating in the grimy Passaic River. He could also feel the fine hair rising at the back of his neck and down his forearms, his anger rising at Garland's hectoring, sarcastic tone of voice. "What do you think is in my file?"

"I don't know," said Garland. "You tell me."

"I can't tell you, you know that."

"I assume it's in your office."

Jay did not answer. Garland in a bad temper was capable of anything, like sending a SWAT team to Jay's office to seize the file.

"You wouldn't *hide* it, Jay?" said Garland.

"I'm not giving it up without a court order," Jay said. "Don't send your people over here without one."

"Don't get yourself into an ethics situation over this," said Garland.

Jay took a breath and looked up at the brown water stain that he fancied took the form of a dragon on one of the tiles in the dropped ceiling directly above his old wooden desk. Al Garland's years of holding all the power in the criminal justice game had made him self-righteous and stiff in his dealings with the enemy: criminal defense lawyers, and others who stood in the way of his conviction machine. Jay and Garland had had a wary but respectful relationship for many years, and Jay knew that it would pay neither to antagonize him nor to try to stroke him. He would do what he felt should be done no matter what Jay said.

"You know I'm entitled to go to court on this," Jay said finally. "The file is privileged. I would have an ethics problem if I *didn't* fight you."

"How long have you represented her?"

"A year and a half."

"Who's the husband's lawyer?"

"Bob Flynn. He's had three. Flynn's the third."

"Why three lawyers?"

"Every time there was a court order for discovery, Powers changed lawyers. He was reluctant to let go of his paperwork."

"He's the big real estate guy, Bryce Powers & Company, correct?"

"That's him."

"Meet me at Judge Moran's courtroom at nine o'clock tomorrow morning. I'll call Flynn," Garland said. "Take care of the file, Jay. I'm only doing this because it's you."

They hung up, and Jay stayed at his desk. The last of the day's sun filtered through the slatted openings of the wooden Venetian blinds that covered the large window behind him, painting horizontal yellow bars on the rows of red and gold-embossed law books that lined the far wall. His secretary, Cheryl, was gone, and the building was quiet. He could hear the occasional car horn honking on Market Street two stories below. Newark had been trying desperately over the past decade or so, with some success, to revitalize itself; but for all its efforts, each evening at around six o'clock, its downtown merchants and professionals and working class people fled to their homes in the suburbs, and the city center, bustling all day long, became eerily quiet while the cops waited for the next teenaged carjacker to go screaming by.

The mellow glow of his corner office did not match Jay's mood. He and Melissa Powers, Kate's twenty-two-year-old daughter—his *client's* twenty-two-year-old daughter—had been lovers for six months. In the midst of their affair, Jay had received documents from Bryce Powers's lawyer that revealed that Melissa and her older sister, Marcy, were each drawing a hundred thousand dollars a year for "maintenance services" from Plaza I and II, large hotel/retail/condo complexes in north Jersey's upscale Bergen County, developed and managed by Bryce Powers & Company. The sole shareholders of a shell company, the Powers sisters were simply receiving an allowance from their father via phony service contracts. All cleaning and other routine services were done by Bryce Powers & Company employees. Over a million dollars had thus been siphoned from Plaza I and II in the past five years. Acutely aware of his obligation to retrieve her share of this money for Kate—to sue Marcy and Melissa for it if necessary—Jay, glad for the excuse, had ended the relationship with Melissa two months ago.

Rousing himself, he dialed the number of Dan Del Colliano, a private investigator and his lifelong friend, who had an office on the same floor as Jay. Jay had hired Dan to do some investigating in the Powers case, and wanted to let him know that he might be getting a visitor with a search warrant. There was no answer.

He then dialed Bob Flynn's number, surprised when Flynn answered. It was close to seven p.m., by which time Flynn was usually on his second Manhattan at the Colonial, a local lawyers' hangout near the courthouse.

"Bob," said Jay, "did you get a call from Al Garland?"

"He just hung up," said Flynn.

"Are you going to court tomorrow?" Jay asked.

"Do I have a choice?"

"What is it with Garland?"

"He's loony tunes, Jay, power mad, you know that," Flynn replied. "Are you worried about fucking the daughter?"

"Yes."

"You deserve it."

Jay could only laugh at Flynn's directness. He did deserve it, he knew. He never should have gotten involved with the daughter of a client, especially one nineteen years younger than him. One whose father was worth seventy-five million, and who sat on a dozen philanthropic and Fortune 500 boards in the tri-state area. The beheading of this man's wife would guarantee a lot of publicity. Jay's name would undoubtedly come up, linked to both Kate and possibly Melissa, who, angry at being dumped, would hold their love affair over his head, a scarlet sword of Damocles. If dropped it wouldn't kill him—he had done nothing unethical—but it would hurt his professional reputation, a lawyer's most valued asset.

He had been thinking recently that there would be no real price to pay for his affair with Melissa Powers. He sat for a moment after hanging up the phone, staring at the dragon on his ceiling, pondering the error of that line of thought.

2.
8:00–11:00 PM, September 1, 2004, Montclair, West Orange

Jay concentrated on the pastel streaks of lavender and pink on the horizon as he drove home, trying, with little success, to distract himself from thinking of the tortured Kate Powers and the terrible way she had died. At home in suburban Montclair he changed into jeans and a polo shirt, made himself a drink, and sat down on his patio with the Powers divorce file, which he had copied in its entirety before leaving the office, certain that tomorrow he would be handing over the original to either Judge Moran or Al Garland. He skipped over the cold financial documents and hot client affidavits that constitute the typical lawyer's divorce file, until he found the folder that contained the fifty-odd letters that Kate Powers had written to him in the eighteen months he had represented her. In a childlike, but oddly graceful script, the sentences often rambling and incoherent, they dealt mainly with Kate's obsession with appearances and her anger at Bryce's emotional and, of late, financial stinginess.

It was Kate's mention of incest in one of these letters, of Bryce's "fondling love for his daughters," that brought Jay and Melissa together. He had felt compelled to interview her, and her denial was both succinct and credible. "My father may be a prick," she said with a smile, "but he's no child molester." Jay had asked her to confirm her statement in a short letter to him, which she did, adding a postscript inviting him to call her for a drink if the mood struck him, which, unfortunately, it did.

The letters, he recalled, contained other, similarly bizarre accusations against Bryce, which Jay dismissed as patently absurd—psychedelic falsehoods dreamed up when Kate went down her rabbit hole of prescription drugs and alcohol. He found nothing in any of them that gave any clue that she feared for her physical safety or her life at the hands of her husband.

Relieved, he set the letters aside and sipped his Scotch. Overhead, the bats that slept all day in the woods behind his small Cape Cod were beginning their nightly aerobatics in search of insects to consume. A beheading, he told himself, was not a crime of passion, not in American culture. Who could have done such a thing, and why? He remembered the Menendez case in California several years back: two brothers had been convicted of shotgunning their parents to death. The motive: the parents' estate. The thought that had been vaguely nagging him since his call from Al Garland now crystallized: Were Melissa and Marcy, princesses with nasty streaks—fearful of losing some or all of their meal tickets via their parents' divorce—capable of such a thing?

Before he could answer this question, or worse, label it as rhetorical, his phone rang. As was his habit, he let it go to his answering machine. When he heard Melissa Powers's voice through the open window behind him, he went into the kitchen to listen, picking up her message halfway through: ". . . the police. I need to talk to you. Call me." He heard her hang up, then pushed the replay button and learned that Bryce Powers was dead, that he had apparently overdosed on his insulin, and that the police had just tracked down Melissa and Marcy to give them the news.

Jay called Melissa on her cell, but there was no answer and no instruction to leave a message. He finished his drink in one gulp, put the legal file away, got in his car, and drove through the last of the twilight to nearby West Orange, where the Powers mansion sat in the lush, gated enclave-within-an-enclave of Llewellyn Park. When he got there, he was surprised to find the house and grounds in complete darkness. Nevertheless, he took his time negotiating the long, curving driveway, assuming he was being watched. He exited his car nonchalantly, but had taken only three or four steps when a loud voice said: *"Stop right there. We're police."* Jay stood still as two uniformed officers, each with a flashlight in one hand and a gun in the other, appeared out of the darkness. Behind them was a plainclothesman whom he recognized as Frank Dunn, a detective at the county prosecutor's office who he had been friends with for years.

"Frank," he said, "it's me, Jay."

Dunn, recognizing Jay, said to the officers, "It's okay. I know this guy. It's the wife's lawyer." He approached Jay. They shook hands, and the officers, tucking their guns away, headed back to the house, the beams of their flashlights stabbing into the darkness ahead of them.

Dunn was an old-timer, waiting to retire, but despite a cynicism that was part native and part acquired after forty years of police work, twenty of them in New York, Jay knew that he took his job seriously; as seriously as anyone who had seen all the faces of human horror and folly—including his own—could.

"You get dumber all the time," Dunn said to Jay.

Jay did not answer. He had no business being at a fresh crime scene, and he knew it.

"What are you doing here?" the detective asked. He lit a cigarette and then handed one to Jay, who, lighting it from Dunn's gold Zippo lighter, caught a brief glimpse of his friend's grizzled face before the darkness closed in on them again.

"Where is everybody?" he asked Dunn.

"Are you kidding, Jay?" said the detective. "Get in your car. Go home. I'll try to forget you were here. You're too dumb to do anything seriously criminal."

Jay smiled at this. When he was a young lawyer, he had faced Dunn—a seasoned and savvy testifier for the state—several times on the witness stand. Though Dunn was a cynic through and through, he was not dishonest and would not lie under oath, even to put a bad guy away. Recognizing this, Jay had not done badly. Afterward, he and Dunn had come to respect each other, to admire each other's style and, despite the age difference—Jay was forty-one, Dunn sixty-two—to become good friends.

Jay, a lean six-three, towered over the detective as they stood close to each other in the dark on the edge of the circular driveway near the large, stately house. His eyes adjusting to the darkness, he could see the outline of the thickly wooded hills behind it emerge in the night sky. Embarrassed, he took a short, hard drag on his cigarette before throwing it to the ground.

"You're right, Frank," he said. "Melissa called me. I thought she might be here."

Jay watched as Dunn put his cigarette to his lips, sucked in smoke, and took it away.

"Fucking pussy," the detective said. "It makes us weak."

Jay smiled. He knew that Dunn, who had been having an extramarital affair for the past five years, was referring to himself as well as Jay.

"We're done, Frank," Jay said. "But her parents are both dead."

"You could have anybody you want," Dunn said.

"I don't think so," Jay murmured. Dunn, his fair face ruined by drink, had often referred to Jay as Attorney Adonis.

"She's with her sister at that fancy Hilton in Short Hills," said Dunn. "You think I give a shit if these rich bastards kill themselves off?"

"You're tired, Frank."

"Fuck."

3.
5:00 PM, September 4, 2004, Montclair

The town of Montclair, one of a closely-linked chain of suburbs to the west of Newark, is known and much praised for its cultural diversity. Point of view being all, Jay Cassio, who graduated from Montclair High School in 1980, experienced that diversity as separateness: Blacks hung out with blacks, rich white kids with rich white kids, middle class white kids with middle class white kids, and everyone else, that is, the handful of lower-middle–class white kids, like Jay Cassio, was left to fend for him or herself. Jay, a terrific athlete, managed to rise above class on the football field, and avoid it at all other times by hanging out with Dan Del Colliano and his friends from predominantly blue-collar Bloomfield, the next town to the east, but light-years away in terms of youthful snobbery.

When it came time to buy a house, Jay, then thirty-two, chose Montclair because its many physical charms were no longer painful, as they were when he was a teenaged outsider, but actually pleasant. The tree-lined streets, the well kept parks, the mansions of the rich, the Mercedes in the parking lot at the Whole Foods supermarket, were the devils he knew. His house, a small Cape Cod, was on a quiet dead-end street that backed onto the South Mountain Reservation, two hundred acres of county-owned park and woodland, the perfect setting for the outsider life he had grown accustomed to living.

On Saturday, three days after his conversation with Al Garland, Jay took a run on a five mile loop in the reservation, mowed his lawn, pulled some weeds, and then, after showering, settled on his flagstone back patio to read and eventually sleep. He woke up, around five p.m., to see Dan Del Colliano, sitting, facing him, on one of his patio chairs, drinking a beer and smoking a cigarette, a newspaper rolled up on his lap.

"Hi," Dan said, smiling. "How are you?"

"I'm good. What's up?"

"You're in the paper."

"I thought so."

Danny handed him the Newark *Star-Ledger*. Jay, groggy from his nap, took it and tossed it onto a nearby low table. "What's it say?" he asked.

"Murder-suicide."

"Anything else?"

"That you're very handsome and the best lawyer in the state."

Jay laughed and, sitting up, rubbed the sleep out of eyes and then ran his fingers through his hair. He retrieved the newspaper, which Danny had folded to the Powers story, under the byline of a reporter they knew named Linda Marshall. Remembering the locustlike swarm of reporters that accosted him and Bob Flynn on the courthouse steps on Thursday morning, he saw the disappointment in the lead paragraph. *Essex County Prosecutor Alan Garland has determined, based on preliminary autopsy findings, that the deaths of the beheaded socialite Kate Powers and her multimillionaire husband are a case of murder-suicide . . .*

In court, Garland said he still wanted the Powers divorce files, but he was much less aggressive. Without objection from the prosecutor, Judge Moran had ordered Jay and Bob Flynn to surrender their files to him so he could decide what information they contained that was relevant to a murder investigation, assuming one was still being pursued.

The announcement by Garland, Linda Marshall's story continued, rendered moot his earlier attempt to confiscate the legal files of the Newark attorneys representing the couple in what was believed to be a contentious divorce . . . Confiscate, Jay thought, recalling his history with Marshall, that's the wrong word, but I like it. Give Garland a whack. He deserves it.

"I've been calling you," Jay said to Danny, settling the paper on his lap.

"I've been busy."

"Doing what?"

"I have a new client."

"So?"

"*So*," Danny answered, "she says she worked for Bryce Powers."

"Who is she?"

"A knockout Spanish broad."

"What's her name?"

"Donna Kelly."

"*Donna Kelly* is *Spanish*? You believe that?"

"It's an alias, who cares?"

"What's her story?"

"She has something she says Powers gave her."

"What?"

"Five hundred thousand in cash."

Jay's brain had still been dull from sleeping, but this brought him fully to his senses. "Seriously?" he said.

"Yes. I'm going to Florida on Monday."
"What for?"
"I'm bringing her the money."
"Where is it now?"
"In a locker at Newark Airport."
"Dan," Jay said, "I don't . . ."
"Get dressed," Danny replied, cutting him off. "I'll tell you in the car."
"Five hundred grand, Dan, come on, it's dirty."
"Her retainer was clean."
"How much?"
"Twenty-five K."

Jay took this number in, remaining silent. Twenty-five thousand dollars was a lot of money for any working class guy, but especially for Danny, who was always on the balls of his ass, swimming in credit card, and, recently, shylock debt.

"Where are we going?" Jay asked, knowing that with a fee like that in hand there would be no talking his friend out of this job, and that he would get the full story later when Dan, a lover of drama, felt the moment was right.

"Remember that hostess at that restaurant on Varick Street?" Dan asked.

"No."

"She remembers you. I ran into her last night. She was with a friend. She said to bring you in tonight, we'd have dinner, the four of us. She says there's no hard feelings."

"No hard feelings for what?"

"She wouldn't say."

Jay, smiling, rerolled the newspaper and threw it at his friend, who fended it off with a forearm. In Danny's dark brown eyes was the sly, mischievous look that even Jay, who had known him for thirty-seven years, could never interpret entirely. *I might be pulling your chain*, it could be saying, *or I might not, take your pick*; or possibly, *I am lying to you for the fun of it and you may never know the truth.* Or, *you're too serious, Jay, so I'm breaking your balls to try to get you to lighten up.* Or any combination of these.

"Okay," Jay said, looking at his watch, "what time?"

"Eight o'clock, but let's go in now. I gotta see a guy."

"What kind of a guy?"

"Just a guy. Come on, get dressed."

Upstairs, Jay shaved and put on khakis, comfortable loafers, and a black polo shirt. Before he pulled his shirt over his head he took a quick look at the six-inch scar that ran vertically down his right bicep, faded to a pale, almost translucent white after thirty years. Danny had helped him get revenge for the infliction of this wound, had nearly killed a black kid twice his size in Newark's Branch Brook Park to do it. He was a happy-go-lucky guy usually, his friend Danny, but he could turn mean in a heartbeat, and there was no stopping him when he got it in his head to do something, like take on somebody twice his size or courier a large amount of cash to Florida for a beautiful woman.

"So who's this guy we're seeing," Jay said once they were out of Montclair and headed east on Route 3, one of a half dozen north Jersey highways that feed cars and buses and people by the thousands around the clock into the glittering maw that is Manhattan.

"Why do you have to ask so many questions?" Danny replied, "It's not good for your health."

Danny was divorced, with two sons, aged fourteen and twelve. He made a decent living from his private eye business, but he liked nice clothes and fancy cars; he liked to eat at good restaurants; he liked to entertain women in style; he liked to pick up tabs; he liked to go to the track, and bet with bookies. With those habits he was always in debt. He had maxed out many credit cards since his divorce five years ago, and could never manage to pay anything but interest on a total debt that was approaching sixty thousand dollars. And Jay knew that he had recently borrowed from a loan shark in Manhattan, a guy that he and Danny had grown up with on the streets of Newark, but who nevertheless insisted on repayment. *They're quirky that way*, he had told his friend at the time.

"Is it the Pretzel?" he asked now.

The Pretzel was Johnny D'Ambola, who, at the age of eight, had been diagnosed with idiopathic scoliosis. His back corkscrewing out of control—hence the nickname—he had been put in a full body cast for six months, which apparently left him a lot of time to ruminate on how he would one day get even with his neighborhood tormentors, Dan Del Colliano being chief among them. He was the loan shark.

"Yeah. But first I gotta see another guy."

"You're collecting for the Pretzel?"

"Right. It cuts down my vig. I gotta do it."

"Fuck."

"You asked."

"I have to know, asshole. You want me to sit around with my thumb up my ass?"

"Don't worry. The guy's a fag."

"Literally?"

"I don't know, but he's a faggot."

Jay did not respond. He had had this kind of conversation with Danny enough times to know that at a certain point further questioning would be fruitless. He had the option of asking to be dropped off someplace, a bar, say, and picked up later. He wouldn't exercise that option in this case, although in the past he had steered clear of some of his friend's more dubious activities, which included low-end drug dealing and the occasional insurance scam.

They were different people in many ways, he and Danny—in most ways, really—but their friendship went deeper than mutual interests or values. Thrown together at age five on the first day of the Newark riots, they had spent the next nine years back-to-back with each other in a long fight for survival as the city rapidly changed from a patchwork of peaceful middle class ethnic enclaves to a no-man's-land dominated by black and Hispanic street gangs. Walking home from school, or to the corner candy store, were dangerous trips in those years.

Once, riding his bike in Branch Brook Park when he was ten, Jay was accosted by two older, and bigger, black boys, who wanted the bike. When he resisted, they slashed his arm with a box cutter. He had made the mistake of going out alone that day. Thereafter he stuck close to Dan, who was a fearless brawler, and who had good tactical sense as well: He knew when to talk, he knew when to cut and run, he knew fence holes and alleys and backyard escape routes all over the neighborhoods they lived in; and if it did come down to a fight, he was a wild man with his fists. No one fucked with Jay if Danny was around, and he was never far off; and Jay never forgot this.

They stopped on Canal Street to put the top down on Danny's leased BMW convertible, and then made their way to Silvano's, a restaurant on Sixth Avenue, where the guy who owed the Pretzel money was the bartender. His name was Al Spano. He was around fifty, tall, with too much wavy gray hair and a potbelly. He owed D'Ambola twenty-five hundred dollars, and had missed his last two weeks' interest, or *vigorish payments*, at two hundred fifty per week. Dan was supposed to collect those two weeks, plus the current week, seven hundred fifty all together. The restaurant had just opened for dinner, and was quiet, with only a young couple sitting at an outside table, having drinks.

Dan parked at the curb in a loading zone in front of the restaurant. He asked Jay to stay with the car, and move it if a cop came along. Jay got out and leaned against the car, and watched Danny enter and take a seat at the bar. At first Spano, who he could see from the waist up, did not seem concerned. Then the fight seemed to go out of him, and he went over to his jacket, which was hanging on a hook behind the bar, took an envelope out, and handed it to Danny. Danny strolled out, and they drove off, this time with Jay driving.

"How'd you do?" Jay asked.

"Okay. I got five hundred."

"He didn't look too worried."

"He wasn't, at first."

"I don't want to know what you said to him."

"No, you don't."

"What *did* you say, tough guy?"

"I told him that because this was the first time he was late, he got to deal with me, that I wouldn't hurt him, but that if I left without the money, the next guy they sent, it would be different. The next guy got paid to hurt people, break bones and so on. I asked him how his family was doing, his two grown daughters, his grandkids. He's a degenerate gambler, the dumb fuck. He won at OTB today and gave me some of it. I was lucky. It was easy."

"Who told you to say all that, Johnny D.?"

"No, he left it up to me."

"How much do you owe him?"

"Five grand. The vig's five hundred a week."

"Five hundred percent annual interest."

"That sounds right."

"Christ."

"When I bring him the money, I'll get a pass on this week's vig. I can use it."

"Can you imagine, the *Pretzel*?"

"Unbelievable. It would give me great pleasure to break his ass, but if I did, I'd be in trouble. He's a made guy."

"I can loan you the money."

"Maybe someday."

"Where are we going?"

"Little Italy. I'll tell you when to turn."

Danny directed Jay to the Abbadabba Italian-American War Veterans Club on Madison Street in what was left of Little Italy, where Johnny D'Ambola hung out every night of his life except for Christmas, Easter, and when he went to Florida, where he owned a nightclub in Hallandale. The city was not as busy as it usually was—it was the Labor Day weekend—but there were still a dozen cars double-parked on Madison Street. Jay double-parked as well, and waited in the car while Dan went into the club. Ten minutes later he came out, and got into the passenger seat.

"That's done," he said.

"Good. How was the Pretzel?"

"He's a jerkoff."

"I'm sure. How come he didn't come out to say hello?"

"I didn't tell him you were here."

"Why not?"

"Because there's surveillance here all the time. You don't need to be on film with these assholes."

"Okay. If you say so. Where to?"

"I told them we'd meet them at the bar at the Four Seasons."

"All the way uptown?"

"It's a beautiful night for a drive."

It *was* a beautiful night for a drive. It was warm. There was a gentle breeze. The sun was setting across the Hudson and, as it did, its last mellow light cast a magical glow on the only real city in the world.

"Tonight you can get your mind off of beheadings and whatnot," said Dan.

"Right."

"One thing."

"What?"

"Let's not talk about Nietzsche, and those guys."

Jay laughed. "I never talk about Nietzsche," he said.

"Well, Hemingway, Schopenhauer, you know what I mean."

"I can't promise."

"These broads are gum chewers."

"They have their place."

"The gorgeous mosaic."

Jay laughed again. He did not think that Dan had been keeping up with the latest in diversity marketing. "I'll do my best," he said.

"That's all I ask. God knows that's all I ask."

"Have we ever had a bad time together?"

"Not that I can remember."

4.
August, 1991, Mexico City

Mexico City's Aztec founders believed that human sacrifice was the only way of guaranteeing that the gods would allow them to continue as a race. Each evening a heart was cut from living flesh to ensure that the sun would rise the next day. On one occasion in the fifteenth century, twenty thousand prisoners were sacrificed over four days as part of the dedication of a new temple to the main god, Huitzilopochtli. Their fetish for offering flayed humans to their gods, and their history as mercenaries and warriors did not, however, prevent the Spanish from conquering the Aztecs in the sixteenth century, nor their gradual demise, via intermingling with their conquerors over the following centuries, as a distinct race. There are no pure-blooded Aztecs among Mexico's population today, although many claim, with pride, to have some of that ancient warrior blood in them, as a means, in some cases, perhaps, of rationalizing conduct not far removed from that of their cruel and violent ancestors.

Polanco and Lomas de Chapultepec, only a few miles to the east of the city center, are, among Mexico City's nearly four hundred *colonias*, or neighborhoods, arguably the finest: Polanco with its smart hotels and shops, its charming residential streets, its Parisian air; Chapultepec with its walled estates and polo clubs and botanical gardens. They stand side by side, the princess and the dowager queen, casting fearless and disdainful eyes on the urban monster that surrounds them.

In these enclaves of the rich lived two of mixed Aztec and Spanish blood, a mother on an estate in Chapultepec, and her daughter in a three-hundred-year-old convent in Polanco. The mother, a spoiled heiress to a *nouveau riche* fortune, did not know that the daughter—the product of a youthful indiscretion—lived nearby, but if she were told, the effect on her life would have been minimal: distasteful, but fleeting and not disquieting, like the bad smells—unavoidable in *La Ciudad de Mexico*—she sometimes encountered on her shopping trips into the city.

The daughter, Isabel Gutierrez Perez—a name chosen from the phone book and placed via a one hundred peso bribe on her birth certificate—had been told that her unwed mother, a servant in a Chapultepec mansion, had died giving birth to her in the summer of 1977, and that her father was unknown, possibly a Mixtec Indian from the south, passing through the great city. The landowners, Isabel was told, represented by one *Senor Hermano*, who visited Isabel from time to time, had given her to the Convent of Santa Maria, where Dominican Sisters ran an orphanage as part of their life of service to Mexico's poor.

Isabel was given these few threads about her past, and no more, when she was five, and as the years passed she wove them into a melodramatic tapestry containing the images of her brave and beautiful parents, "Rosalita," saintly in life and in death, and "Miguel," working the land, trying desperately to save enough money to send for his daughter. These images she clutched fiercely to her heart until 1991, when, at the age of fourteen, she was forced to abandon them forever.

For as long as she could remember, Isabel received visits from *Tio Hermano* once each year on her birthday. A large, impressive man who smelled of a sweet cologne and whose dark, wavy hair turned a distinguished silver as the years passed, he brought her small gifts—a coloring book, plastic beads, a cheap doll—and sat with her and Sister Josefina for a few minutes in the convent's hushed courtyard, their conversation gently monitored by a weathered statue of Our Lady of Guadalupe gazing not at them but at the bloodred roses strewn at her feet. Isabel was at first awed by these visits. They gave her hope, and they conferred a status on her that the other children did not have: She might be *wanted*. Nothing came of them, however, and the void in her life where her parents should have been grew bigger with each passing year. She receded, even on her birthday, in the presence of larger-than-life Uncle Herman and demur Sister Josefina, into her isolation and loneliness. But after his visit on her thirteenth birthday, in 1990, Uncle Herman came twice more: at Christmas, when he brought her a simple but very beautiful pearl necklace, and at Easter, when his gift was a bouquet of spring flowers and a lovely white dress for her to wear at her confirmation ceremony.

Isabel, as any curious teenager would be, was eager to experience the world beyond the convent, a world she had seen only in small glimpses through the distorting prism of smuggled magazines and the occasional television show the girls were allowed to watch; but the idea of scheming to escape, to meet boys, did not appeal to her as it did to some of the other older girls, who were reacting to the stirrings of womanhood in their bodies.

Isabel had no enemies, nor any close friends among these girls. She stood aside, as she had been doing since she was a child, and watched their girlish exuberance play itself out among the tall columns, and in the quiet corridors and austere common rooms of the orphanage. Fingering the pearls in her room, she prayed that they were a talisman of her freedom. She had no way of knowing how expensive they were, but they glistened against her pale olive skin, and it was obvious, even to her inexperienced eyes, that these were different from the trinkets that she had been given in the past. She had never been mistreated or lied to and so she did not fight off the question that came naturally to her mind in the light of Uncle Herman's gifts and extra visits: was it not possible that he had come to have some affection for her, and would help her find her place in the world beyond the convent's massive wooden gates?

As Isabel approached her fourteenth birthday her breasts rounded and filled to a heaviness that was at first disturbing; her long, coltish legs turned shapely and her rear end plump and high and firm below a trim girlish waist. Her face remained angelic, but beneath its layer of baby fat her features were fine, her eyes a breathtaking blue, her lashes long and black like her lustrous hair. In short, she was a beautiful, exotic child in the body of an even more beautiful and exotic woman. She was not unaware of these changes, had seen the way people—the other girls, the sisters, the occasional visitor—had looked at her. There was, however, nothing in her life experience that would enable her to connect them to Uncle Herman's heightened interest. But they were. Uncle Herman saw them coming when he visited Isabel for her thirteenth birthday in August of 1990, and confirmed them on his Christmas and Easter visits. On her fourteenth birthday he took her away.

The nuns made no objection. *Senor Hermano* had donated five thousand dollars to the convent each year that Isabel was with them. When he told them that she would be going into service with a good family with close government ties, the sisters felt they had done well for Isabel. Not every orphan who came to them entered the Order, especially ones as beautiful as Isabel. They did not permit the absence of legal nicety in her initial placement and her final departure to disturb them. *Senor* seemed like a good man and his money had fed and clothed dozens of children over the years, and they were grateful for his promise that it would continue.

In July, Sister Josefina and Sister Adelina took Isabel to a small retreat house owned by the Order in the hills above Puerto Angel, a tiny, impoverished fishing village on Mexico's southern Pacific coast. There they explained *Senor Hermano*'s plans to her. Afterward, as she walked the beach and climbed into the hills with a local peasant boy who had become her friend during prior visits, she silently thanked the Virgin of Guadalupe for her good fortune, and allowed herself for once to envision a happy future not as a dream but as a reality.

5.
3:00 AM, Sunday, September 5, 2004, Montclair

"I think I'm in love," Danny said.

They were sitting in padded outdoor chairs on Jay's patio, a small coffee table between them, on which rested, as if composed for a still-life painting, an old-fashioned aluminum espresso pot, a bottle of Remy Martin, an ashtray, and a pack of unfiltered Camels. Danny had lit a candle he found in the kitchen to complete this scene. It was three a.m. In the distance they could hear the splashing of the stream that meandered through the reservation, coming only a few hundred feet from Jay's property line before swinging back into the woods. An awning of stars shone down on them through a crystal clear night.

"Not with Gloria?" Jay said.

"No, but she's interesting."

After drinks and dinner and more drinks they had put their dates, Gloria and Candy, in cabs and headed back to Jersey.

"You can have Candy, too," Jay said.

"Do you remember her now?"

"Yes."

"You told her you were on the United States Supreme Court."

"I remember."

"She checked it out."

"I didn't think she'd take me seriously."

"She's crazy about you."

Jay did not answer. Candy, in her late twenties, was tall and beautiful, with a great smile. She wasn't pushy, not looking for a commitment, just a fun night, maybe a few more. There was no click, and that was it. It had been almost three years since he had last had a serious girlfriend, a long time between clicks, he knew. He liked being alone, he would tell himself. An only child, he had lost both of his parents at once in a plane crash. Danny had a theory about the effect this trauma had on his life, but he rarely brought it up, just as Jay rarely mentioned his friend's shortness of stature—he was five-seven—not even to tease him about the platform cowboy boots he'd been wearing since he was a teenager. It was the things not said, Jay knew, that made for a great friendship.

"Maybe I'll call her," he said finally.

"I'm worried about you," Dan said.

"Why?"

"Because I know you won't call her. You didn't even ask for her number."

"You can get it for me."

"Do you want it?" Dan asked.

"Not really."

"Jay," Dan said, "she's a fucking knockout. Every guy we know would kill his mother just to be with this broad."

"You'll have to find me somebody else. You always do."

"What happens when I'm not around?"

"You'll always be around."

"Don't be so sure. I might run off with Donna Kelly."

"Is that who you're in love with?" Jay asked, laughing.

"The new client? That you just met yesterday?"

"Yes."

"Tell me about her."

"I put her in her mid-twenties," Dan said, "about five-seven, a hundred and twenty-five pounds. Slender, but voluptuous—a great rack—an unbeatable combination."

"What about the face?"

"That's the best part. Long black hair, dark complexion, blue eyes. Strong, classic features. I said she's Hispanic, but I'm really not sure. Those blue eyes . . . You'll die when you see this broad. She's an absolute knockout, and very classy."

Jay did not put much credence in this description. Danny's women were always more beautiful, and occasionally more "classy"—meaning in his friend's lexicon that they had minds as well as bodies—before he slept with them.

"What's her story?"

"She says that Powers gave her the cash to hold for him about a month ago."

"Where's she from?" Jay asked.

"Florida," said Danny. "She was managing a property in West Palm Beach for Powers."

"Were they lovers?"

"She says not. She would fly up for monthly property managers meetings. After the last meeting he took her out to dinner, and asked her to keep the cash for him."

"What does she want from you?"

"I'm supposed to bring the money to her in Florida on Monday."

"Which you'll happily do."

"Of course."

Jay had fought tooth and nail for what lawyers call discovery in the Powers divorce case, which, as it was provided grudgingly in small pieces by Bryce Powers's lawyers, he scrutinized thoroughly under the old legal maxim, *if you're trying to hide something it must be damaging*. Powers had gone to work for Gentex, a huge international real estate developer, right out of Harvard Business School, at the age of twenty-one. By the time he was thirty, he was a vice president, in charge of government relations for all of Central and South America. Chief Executive Officer had clearly not been out of the question for him. But he left, and used his carefully guarded savings and contacts to start Bryce Powers & Company. True grit, Jay had thought, sincerely, until recently.

"Powers lived in Mexico City," he told Danny, "for about five years. He worked for a very big international developer, skyscrapers, things like that. He must have met some important people. He was in charge there eventually. Don't take this lightly, Del."

"What?" Danny asked.

"Come on."

"I'll die with my boots on," said Danny, smiling, sipping his liquore-laced espresso.

"Do you know anybody in Florida?" Jay asked.

"No," said Danny, "but Frank Dunn has a buddy living there, another ex-New York cop, who's supposed to have friends in the Miami Police Department."

"What good will that do you?"

"If I get in trouble, I'll call him. But I won't get in trouble. Don't worry, this is not the French Connection."

"How did she get your name?"

"She says you recommended me."

"I don't know her, Dan."

"She was in Jersey this week, for a property managers meeting scheduled for the day after the massacre at the Powers house. She read in the paper that you were representing the wife. She says Powers told her what a prick you were. She liked that about you. She called your office and Cheryl gave her my name and number."

"I don't buy it. I mean, she hardly knows Powers and he's trusting her with a half million dollars in cash?"

"I don't either, actually."

"Why can't she get the money herself?"

"I think the idea is that other people are interested in it."

"Besides her."

"Right."

"Maybe you should have someone else with you."

"I'll be fine."

"What's your take on it?"

"I think Powers was banging her. Anybody would. And together they were stealing the company's money. Maybe they were planning on running away."

"Then why would anyone else know about the money?"

"I've already spent half my fee, Jay. I can finally catch up. Fuck the rest."

"Why not just skip it altogether, then? Keep it all?" Jay knew that his friend was a petty, not a real, thief. He would make an honest effort on behalf of Miss Kelly. Honest according to his own somewhat flexible standards. He also knew that Dan had smiled his way through more dangerous assignments, not so much fearless as oblivious to fear, and that no amount of talk, sarcastic or otherwise, had the slightest chance of persuading him to change his approach to his work or his life. He watched as his friend of thirty-seven years shook a cigarette from the pack, lit it from the candle, took a deep drag, and then blew the smoke up into the night sky.

"She's hot for me, Jay," Dan said, smiling his insane devil's smile. "I can feel it in my bones."

"Christ."

"Well, some of us still like to get laid."

"Just be careful, okay, asshole?"
"Don't worry, I'll wear a condom."
"Christ."

6.
2:00 AM, September 12, 2004, Montclair

A week later Danny was dead, shot twice in the head; his body, tied at hand and foot, found in a room at the South Miami Beach Motor Hotel. Frank Dunn showed up at Jay's house at 2:00 a.m. to break the news. Dunn had gotten a call from his friend in Miami, Angelo Perna. Multiple burn wounds had been found on Danny's hands and feet, and his testicles were grossly swollen and pulpy. Dunn found a bottle of Jameson in Jay's liquor cabinet, and by three a.m. it was finished. It had been Dunn's first drop of liquor in ten years.

Jay did not drink. Judge Moran had returned the Powers divorce file to Jay's office on Wednesday after Al Garland had determined that the deaths of Bryce and Kate were definitely murder-suicide. But the copy Jay had made before going to court last week was still in the small second bedroom he used as an office. He managed to lay Dunn out on the couch, and then he sat and carefully began to reread Kate Powers's letters, hoping to find some reference to the beautiful Hispanic woman, aka Donna Kelly, who had lured Dan Del Colliano to his death.

He found none, but one or two letters he now read in a different light. In one, Kate mentioned an affair Bryce was supposed to have had while they were living in Mexico City, with the daughter of a well connected, patrician type family. His "fouling of the royal nest," as she melodramatically put it, had led, she claimed, to Bryce's resignation from Gentex and their sudden departure from Mexico. Bryce Powers & Company was capitalized, according to Kate, with hush money from the woman's father. This was supposed to have happened in the mid-seventies, clearly eliminating Donna Kelly, in her mid-twenties according to Danny, as Bryce's lover. Was Kate raving? Was an affair in the high end of Mexican society such a scandal in the seventies? In several other letters Kate spoke of Bryce's "friends" in Bogotá and Panama, of the many supper parties they attended in Mexico City with the "biggest drug dealers in the world and their front men."

Putting the letters aside, Jay recalled that Bryce's first syndication in 1977 was a deal in southwest Texas, and that the four general partners, except for Bryce, had distinctly Latin names, which would not be unusual given the location of the property. He pulled the documents relating to that deal and found that the property, a two hundred unit garden apartment complex called Lantana Gardens, had been valued at twenty million in 2004. Assuming a conservative rate of appreciation, the purchase price for the property would have probably been around eight or nine million. How had Bryce come up with his share? Or enough collateral to make a bank comfortable, assuming there was some financing in the beginning?

The next few deals were also in Texas, but after that, properties were purchased in Florida, Delaware, Arizona, New York, and New Jersey, Bryce's eventual home base. In the mid-eighties Plaza I and II were built. They were Bryce's ultimate achievement, establishing his net worth, at the time of the divorce, at around seventy-five million. Why, then, was he dicking around with five hundred thousand in cash just before he died? Why bother? Jay looked again at the Lantana Gardens partnership papers, and found that the other managing partner, besides Bryce, was one Herman Santaria. "H. Santaria" was the co-managing partner on the other Texas properties as well. Managing partners, Jay knew, were the ones with the real control over real estate syndicates set up as partnerships.

H. Santaria did not appear as a partner in any deal outside of Texas, but every Bryce Powers & Company property, forty-three in all, listed *H.S. Company* as a maintenance contractor receiving close to a million dollars per year in all for its services. It took no great power of deduction for Jay to see the distinct possibility that Herman Santaria, aka H.S. Company, had the same phony deal with Bryce as did Melissa and Marcy, only on a much larger scale. So who was Herman Santaria, and what grip did he have on Bryce Powers?

And then, of course, there was the cash. The properties were run as separate businesses, with each having several bank accounts, including a rent account, a payroll account, a general operating account, and a trust account into which deposits from investors were made and dividends distributed. Bryce Powers & Company was the manager of all forty-three properties, which gave it, by contract, exclusive control over some 172 bank accounts. The cash flow was about forty million per year. In addition there were Plaza I and II, which also maintained several bank accounts and which had a total cash flow of about ten million per year. Jay did not know much about money laundering, but any beginner could see that having control of 172 bank accounts would not be a bad idea for someone interested in doing it.

Jay and Danny were five years old when their paths first crossed on a deceptively lovely summer day in 1967. Neither the past nor the future exist, only the present, but in Jay's present, making coffee in his quiet kitchen, was Danny; running headlong down Sheffield Street in their old neighborhood in Newark on the day they met; pitching from a comically big windup during their stickball games; ordering drinks for the bar at Tierney's, their hangout in Montclair; making tomato sauce in the kitchen of his apartment; reciting lines from *Scarface* and *The Godfather*, his favorite movies: brash, confident, swaggering, the devil in his eyes and in his smile. These and more were the images embedded in Jay's heart, in the here and now. Beyond these images he could not see, did not want to see.

7.
9:00 PM, July 12, 1967, Newark

"What were you doing in the church?" A.J. asked.

Jay was silent.

"Did you see the cop who was shot?"

"Yes."

"That was Phil Franco."

"I know."

"He's dead."

Silence.

The police had let the mourners leave the church, along with Jay and Danny, who had appeared suddenly in their midst, at around six p.m. *Run*, Danny had said, and before the cops could say or do anything, Jay was halfway home and Danny was dashing around the perimeter of the projects toward his apartment building on Eighth Avenue, where, he had casually mentioned to Jay while they were holed up in the bell tower, a "spic and a shine family"—whatever *they* were—had just moved in.

"The school said you were missing," his mother said.

"I spoke to your friend's father," said A.J. "We were just about to go looking for you."

On the table in front of Jay was a dish of *spaghettini marinara*, a favorite of his, with several chunks of his father's bread on a plate next to it. He was hungry, but he hadn't touched it. His parents were making him too nervous.

"What else did you see?" his father asked.

"I saw the guy on the roof."

"The guy with the rifle?"

"Yes."

"You saw him shooting?"

"Yes."

"Did you see Phil get shot?"

"Yes."

"Son of a bitch," said A.J., softly. Jay watched his father's eyes go flat, look inward, if that was the right way to describe it. Sadness, Jay thought. Every day for as long as Jay could remember, Phil Franco had stopped by the bakery to buy bread to bring home to his family. Jay had listened in occasionally as Phil and A.J. had spoken about grown-up things. They were friends, he thought now. My father had a friend—and lost him. These thoughts were like small claps of thunder in his brain, marking something he would think about later, lying in bed.

"We'll go to the funeral," A.J. said.

"Me?" said Jay.

"Yes. When people die, they're laid out in a funeral home—it's called a wake—then they're buried in a cemetery. You saw Phil die, you should see him buried."

Silence.

Jay turned his attention to his mother, who had said little since placing Jay's food on the table. She was looking around the small kitchen. Jay followed her gaze as it swept in a few seconds over the things that he had seen her wipe and scrub and clean every day of his life: the gas stove, the new refrigerator, the worn linoleum floor, the chipped enamel sink. He paused with her to look through the window above the sink at the television antennas on the rooftop of the three-story tenement behind theirs, the hot summer breeze rustling her gauzy yellow curtains.

Carmela taught something called *Greek mythology* at the local junior high school, two blocks away. Occasionally Jay had watched with pride as one of her students, passing her on the street out front, would say, "Hello, Mrs. Cassio," or "Good morning, Mrs. Cassio." Until tonight he had thought that her air of calm authority was a permanent part of her, like her beautiful brown eyes or her wedding ring. Tonight he could see she was afraid—of the city going up in smoke, yes, of course, but of something else, too, something worse; something he would only much later identify as the prospect of poverty and loss of hope.

"I think that's a good idea," she said to Jay, finally, her face recomposed, reassuring him with her eyes, "You can meet Phil's wife, and tell her how brave he was."

Jay looked at his mom and nodded, trying to understand this thing called a *wake*, where a dead person was *laid out*, and where he was supposed to say something to Phil Franco's wife, whom he'd never met. He couldn't imagine any of this, but he trusted his mother implicitly and was not afraid. Years later he would come across the concept of grief counseling and recall that, in two or three sentences, his parents had given him all he would need to deal with the strange mix of exhilaration and anxiety that had been pressing on his heart since witnessing the cold-blooded killing of the cop Phil Franco.

"Your friend's father says you went to the church to pray," said A.J., who had called Dan's dad as soon as Jay walked in the door.

Jay stared at the Formica tabletop, suddenly fascinated by its squiggly yellow and blue lines.

"Look at me, Jay," A.J. said, and Jay, knowing he had no choice, did. He saw not anger on his father's face, however, but fatigue and relief, and perhaps the beginning of a smile.

"Is that right?" A.J. said.

"Why not?" said Carmela, coming swiftly to Jay's rescue. "Anybody would want to pray at such a time."

Jay knew what lying was, and that it was supposed to be a sin, but it was by his suggestion that they conspire to lie together—a compact that by its nature excluded the rest of the world—that Dan had offered himself as a friend. What was the committing of a *sin* against an abstract and lifeless *God* compared to the betrayal of a flesh and blood friend? Nothing. And so Jay held his father's gaze, prepared to lie, exhilarated at the thought of having a friend and a life separate from his parents.

"Don't answer," said A.J., giving way to a full-blown smile. "Nothing could be more absurd. But somebody had balls to think it up."

At seven o'clock, after drinking a cup of hot milk laced with a teaspoon of whiskey, a guaranteed restlessness remedy usually reserved for Christmas Eve, Jay was in bed. Carmela sat next to him for a minute or two until he pretended to be asleep. After she left, he lay there and listened as she and A.J. sat in the living room of their tiny apartment watching the looting and burning of their city on television, occasionally murmuring something to each other he could not hear.

He fell asleep thinking of friends lost, Phil Franco, and found, Dan Del Colliano, his exhilaration finally giving way to his exhaustion.

• • •

A.J. and Carmela Cassio were stunned by what they saw on their television that night, especially the images of rifles sticking out of windows at the Columbus Homes and the sacking and torching of Big Red's on nearby Mount Prospect Avenue, the last supermarket in the Ward. During a commercial break, A.J. called the two young men who helped him make the bread every night at the bakery and told them not to come to work that night, and possibly for another day or two. An unbroken string of nights, going back to 1903, in which bread had been made at Cassio's, had come to an end.

If you had an aerial view of the city that night, as New Jersey's governor Richard Hughes did for example, from a helicopter, you would have seen buildings and cars burning; people smashing windows and looting stores and dancing around bonfires in the streets; the streaking overhead lights of police cruisers and ambulances; and the smoke from tear gas as the police tried to flush snipers from buildings in neighborhoods thick also with hatred and tension and fear. You would have seen all this, and more, but you would not have seen A.J. Cassio sit up abruptly in his bed at two thirty, his usual rising time, and begin to fumble for his slippers, nor his wife rise also, to gently place her hands on his shoulders and say softly, "Jay, you forgot, you're not making bread tonight," nor A.J. grunting and shaking his head as Carmela slipped off her nightgown and encircled her husband's body with her arms, pressing her breasts against his back while caressing his chest and stomach and loins and, pulling him down beside her, murmuring, "hold me Jay, hold me, sweetheart . . ."

8.
10:00 AM, September 17, 2004, Newark

Jay gave the eulogy at Danny's funeral mass, held at St. Lucy's, still standing amidst the rubble of the old neighborhood, including the rubble that filled the empty lots where the Columbus Homes—demolished in 1994 by the same federal government that built them—had once stood. He kept it simple, speaking of Danny's love for his mom and his two sons, his loyalty to his friends, his contagious smile. Kay Del Colliano, dressed in black, sitting in the front pew next to the casket, an arm around each of Danny's boys, had had a hard life, and now had lost her only son. At the wake she had told Jay that she was afraid that Dan's ex-wife—class conscious and ashamed of her Italian roots—would not let the boys see much of her now that Dan was gone.

"Your son—and your father," Jay said, looking at Kay and the boys, "lived every second of his life to its absolute fullest. I never saw him back down from a fight. I never saw him do anything halfway. If he was afraid of anything, I never knew about it. I often wondered where his energy, his happy spirit, came from, especially in a world where many see only sadness and misery. I now realize that Dan was a gift—from God, from the universe—to all of us who knew and loved him. But great gifts are not meant to last forever. We were lucky to have him as long as we did, and we will need each other now more than ever before. Danny will speak to me always. I know that I will see him again one day, recognize him instantly, and smile . . ."

Jay was no stranger to sudden death or change. His parents had been killed on their way to his law school graduation in San Francisco in 1987. The universe had stopped that day for Jay, and never really started moving again. Numb, he married his girlfriend at the time, whom he did not love and barely knew. Unhappy, childless, they were divorced a year later. Jay moved into an apartment in Montclair, but spent most of his time at work, finding refuge in an ethic of sacrifice that almost, but never quite, defeated the demons of heartache and loneliness that haunted him.

Quietly, without ever speaking of it, Danny fought these demons with him. He knew, somehow, that pain cannot be conquered, only endured, but he also knew his friend, knew how harmful Jay's natural tendency to isolate himself and brood could be in the wake of such a loss. And so, knowing that he was the only person capable of it, he forced diversions down Jay's throat, dragging him to golf in Florida, to fish in the Sea of Cortez, to gamble in Las Vegas. One night in New York with Danny, Jay met an adventuresome, sexy redhead who he dated for a year, a year in which his heart returned more or less to normal. By living, we outwit death, but who would help Jay outwit it now that Danny was gone?

Jay did not ride in the funeral cortege after Danny's mass. Frank Dunn asked to be taken on a quick tour of the neighborhood before heading to the cemetery, and Jay grimly complied. Dunn stared silently as Jay pointed out the tenement on Seventh Avenue that had housed the family bakery and three generations of Cassios, now a boarded-up shell; and the duplex on Garside Street where Jay and Danny lived side by side, with their families, for eighteen happy months from 1970 to 1971.

They headed out of the city toward Bloomfield, where Danny would be buried in Glendale Cemetery, next to his father. On the visor of Jay's car was a postcard he had received from Danny the day after he learned of his murder. "Finally made it to Jupiter before I died," it read. "Not at all like the other planets. Miss Kelly says hello . . . Dan." Jay had brought it with him to the church, thinking he might use it in his eulogy. In the end he decided not to. These were Dan's last words to him, which he would keep to himself.

"That was a nice thing you said about needing each other more now," said Dunn.

"Thanks."

"I don't think it will work, though. The ex-wife's a bitch."

"I know."

"Do me a favor," Dunn said.

"What?"

"Have a drink with me after the funeral. I believe I'll need one."

9.
July 1967 – July 1976, Newark

Jay got a new bike for Christmas, 1972, a shiny red and white beauty that stood in the basement of the Cassios' new apartment through a stormy winter and a cold, rainy spring. In late May the weather broke and, after school one day, he decided to take it to Branch Brook Park, whose endless, winding cinder paths had been calling his name for four long months. The day was warm and beautiful, and the park was only three blocks away. His father was asleep, and could not be woken to ask permission, and his mother was far away "at work."

He rode like the wind for a half hour before he was hailed down by two teenaged black boys who he thought wanted to talk. Before he could come to a full stop one of them punched him squarely in the mouth, knocking him to the ground. Instead of trying to get to his feet, he rolled over and spread himself over his bike, which had toppled over next to him, one hand in a death grip on the handlebars, the other enmeshed in the spokes of the rear wheel. The two boys pounded him with their fists and feet for a minute or two, but he clung all the tighter, hoping they'd go away or that someone would come to his rescue. Then he felt a sharp pain down his right upper arm. Without thinking, he grabbed his bicep and soon his hand was full of blood. At the same time the boys flung him to the side of the path and were gone, with the bike, which he never saw again.

The next day Kay Del Colliano, who lived four blocks away, came over to commiserate with Carmela, bringing Danny, who laughed when he saw Jay's swollen lip and missing tooth.

"How many were there?" Dan asked. They were sitting on the porch of the Cassios' sagging duplex apartment on Garside Street, eating ice cream, one of the few things Jay would be able to eat for the next week or so.

"Two."

"How old?"

"I don't know. One was big."

"Did you hit back?"

"Yes," Jay answered, lying.

"That was dumb," said Danny. "It was two against one. You should have just covered up, or run, and let them take your bike. It's only a bike."

A faint smile—his first in twenty-four hours—crossed Jay's face as he looked at his friend. Danny was smiling, too, the wicked smile that by now Jay had seen many times, but could never quite get used to.

"I know a way to get even, though," said Dan. "But first you have to get better. It can wait a week or two."

Two weeks later Jay and Dan went to the park, and Jay rode Dan's bike on the same cinder path for an hour while Dan crouched in the bushes nearby. They did the same the next day, and the next. On the fourth day, the two bike thieves appeared on the path.

"Motherfucker," said the bigger one, smiling, as Jay came to a stop. "The boy brought us another bike." The smaller of the two—still a head taller than Jay—stepped up quickly and shoved him off the bike, but Jay was holding a baseball bat at his side, which, taking a stance and rearing back, he swung as hard as he could at the boy who had punched him in the mouth two weeks ago, hitting him in the elbow, which snapped in two. As this was happening, Danny flew out of the bushes and headbutted the bigger boy in the chest, knocking him to the ground and flinging himself on top of him. Jay stood still as Danny—ten years old and all of five-two—pounded the boy's face, his fists working furiously, like pistons gone haywire. The first black kid, his forearm dangling from his elbow joint, seeing this, fled. When Danny got to his feet, his dark face was flushed, his eyes wild. Jay stared at him, getting the only glimpse of the devil in Dan Del Colliano he'd ever need to see. The boy on the ground was half conscious, his face swollen and bruised.

"Who's a motherfucker, now?" said Dan, kicking him in the ribs and spitting on him. "You are, you motherfucking cocksucker. I've got two brothers bigger than me. If you try something again, they'll fucking kill you, and they'll burn your fucking house down with your family in it. *You're the motherfucker now!*"

• • •

The riots left Seventh Avenue and its environs in ruin, and A.J. was forced to abandon the bakery, leaving behind the new ovens and counters he purchased in 1965, but taking with him the nine thousand dollar note he signed to finance them. He also lost the four-story tenement that housed Cassio's, inherited from his father in 1962. Two of the apartments were already vacant, and the remaining two tenants fled after the riots. His new tenants, when he could get them, either destroyed their apartments or didn't pay their rent, or both. He had three thousand dollars in savings, which he used to make repairs, but when this money ran out, he fell behind on his taxes and, after trying with no success to sell the building, in 1972 he deeded it to the city.

He had moved only once in his life, in 1957, from the second to the fourth floor of his father's building with his new bride, but in the years from 1967 to 1976, he moved his family four times, each time to an apartment in smaller and smaller Italian-American enclaves within the Ward. Carmela did not complain, but those years aged her, and sometimes, when she didn't think he was looking, he saw something close to despair in her eyes. Though he seemed outwardly the same—steady, methodical, optimistic—A.J. Cassio was not a happy man as he set out, at the age of forty-one, to rebuild his life.

He took a job in the bakery of an A&P supermarket in nearby Belleville where, in a midnight-to-eight a.m. shift, he made white bread and party cakes for mass consumption. Carmela tried to resume teaching English and Greek and Latin Mythology at Webster Junior High in the Ward, but she quit after a forearm from a two hundred pound fourteen-year-old girl broke her jaw one spring day in 1968. In the fall she began substituting in grammar schools in the city. They did not intend to stay in Newark as long as they did, but the rents were cheap, and it took them a long time—seven years—to pay off the loan for the ovens and put aside money for the down payment on a house.

In July of 1976, one of A.J.'s coworker's at the A&P told him about a house that was for sale in his neighborhood in Montclair. The owner was a woman whose husband had died, and who was moving in with her daughter in a house on the same block. She was willing to take back a mortgage, at less than the market rate, so that she could have a steady income to supplement her Social Security, and she did not require much of a down payment. When A.J. and Carmela went to look at the house, Jay in the backseat, they made a wrong turn and saw parts of Montclair that left them speechless: spectacular homes with broad lawns running down to leafy avenues presented themselves in all their splendor. Only the very rich could live in such mansions, they thought, and they were right, but the house they looked at was in a modest neighborhood, a few blocks from Bloomfield Avenue, a busy thoroughfare that ran for miles through the thickly populated suburbs west of Newark. The house, a yellow ranch with three bedrooms, a fireplace, two tall pine trees in front, and a quiet backyard, was more than A.J. and Carmela had let themselves dream of, and they made the deal immediately. By the middle of August they had moved in, and their last nine years in Newark were soon a distant memory.

Earlier that summer, the Del Collianos had moved out of Newark as well, but under different circumstances. In March, Dan's dad, Dominick, a gambler with a violent temper, had been killed, presumably by loan sharks or bookmakers, his body found in the trunk of his car in the parking lot of a discount store in Kearny, a factory town on the banks of the Passaic River. To Kay, her husband's death could not have come a minute too soon. The week before, Dan, who had just turned fourteen, had intervened while Dominick was slapping her around the kitchen of their apartment, and Dan had wound up with a broken nose, blood streaming down his face as he and Kay watched Dominick fling himself out the door.

Two weeks after he was buried, a representative of Dominick's mason's union appeared at Kay's door with a check for twenty-five thousand dollars, the proceeds of a life insurance policy that the union gave as a fringe benefit to all of its members. A fatalist, like many Italian-American women of her generation, Kay saw in her husband's death, and the miraculous life insurance policy, the hand of God at work, compensation for putting up with an abusive husband for fifteen years. She used the money to buy a small house in Bloomfield, where her son would no longer have to run the streets and where she planned on living out her days in peace.

Jay did not mind the smaller and smaller apartments and the successively more crowded neighborhoods they lived in those post-riot years in Newark. He did not learn until years later the price in lost pride that his parents paid as they watched their friends move to the suburbs to raise their children among trees and lawns and safe schools. Jay was too young to know about those things. He *did* know, however, that his friend Danny's father, Dominick, was violent, and beat his mom, Kay. He had heard Danny say many times that he planned on killing Dominick when he grew up; and Jay, knowing Danny, believed him. So, although he was sad to see his friend go, he was relieved that he would not have to commit murder. At the time Jay thought it possible that he would never see Danny again. But the following Saturday—and every Saturday that summer—Dan rode his bike to Newark, and he and Jay played stickball in the schoolyard. In August the Cassios moved as well, and though the boys went to different high schools, Jay stopped thinking that he might never see Danny again, that their friendship would not last forever.

10.
2:00 PM, September 27, 2004, Newark

Jay took a week off after the funeral. On the following Monday he put on a lightweight summer suit, white shirt, and dark tie and went to work. Cheryl, a single mother with problems of her own, smiled quickly when he walked in and then returned to her typing. She had taken care of the office while he was home, putting everyone and everything off except for Melissa Powers, who had insisted on an appointment for today. He looked around his office for a moment and listened to the traffic below. The week's mail, opened and sorted by day, was in a folder on his desk. On top of it were his calendar for the week and reminder notes. The case files that needed attention were lined up on the floor to his right, next to the large potted plant that Kay Del Colliano had sent him eight years ago when he left his former law partner, then under indictment for attempting to bribe a cop, and started his own practice.

Everything looked and sounded the same.

On the keyboard of his computer was a large note from Cheryl: "Melissa Powers coming in at eleven." Jay looked at his watch—it was ten thirty—and opened the mail folder.

Melissa arrived promptly and, after greeting Jay, settled—slowly crossing her long, tanned legs—into a chair facing his desk. She had on a short white skirt, gold leather sandals, and a light cotton pullover blouse. At twenty-two, her large hazel eyes deceivingly innocent, she did not need makeup and wore none, except for a hint of red lipstick.

"I'm sorry about Danny," she said. "I tried calling."

Jay nodded. He had not picked up the phone at home except for Cheryl. "Thanks," he said.

Jay had gone to the Hyatt in Short Hills to meet Melissa and Marcy on the night of their parents' deaths. They had a drink in the plush lounge on the twentieth floor, overlooking the lights dotting northern New Jersey's rolling hills. He had not slept with Melissa that night, although she wanted to and he had been tempted. He did not blame her, knowing from experience how powerful an antidote sex was to grief, powerful but extremely temporary. He remembered seeing the Powers sisters' thoughts in their eyes as they sipped their drinks. He knew what they wanted: their parents' money, all of it, and as quickly as possible. He also knew the obstacles they faced.

"What's up?" he said.

"They've put a freeze on all of my father's assets."

"Mesa Associates?" Jay said.

"Yes."

Jay knew from the discovery in the now moot divorce case that Bryce Powers had been funding, out of his own pocket, a disastrous townhouse/golf course development in Arizona. Whatever could go wrong, had: the general contractor had filed for bankruptcy, the subcontractors had walked off the job, the bonding company was claiming fraud, the town fathers were upset; and somehow Bryce's people had overestimated the market: sales were slow at first and recently nonexistent. Powers had kept it from failure, but still, at the time of his death, it was over six million dollars in the red. His investors, all general partners, could not be expected to be happy about being potentially liable for a debt in excess of ten times their initial investment. They would certainly try to do something about it, that is, shift the blame to Bryce, hence the jeopardy to the Powers assets.

"What kind of a freeze?" Jay asked.

Melissa had been holding some papers in her lap, which she handed to Jay. "We were served these this morning at the house."

Jay glanced at the top document, an Order To Show Cause and Temporary Restraining Order, knowing that the fifty pages below it would be affidavits from irate partners.

"What about Plaza I and II?" he said.

"The partners are having a meeting next week. They've actually invited us."

Jay knew that the partners in Plaza I and II were the same, for the most part, as those in Mesa Associates. Bryce had made many people wealthy over the years. No one challenged how he ran his business, not even those who knew about or guessed at his daughters' illegal "maintenance" contracts. They all wanted to be invited back into the next deal. But Bryce was dead now and, given the amount of money involved, lawsuits against Melissa and Marcy and the Powers estate would be sure to follow.

"Don't go," Jay said.

"What will they do?"

"They'll want you and Marcy to repay the money your father paid you every year."

"All of it?"

"You didn't do anything to earn it. It was a total scam."

"Can you represent us?"

"Yes," Jay answered. "I can, but it'll be expensive."

"How long will it take?"

"A year, more or less."

Melissa remained serenely silent, occasionally stroking her long, honey-colored hair from her face, while Jay explained some of the issues he anticipated would come up in the case, and told her that she stood to lose a substantial portion of her share of the estate in settlements and attorney's fees. He could see her calculating her net share as he spoke.

There had been no real romance in Jay's affair with Melissa, no emotional connection to help him rationalize what he had done. Was this good or bad? He did not know. Certainly falling for Melissa Powers would be painful. But then again he only dimly remembered the joy and the pain of being in love. He was not surprised now to see Melissa's flawless amorality serving her so well in the face of the horror of her parents' death. She had her way of surviving.

Did he? This was another thing he didn't know.

When Melissa left, he looked at his watch. Noon.

11.
5:00 PM, December 3, 2004, Newark

"Jay, John Parker, how are you?"

"Yes, John. I'm fine, thank you, and you?"

"Good, thanks. I'll tell you why I called. We just had a call from an attorney in Houston. He says he represents the Santaria family. Apparently you sent a subpoena to a Herman Santaria. Is that right?"

Parker was a senior partner at McCrae & French. He was representing Chemical Bank, the executor of Bryce Powers's estate, in the suits started by Plaza I and Plaza II and Mesa Associates. Jay had filed answering papers for Melissa and Marcy and, in October, over two months ago, using the lawsuit as a vehicle, had in fact sent a subpoena *duces tecum*, that is, for documents, to Herman Santaria, at the post office box in Houston given as his address in the Lantana Gardens partnership agreement.

"Yes, that's right," he replied.

"Well," said Parker, "then I'm puzzled. I mean, I assume you know the subpoena is not valid, and that whether it is or it isn't, we should have had notice."

Parker had a junior partner and senior associate working with him in the cases. For him to make this call, his first personal communication ever with Jay, meant that the "Santaria family" had a lot of clout.

"Who's the lawyer in Houston?" Jay asked.

"His name is Reid McKenzie, but you haven't answered my question."

"You didn't ask a question." Jay was playing for time. He could think of no plausible excuse for taking a step that was in blatant violation of the New Jersey Court Rules, that is, serving a subpoena beyond the state's jurisdiction, by mail no less, and without notifying his adversaries.

"Look, Jay," said Parker, whose reputation as a stuffy but brilliant lawyer, still in his prime in his mid-fifties, Jay knew well. "People tell me you know what you're doing, so I don't believe it was incompetence or stupidity that prompted you, but I'm here to tell you that if it happens again, you will wish it didn't. They're talking about suing you right now, and going after your license."

"Nothing would come of that, John, you know that."

"Probably not," replied Parker, "but they sound like they would see it through, and in high style. You know the headache that would cause you."

"I made a mistake," said Jay.

"Yes," said Parker, "you did. I assume you thought they'd simply respond, like some country bumpkins."

Jay did not answer. He had not expected Herman Santaria to respond "like some country bumpkin" to his request for numerous documents, including all of the invoices and contracts relating to work done by H.S. Company for Lantana Gardens and the other three Texas properties owned and managed by Bryce Powers & Company. He thought it possible that Herman Santaria did not even exist.

"How did they get your name, John?" Jay asked.

"They called to retain me, actually, to quash the

subpoena, if that became necessary. I know Reid McKenzie from American Bar Association business. I told him I represented Chemical Bank in the case, and so couldn't handle a suit against you. I calmed him down, Jay. They need to know it won't happen again, that's all."

"It won't."

A pause ensued. Jay, his reputation in mind, would like to have told Parker why he sent the subpoena out. Actually, he hadn't been exactly sure why he had done it. Until now.

"Who's Herman Santaria?" Parker asked.

"He's a managing partner," Jay replied, "in one of Bryce Powers's properties in Texas, Lantana Gardens."

It was not hard for Jay to guess what Parker was thinking. Chemical Bank would be applying for a huge executor's commission when the Powers estate was ultimately settled, and would receive trustees fees many years into the future. Only two partnerships of a total of forty-four were involved in the current lawsuit. If any of the others were unhappy, if they had claims that had merit to them against Bryce Powers, the corpus of the estate could be substantially reduced, and Parker's client's cash flow with it.

"I'm sure you had your reasons, Jay," Parker said. "But I assume I am authorized to tell McKenzie that the subpoena was a mistake, and that it won't happen again. Am I right?"

"Yes, of course," Jay replied.

"Good," said Parker. "We've got enough on our hands, don't you think?"

"I do," said Jay.

Jay put the phone gently down onto its cradle, and slowly looked around his office. The legal files that needed attention in September were still lined up next to Kay Del Colliano's plant. Others were piled on each of the client chairs facing his desk, and more on a table under the window to his left. In front of him on his desk was the memo pad that Cheryl used to record his telephone messages, opened to the Thursday before. For a moment he could not remember the current day of the week, and then realized it was Friday. The top message on the pad was from an assistant county prosecutor asking him to call her back to discuss the possibility of a deal in a drug case he was handling. Cheryl had written "# 2" under it in parentheses. The next message was from a law clerk at the federal court in Newark telling him that the adjournment he had requested in a product liability case had been granted. Under this Cheryl had written "Notify client, expert, etc.?"

Earlier in the day, Danny's mother had called to tell Jay that the police were allowing access to Dan's office and apartment, and to ask him to go through both, and to do whatever had to be done to wind up Dan's affairs. Jay had quickly agreed. It would give him something to do. Looking at the barely touched law artifacts lying around his office, the irony of this thought had not escaped him, but subtleties, like irony, had not been very important to Jay in the last two months. His work ethic had turned out to be a fraud, betraying him when he needed it most. Although, thinking about the strangely menacing quality of the call from John Parker, the dormant lawyer in him stirred. Herman Santaria had something to hide, and had the juice, or thought he did, to keep it hidden.

Before leaving the office, Jay went online and Googled Reid McKenzie, who, he quickly found, was a name partner in Smith, Dillon & McKenzie, a Houston firm of some 430 attorneys, with offices in Dallas, Austin, and Mexico City.

12.
6:30 PM, August 25, 1991, Mexico City

Herman would have preferred to break Isabel gently into her new life. After all, she would be in it a long time. But Rafael, when he saw her in Herman's apartment the day she arrived from the convent, still wearing her school uniform—a pleated navy blue skirt, a white blouse, white socks, and penny loafers—was of a different mind. And why defy Rafael—a rising and brilliantly corrupt star in the PRI, the all-powerful Institutional Revolutionary Party—who would shepherd Herman's brother, Lazaro, an idealistic young lawyer, to the top or very near the top of the government? So near that Herman and Lazaro and their children and grandchildren and great grandchildren would never have to worry about money and all that it could buy.

Herman was also concerned for the girl, not that she would lose her innocence to a jaded, fifty-year-old politician, but because she was such an exotic flower, and might wilt and never recover from the shock of being fucked for the first time by Rafael, a pig who found his only sexual pleasure in brutal "love" with young girls, especially virgins when he could find them. They were partners, were they not, in the matter of Isabel, as they were in many other matters, and had they not spent good money in cultivating her from a seedling? But this argument, discreetly made, fell on ears made deaf by the drumbeat of lust.

Herman did defy his partner on one minor point. On the evening of her first "date" with Rafael, he tried to prepare Isabel for what lay ahead. He did this to give her some means of softening the blow she was about to receive. She was an incredible beauty, a treasure, but would be of no use to them if she broke down mentally and retreated into a more or less permanent state of semishock as he had seen some girls do in the same situation.

Rafael wanted to actually rape his virgins, and did not want them spoken to beforehand. Some, taken from the streets or from the dirt of the countryside, had felt some of the world's harshness and were able to recover, but others, from orphanages or bought from good peasant families, were mortally wounded in their spirit, and had to be disposed of. Herman did not want to lose Isabel to that fate, and so he sat her down in the living room of his spacious apartment overlooking Alameda Central—Mexico City's answer to Central Park—about an hour before his bodyguard, Stefan, was scheduled to take her to meet Rafael, and her destiny.

• • •

"Do you know what sex is, Isabel?"
"Yes."
"And love?"
"Yes."
"They are not the same, do you know that?"

Isabel did not answer. She was wearing blue jeans—her first pair—with white sandals, a shimmering silk blouse, a new bra, and tiny new panties, all purchased for her by Uncle Herman on a shopping trip he had taken her on earlier in the day. American jazz was coming softly from the apartment's hidden speakers. But the music was not soothing or distracting, and the new clothes were beginning to be not so exciting. Uncle Herman had insisted on watching her change into them.

"You are a very beautiful and desirable young woman, do you know that?"

"I am happy to be here."

"You will be meeting Senor de Leon tonight. Stefan will take you."

In the three days that Isabel had been living with Uncle Herman, there had been no mention of her working as a servant, or training as a nanny, as Sister Josefina had told her would be the case. There had been television and good food and an occasional exchange with Stefan—a dark and muscular giant—and then today's shopping, exhilarating until she was made to disrobe while Uncle Herman sat on her bed and watched, turning her this way and that with his hand from time to time.

"Rafael will have sex with you," Uncle Herman said. "It will hurt, and you will bleed, but it will not kill you. It happens to all young girls, it is how they become women."

Isabel knew that she had not sinned, had done nothing to earn the strange nauseating mix of fear and remorse churning in her stomach—nothing to offend God. And yet she must have offended Him, must have sinned, must be a truly bad person in the sight of all the saints and martyrs, and the Blessed Virgin, to whom she had promised her purity on many occasions. Otherwise how could she feel so evil, with such sickness in her heart? How could she be chosen to do a thing like lay in love with someone like Senor de Leon, who was old and smelled of cigars and whose thin lips seemed always to be wet with saliva?

"But you have already seen me," she said, raising her beautiful eyes to meet Herman's, hoping to find in them a reprieve from the vast emptiness that had so suddenly replaced all of her childish dreams and longings and complaints. "I would rather marry you."

"You will not marry Senor de Leon, Isabel."

"I know. I meant . . ." She could not find the words for what she meant, embarrassed, and shocked, that she had mentioned marriage.

"After tonight you will have sex with Rafael a few more times, and then no more. Soon, but not too soon, you will have sex with other men, at my command, and only at my command. You will live here for a while, but eventually you will have your own place. You will have beautiful clothes and money, all that you may need. You will work for me, and I will pay you and protect you. As long as you do as I say, you will come to no harm, you will have a good life, far better than most orphan children ever dream of. But if you defy me, or try to run away, I will find you and you will be hurt. Your face will be cut and your body. You will be killed."

Isabel took advantage of the one defense available only to children and the simpleminded: she put aside her pain, locked it away, and released the key into the cosmos. Herman—he was no longer Uncle Herman—had done her a favor, and on some unconscious level of her being, she knew that he had. He had allowed her to anesthetize herself against the deep wound that Rafael was about to inflict. Afterward, when the anesthesia wore off, she would find a way to deal with her new life. She would survive. She did not know— what child does?—that someday someone would pluck her cast-off key from the seemingly haphazard currents of the universe, insert it into her heart, and unlock her many secrets, down to the last one.

"Do you understand?" asked Herman. He had been intensely searching her face, thinking perhaps that she would cry, but she had already retreated into herself. She saw that he was pleased, and it occurred to her that there was safety in such retreat, survival.

"Yes."

"One last thing."

"Yes."

"Rafael will expect you to be surprised, unprepared. He does not know that I have spoken to you as I have. You must act accordingly."

Isabel stared into Herman's face and nodded, and by that nod, she made her alliance with evil, but what else could she do? Had not Herman betrayed Rafael in this small respect in order to help *her*? And would not this knowledge be an advantage to her someday, when she began to fill the place where her soul—now lost forever—used to be?

There was a knock, and the door that led to the kitchen and back rooms of the apartment swung open and Stefan entered the room. Dressed in the simple black suit, white shirt, and thin black tie of a livery driver, stalwart, of few words, Stefan gazed at his watch and said, "It is six thirty, senor, senorita."

13.
2:00 PM, December 5, 2004, Newark

It was good to see that the yellow crime scene tape, in the form of a large *X*, had finally been removed from Danny's office door. "No Danny," it said to Jay every day as he passed it on the way from the elevator to his own office. No Danny. No smiling face. No voice of irrational reason in a world filled with posers and bullshit artists of every stripe. No Danny.

The door was not locked. Inside, Jay first saw the three cardboard boxes sitting on his friend's cheap metal desk, then scanned the fifteen-foot-by-fifteen-foot one room, one closet office, and saw that Dan's pictures and college diploma were still on the walls, and his books still on the two small bookcases that flanked the desk. One of the pictures was of Jay and Dan sitting at a fire on a beach at the Jersey shore, the light from the flames dancing in their eyes as they smiled at the camera. The picture of his two sons that Dan kept on the top of the filing cabinet behind his desk was not there, but Jay expected to find it somewhere in the office.

Taking a deep breath, he sat in the tired leather armchair behind Dan's desk and confronted the boxes. On top of the middle box was a Seizure/Return notice from the Essex County Prosecutor's Office, indicating the date the enclosed materials had been taken, the date they were returned, and the word *Zero* under the heading *Items Retained*. The "enclosed material" had been crammed randomly into the boxes, and the first thing Jay did was separate the contents into three piles: client files, banking, and miscellaneous. It did not surprise him that there was no Donna Kelly among the fifty or so client files. Most of Danny's client information he kept on scraps of paper that he threw away as soon as the case was over. Really important data made its way into the small address and date book that he kept with him at all times, and which was not, according to Dan's mom, among the items sent north by the Florida police. There was no record of a recent deposit of twenty-five thousand among the banking documents, some pages of which seemed to be missing, which was not unusual for Dan, who looked on record keeping as something people took much too seriously.

Dan's business account had just under two hundred dollars in it. He had no receivables, and bills due totaling around two thousand dollars, including two months' rent at six hundred per month. Jay closed up the boxes, sat back, and lit a cigarette. It was a cold, damp Sunday afternoon. Below him, Market Street, raucous during the week, was quiet. Before leaving, he went through the closet, the filing cabinet, and the desk, where, in a bottom drawer, he found the framed picture of Dan's boys—Dan, Jr. and Michael—wearing Yankee caps, smiling shyly at the camera. The glass facing was cracked diagonally. As Jay began to remove the photograph, he felt the cardboard backing begin to move and, slipping it from the cheap metal frame, he found a thick envelope between it and the boys' picture. In the envelope was eleven thousand dollars in cash, in hundred dollar bills, and a piece of lined notepaper, on which was written, in Danny's handwriting, "If you find this, give it to my boys. *Don't* pay my debts with it." Smiling, Jay put the envelope in his jeans pocket, and the picture in one of the boxes.

He loaded the boxes, wall hangings, and books into his Saab, and headed to the Colonnade Towers, twin, glass-skinned high-rises only a mile or two away, built at the edge of Jay and Dan's old neighborhood after the Newark riots. He parked in the underground garage, rode the elevator to the tenth floor of Building A, and let himself into Danny's apartment with the key given to him by Mrs. Del Colliano. Leaving the door open—the apartment was hot and stuffy—he went around opening windows and drawing curtains, and then sat in an overstuffed chair and looked through the living room's glass wall down into a section of Branch Brook Park that contained an old-fashioned circular reservoir, empty since before he was born, where he and Danny had played endlessly as boys. His reverie was broken by a deep voice, quite nearby.

"Excuse me, young man, do I know you?"

"I don't think so," said Jay, getting to his feet. "Are you Bill Davis? I'm Jay Cassio, Danny's friend."

Jay's interrogator, a black man in his sixties, with short salt-and-pepper hair—more salt than pepper—and a thick, neatly trimmed mustache of the same mix, said nothing. About six feet tall, wearing a dark cardigan sweater buttoned over a substantial potbelly, he stood in the doorway and stared at Jay, whose appearance, he suddenly realized, was not one to inspire confidence. Sleeping badly, if at all, of late, going days between shaves and showers, his hair longer than usual, there was a mad look to him that he now saw reflected in Davis's wary eyes.

"I'm a lawyer," Jay said, reaching for his wallet to produce one of his cards. "Dan's mother asked me to handle his estate. All this stuff will have to be sold or given away."

They both looked slowly around the apartment, at the open, well stocked kitchen—Danny was a great cook—the comfortable living room, the Persian rug beneath Jay's feet, the television and stacks of magazines and books, the artwork on the walls—Danny's home—and then back at each other.

"Didn't I see you at the wake?" Jay asked.

"I was there."

The black man took the card from Jay, read it, and then walked over and extended his hand.

"I'm Bill Davis," he said. "I'm sorry to be so stiff, but it's not every day your neighbor is murdered, with people traipsing in and out at all hours."

"The cops, you mean?"

"How about I stand you a drink, Mr. Cassio? You look like you could use it."

"Call me Jay."

"Jay."

"Sure."

"Is bourbon okay?"

"A little ice."

Davis left and returned a few minutes later with a bottle of Jack Daniel's and two cut crystal rocks glasses, one with ice in it. He sat on the couch, placed the bottle and glasses on the coffee table in front of him, and poured three fingers neat for himself and a healthy splash for Jay, who had returned to his easy chair.

"So how did you know my name?" Davis asked, reaching with his glass to touch Jay's.

"Danny mentioned you moved in over the summer."

"He brought me a bottle of bourbon as a welcome."

Jay did not respond.

"We're drinking the last of it."

"I saw you with your wife at the wake," Jay said. "I'm sorry if I scared you."

"You didn't scare me, but a couple of others have."

"What do you mean?"

"There were two punks here," Davis said. "Mexicans, I think. I was coming back with groceries. The police tape was down, so I pushed the door in, like a fool."

"When was this?"

"Couple of weeks ago."

"Dan owed a shylock some money."

"How much?"

"A few grand."

"These were no collectors of a few grand. They were reptiles."

"What did they say?"

"They were looking for Danny's girlfriend."

"He didn't have a girlfriend."

"A beautiful Mexican woman. They showed me her picture."

"Had you seen her before?"

"Never."

"What did she look like?"

"Long, dark hair. Beautiful face. She looked like Sophia Loren. They don't come more beautiful than that."

"How old?"

"Mid-twenties."

"How old were these two guys? What did they look like?"

"The same, mid-twenties. They might have been twins, shiny black hair, swarthy. Eyes like snakes. They said the girl was their sister. They hadn't seen her for a few weeks. They were worried about her."

"Did you get their names?"

"You must be kidding."

"Do you have the picture?"

"They never let go of it."

"Did you call the police?"

"Of course, and who shows up but the FBI. Special Agent Chris Markey."

Jay had not been convinced that the two Mexicans Davis described were quite as scary as they appeared to the old man, nor that they were involved with Danny in anything but one of his low-grade schemes. Possibly Danny had hired them to dump a car for a friend, and they were looking to collect their fee. Possibly they didn't know he was dead and were looking to buy, or sell, some dope. But the FBI was not interested in small-time insurance fraud, or the occasional five hundred dollar marijuana deal. They investigated interstate criminal activity and crimes under federal law. How did Danny's death, and these two Mexicans, fit into that?

"What did he want?"

"He asked a lot of questions, the same as you."

"Did these guys kill Danny?"

"He didn't say, but he showed me pictures, and it was them."

"Did they threaten you?"

"No, but one of them had a gun."

"He pulled it?"

"No. His jacket slipped open and I saw it in his belt. To me they were stone killers. Dead inside."

"Did Markey leave his number?"

"I have it in my apartment. I'll give it to you before you leave. Another drink?"

"Sure."

Davis poured, and then said, "What was it you were looking at so intently when I came in?"

Jay sipped his drink. From where they were sitting they could both see clearly into the park below.

"See that dried-up reservoir down there?" Jay said. "Danny and I played there when we were kids. It was our private Coliseum. We used sticks for swords, and garbage can tops for shields. We would approach each other from opposite ends. I could always hear the crowd cheering wildly. The emperor didn't know I was his bastard son. We pummeled each other. I was taller, bigger, but it didn't matter. It was impossible to get him to quit. Sometimes he won because I could no longer lift my arms. On the rare days when I got him to cry uncle, he would get up and smile as he dusted himself off, and I always wondered if he was letting me win . . ."

Jay stopped himself, embarrassed, and looked over at Davis, who was staring down at the reservoir, caressing his glass.

"This neighborhood has changed, Jay."

"The whole city has."

"Dan had to have a lot of balls," Davis said. "He was the only white guy in either building, and most of us blacks are afraid to go out at night."

"The rent was cheap," Jay replied, "and he grew up here. He felt he had a right to come back. And he wasn't afraid of the things you and I are afraid of."

"I'm sorry you lost your friend."

"Thanks. And thanks for the drink. You were right. I needed it."

14.
7:00 PM, December 7, 2004, Montclair

Jay spent two hours in Dan's apartment making a list of its contents for Kay Del Colliano. At home he opened his own bottle of bourbon and drank until, unnoticed, night fell and he was asleep on the couch in his living room. The next morning, at his office, he called Linda Marshall, the *Newark Star-Ledger* reporter. He told her about his talk with Bill Davis, and asked her if she felt it was worth a call to the FBI to find out if they were in fact investigating Danny's death, and if so, why.

Jay had seen Linda at Danny's wake, where he had related to her Danny's story of Donna Kelly and the five hundred thousand dollars that was an obvious link between Dan's murder and the deaths of Bryce and Kate Powers. Linda had written a story in which she related the reasons for Dan's trip to Florida, attributing her facts to an unnamed, nongovernment source, and questioning the quick labeling of the Powers deaths as murder-suicide. The story noted that the prosecutor's office had refused comment, except to say that the case had been thoroughly investigated and closed on solid scientific grounds.

When Jay's former law partner, Dick Mahoney, was under indictment eight years ago, Marshall had written a story recounting Mahoney's lawyer's claim that Jay had been the one who had offered the bribe to the state trooper. This was ridiculous on its face since the trooper had been wired and had identified Mahoney as the briber. Marshall had made it clear that the accusation was absurd, but the story had nevertheless angered Jay, and he had let the reporter know it when he saw her a few days later in the courthouse, one of her regular beats. When Mahoney abandoned the claim at his trial, Linda wrote a story condemning both Mahoney and his lawyer, in which quotes from Al Garland, calling them "artists of deception" and "frauds upon the court" appeared prominently. Jay took her out to dinner to thank her, and to apologize for his earlier outburst—he had called her naive and a hack, easily used by Mahoney's lawyer to sow confusion.

They had been friends ever since. Now married with two small children, juggling a career and a family, Marshall was well respected for her fair and thorough reporting, and had twice been nominated by her paper for Pulitzer Prizes for investigative series she had done. She said she would be happy to check the story out.

Jay was at home, having Jack Daniel's on the rocks for dinner, when Linda called him back.

"Jay? It's Linda."

"Hi. That was quick."

"It doesn't take long to get a flat denial."

"They denied it?"

"Yes."

"Who'd you speak to?"

"I asked for Markey. A PR person called me back."

"And said what?"

"'The FBI is not investigating the murder of Mr. Del Colliano.'"

"What did you say?"

"I told her that I had it from a reliable source that they were, that in fact Special Agent Chris Markey of the Newark Field Office was working on it."

"And?"

"She said my source is wrong."

"You didn't mention Bill Davis."

"No, you told me not to."

"Did you talk to Davis?"

"Yes, he confirmed it."

"You didn't believe me?"

"I had to get a confirmation, Jay. Don't get testy on me."

"Now what?"

"I'm writing a story for tomorrow's paper relating all this, and again raising the issue of the connection between the Powers deaths and Danny's killing."

"Good. I have something else for you. Bryce Powers worked in Mexico City in the seventies. He was in charge of commercial development for an international real estate company, Gentex. Now two Mexicans show up at Danny's apartment."

"Is Gentex still in business?"

"Yes."

"Anything else?"

"It has to be off the record."

"Sure."

"Kate Powers wrote me a bunch of letters telling me that Bryce was bribing government officials in Mexico, and that he had close ties to some big-time drug dealers."

"Do the police know this?"

"I don't think so. My file was returned by one of Judge Moran's court officers. It didn't even look like it was opened."

"Why do you want this off the record?"

"Because I represent the daughters in lawsuits against them and the estate. Any damage to Powers's reputation would hurt my clients."

"Did you use the letters in court in the divorce?"

"No."

"Who was your adversary?"

"Bob Flynn."

"Does he know?"

"I told him about them, but I didn't send him copies."

"Why not?"

"I wasn't going to use them in the case. Kate wasn't in her right mind. She was drunk most of the time, and drugged out. I thought the letters were worthless."

"Can I call Flynn?"

"I'd rather leave him out of it."

"Okay, he's out of it."

Even if Linda confirmed the existence of the letters via Bob Flynn, Jay would still be her original source. To his relief, she clearly understood that he could not let her make an end run around his ethics issue.

"I'll have to use your name, though, Jay," she continued, "regarding the FBI's involvement. I already talked to my editor. The story needs credibility, especially since I'm naming Markey and quoting the FBI's denial. I'm identifying Davis, but that won't be enough against the word of the FBI."

"Did you clear that with Davis?"

"Yes. Those two Mexicans scared him, and he feels like he's being a good citizen in helping to track them down. Plus, he really liked Danny."

"Who didn't?"

"Can I use your name?"

"Of course."

"What will you do with them? The letters?"

"First I have to get rid of Melissa and Marcy as clients. They're making me sick."

"Your judgment is no longer being clouded by lust."

"Right."

"Then what?"

"I'm not sure. Maybe I'll give Agent Markey a call."

"Can I see the letters, off the record for now?"

"Stop by my office tomorrow. And one last thing."

"Yes?"

"If you win a Pulitzer Prize on this, then all comments about my relationship with Melissa Powers have to stop. Is that a deal?"

"That's a deal. One last thing."

"Shoot."

"Does Frank Dunn know about any of this?"

"I've told him about the letters, but not my talk with Bill Davis."

Jay looked down at his drink, which he had stopped sipping during his conversation with Linda, and which was now mostly melted ice. After a couple of nights of quiet and murderous drinking with the detective, Jay had stopped returning Dunn's calls, and avoided the places where he might run into him. Dunn and Danny respected each other's nerve, realistic take on life, and intolerance of phonies, but there was also a natural tension between them that did not take too long to spring up when they were in each other's presence. Danny's cockiness irritated Dunn, and Dunn's secretiveness irritated Danny. They often provoked each other to anger while Jay watched, trying not to smile. Next to Jay, Dunn probably knew—and loved—Dan as well as anyone, and it occurred to him now, for the first time since Dan's death, that Dunn had sustained a loss, too, and that *he* possibly needed comforting. God placed self-pity, it has been said, next to despair, the cure beside the malady.

"Jay?" Linda's voice came to him over the wire.

"Yes?"

"How are you?"

"I'm okay, Linda. I'm getting better."

15.
6:00 PM, December 8, 2004, Newark

Frank Dunn had not been involved in the hands-on investigation of the Powers case. That had been conducted by the two homicide detectives attached to Al Garland. But he had talked to them, and he had read the file, and he was not comfortable with the rapidly reached conclusion of murder-suicide. Normally he would not care, especially in a case involving the death of two rich socialites. But the Powers murder-suicide was linked, via Donna Kelly, to the torture and death of Frank's friend, Dan Del Colliano. And so he took an interest. Naturally, he related Jay Cassio's account of Donna Kelly, her cash, and her hiring of Danny, to Ralph Greco, the detective in charge of the case, the obvious point being: where there is five hundred thousand in cash floating around, there is a motive to murder. Greco took a statement from Jay, but was not inclined to reopen the case.

On the surface, Greco's reasons were sound. There was no sign of forced entry into the Powers house; they had found a bloody kitchen knife with Bryce's fingerprints on it; Kate's headless body had been found in her bed, the sheets a bloody mess; Bryce's body had been found slumped at his desk, his insulin paraphernalia and hypodermic needle nearby; the autopsy on Kate's body had revealed traces of the antidepressants Prozac and Haldol, as well as a very high blood-alcohol level.

Greco and his team quickly discovered that Mesa Associates had been losing money. They knew about the contentious divorce. They surmised that Bryce had found Kate passed out, as usual, in her bed, had beheaded her, driven to the river, only a few miles from their home, dropped the head in, returned, and calmly injected himself with five hundred cc's of insulin, enough to kill an elephant. Yes, they had found some cash deposits in some of Bryce Powers & Company's banking records, but didn't tenants frequently pay their rent in cash, especially garden apartment tenants?

In Florida, Danny had last been seen by the clerk at the South Miami Beach Motor Hotel when he checked in, alone, on the night he was killed. His body had been found the next morning by a cleaning woman. There were no prints in the room that matched anything on record, and no one had heard or seen anything unusual. Seven Donna Kellys were listed in the phone books for the Dade and Broward County area, but none matched Danny's description. There was no record of a Donna Kelly working currently or in the past for any of Bryce Powers's companies or properties.

The Miami Beach PD's working theory was that Danny was carrying stolen drug money and had been killed by its rightful owners, with a little torture thrown in to see if they could find out who he was working for. But, with no description of the killer or killers, no weapon, and no leads of any kind, a quick resolution was not likely.

The Florida findings Frank learned from his friend, Angelo Perna, who had been advised of the status of the case by his contact, a homicide detective at the Miami Police Department. One thing that Angelo told Frank intrigued him, that is, that the FBI had taken an interest in the crime, that a Special Agent Chris Markey had reinterviewed the clerk at the hotel, and even visited Jupiter, where Danny, because of his postcard to Jay, was known to have been.

Now Frank reads in the paper that the same Agent Markey is investigating Dan's murder in Jersey, looking for "two swarthy young Mexican men"—who he has photographs of—and that Jay Cassio is the person who has uncovered this. Frank had been in law enforcement long enough to know that the FBI would be furious that such information had been disclosed to the public without its consent. Sipping his scotch at his usual back booth at the Colonial, the *Star-Ledger* opened to Linda Marshall's bylined article, on the table in front of him, Frank was fairly certain that the FBI, whose denial he did not believe for a second, had made a major mistake in not talking to Marshall. It was always a pleasure to see them suffer, especially when it was their own arrogance that brought them low.

• • •

Lost in his thoughts, reading his paper, Frank barely looked up when Jay Cassio sat down across from him, a scotch over ice in his hand. Frank continued to read the paper. He looked at Jay a couple of times, but otherwise just read and sipped his drink and smoked his cigarette. The minutes passed. Finally Jay touched his glass against Frank's and said "Your enthusiasm is overwhelming."

"Always a pleasure to pass the time of day with you, Jay," Frank said. "What's on your mind?"

"Nothing, what's on yours?"

"I was thinking," Frank replied, "of how pissed off Special Agent Chris Markey is at you at this moment."

"He should have spoken to Linda," said Jay. "He could have spun it his own way."

"They don't like it when their mistakes are made public."

"It's good to know they're doing something."

"That I agree with."

Jay took a sip of his drink and remained silent.

"Al Garland wasn't too happy, either," Frank said.

"You talked to him?"

"Early this morning."

"What did he say?"

"He says you're a troublemaker and a wise guy. He was trying to be calm, but you could see his eyes starting to bulge."

"What's his problem?"

"Markey, probably."

"Speak of the devil," said Jay, looking over Frank's shoulder. Al Garland, lanky, wearing thick glasses, an ex-Marine still with a military haircut, approached and stood in front of the booth.

"Jay, Frank," Garland said, nodding to each of them. "Can I join you?"

"Sure," Frank answered, sliding over to make room for his boss.

"You want a drink, Al?" Jay asked.

"No, I can't stay."

"So how are you?" Jay asked the prosecutor, eying him across the table. "I haven't seen you since the wake."

"I'm good," Garland replied, "but I don't like the article in the paper today."

"Why not?"

"It's obvious you called Linda Marshall."

"The last time I checked it wasn't a crime to talk to a reporter in this country."

"It makes you look bad," Garland said, "like you're trying to stir up trouble."

"Is the FBI investigating Danny's murder?"

"They say they're not. I believe them."

"Al, we know each other a long time," Jay said. "Don't bullshit me. Up or down, yes or no, you'd know if they were on the case."

Frank Dunn had worked for Al Garland for five years. The brunt, on several occasions, of the prosecutor's wicked temper, he was expecting it to flare now, and would not be unhappy if it did. A good melee, he had always felt, was the equal only of a good drunk when it came to clearing a troubled head. Taken together they worked wonders. He was surprised therefore at the tone and substance of Garland's reply.

"I didn't come over here to argue with you," Garland said. "I came over to ask you, as a favor, not to call any more reporters. You're involved with the estate, you're representing the Powers sisters. If you come across anything in either case, call me, don't go to the papers."

"You're patronizing me, Al," Jay replied. "I can't believe it."

"I'm not," Garland answered. "You've got it wrong."

"I'll tell you what," Jay said, "you give me your word that the Powers case is closed, and that the FBI isn't working on Danny's case, and I'll promise to come to you with anything I come across."

"The Powers case," Garland promptly replied, "is closed, and as far as I know the FBI is not working on Danny's case."

Jay sat back in his seat, his body language very open and innocent, and nodded.

"Is that good enough?" Garland asked as he rose to leave.

"Of course," Jay answered.

"The new Al Garland," Jay said after the prosecutor left.

"You pushed him pretty hard," said Frank.

"I wanted to see how far up Agent Markey's ass he was."

"Pretty far, it seems."

"I'm sorry you were in the middle like that."

"Don't worry about it."

"You work for the guy."

"I'm thinking of quitting."

"Quitting? Why?"

"I spoke to Lorrie today. She says the kitchen knife *could* have been the murder weapon, but she thinks it was something heavier and sharper. A machete maybe."

"Did she tell that to Garland?"

"Yes, but he wasn't interested. He says it's speculation. He knows you can't take castings if the entire head is severed."

"He's probably right."

"That's not all Lorrie had to say. She did a liver stick on both bodies. She says they died within minutes of each other."

"Is she sure?"

"The numbers don't lie."

"What did Al say to that?"

"He said he'd think about reopening the case, but that was two months ago."

"Why did she wait so long to tell you?"

"She knew how I felt about the case. She was afraid I would do something rash."

Frank could see that Jay was having trouble covering up his astonishment at hearing him mention Lorrie Cohen, the Essex County Medical Examiner, who Frank had been having an extramarital affair with for the past five years. He assumed that people knew of the affair, but he had never mentioned Lorrie to his friends. This was as close as he had ever come to acknowledging the relationship.

"Maybe Garland is working the case secretly," Jay said.

"I don't think so," Frank answered. "Ralph Greco just got back from a two week trip to Italy."

"We could call Linda Marshall."

"We can't. It would lead back to Lorrie. She'd lose her job, her pension."

"That leaves the FBI."

"Right."

"I could call Agent Markey," said Jay. "I've got the letters. It's my civic duty."

"You just told Al Garland you'd go through him."

"Fuck Al Garland."

"If you say so."

"There's one more thing."

"What?"

Frank listened carefully as Jay told him about Herman Santaria, the bogus subpoena he had served, and the high-powered, almost menacing response it had drawn.

"Jesus," Frank said when Jay was finished.

"Maybe Angelo Perna can get a line on Santaria," said Jay.

"And get himself killed for asking."

"Are you serious?"

"I am," Frank replied. "Why didn't you tell me about this Santaria character sooner?"

"I did it on a whim," said Jay. "I didn't expect any response at all."

"The response could have been a bullet to your head."

"Fuck."

"Stop with the whims. We're not playing chess here."

"What's got into you?"

"Jay, let me give you my take on this. I've been thinking about it hard since I read Linda's story. Powers's career is not what it appears to be. Let's say he acquires some nasty partners along the way. Let's say he starts stealing from them, or they think he does, which amounts to the same thing. They behead his wife, while he watches, but he doesn't tell them what they want to hear, like *where's our money?* So they kill him, which they would have done, anyway. Donna Kelly, who he's probably fucking, is holding some of the stolen loot. She hires Danny to help her get away with it, but somehow Danny's caught and killed. She gets away, which looks suspicious to me, like maybe she set Danny up.

"Now you tell me about the Santaria family. Isn't that what Parker said, 'the Santaria family'? Not, 'Herman Santaria'; 'the *Santaria family.*' That sounds mafialike to me. They're probably big-time drug dealers in Mexico and Central America. They're Powers's nasty *partners*. But he fucks them, and they kill him, and Danny gets caught in the crossfire, the poor bastard. So this is who you, bright young guy that you are, *serve a subpoena on*. You're lucky, Jay. They think you're ignorant, that you're just looking for records in some dumb-ass lawsuit in New Jersey. If they thought otherwise, they wouldn't have been so polite about the way they threatened you. If you surface again, they'll put two and two together, and they'll come after you."

"I *have* surfaced again," Jay said. "I was on page three of the *Ledger* today, talking about two Mexicans caught in Danny's apartment."

"Do you have someplace you can stay for a few nights?"

"I'm staying in my own house."

"Well then stay off the booze, and the Valium, or whatever it is you're taking. You need to be alert."

"What are you talking about?"

"It's pretty obvious, Jay."

It had also been obvious to Frank that Jay had been

avoiding him, which ordinarily would have been acceptable, as it was his view that most of what the world called suffering was not suffering at all but just life, and was best dealt with alone and in silence. He had stepped out of character in his attempts to *be there*—a phrase he hated—for Jay, which for the most part meant a night of drinking and passing out, but even he, with a terrible marriage and no kids, had Lorrie. Jay had no one.

"What about Santaria?" Jay asked.

"I'll take care of it."

"How?"

"Dick Mahoney owes me a favor. His wiseguy friends will tell us who Santaria is."

"What are we doing, Frank?"

"*We're* not doing anything. *You're* going back to your law practice, and your life. I'm going to get to the bottom of this, and then I'm going to shove it up Al Garland's ass."

"What does Angelo Perna say?" Jay asked.

"Perna doesn't smell any rats."

"In Miami. But you do here."

"All over the place."

"That's not unusual for you."

"They're coming out of the woodwork."

"So you'll talk to Mahoney?"

"Yes. He's at the bar right now, with Bob Flynn. He must have slipped in while I was unnecessarily listening to you. When's the last time *you* spoke to him?"

"Five years ago."

"How do you manage that?"

"We avoid each other."

"I hear he's doing well, for a rat-bastard."

"I'm not surprised."

16.
3:00 PM, December 9, 2004, Newark

On his way into work the next morning, Jay stopped at his bank and put the originals of Kate Powers's letters in his safe-deposit box. The day before he had made copies for Linda Marshall, who had stopped by to pick them up, and who had repeated her promise to keep them off the record until she heard otherwise from Jay.

At the office, Jay called the FBI in Newark and asked to speak with Agent Chris Markey. He was run around a bit, but eventually spoke with Agent Phil Gatti. Jay told Gatti that he had information concerning the Del Colliano investigation in Florida and the Powers investigation in Jersey. Gatti, irritated at Jay's refusal to speak with anyone except Markey, took Jay's name and number, but did not say whether Markey, or anyone else, would get back to him.

That afternoon Jay was working at his desk when Cheryl came into his office to tell him that an Agent Chris Markey of the FBI was in the waiting room and wondered if he could have a word with him. Markey, blue-suited, trim, a flinty fiftyish, took one of the two client chairs facing Jay's desk after Cheryl showed him in and he and Jay had shaken hands. Jay sat back in his swivel chair, but before he did he looked out of the window behind him and saw that the afternoon sky was darkening and that snow was beginning to fall.

There were no preliminaries.

"How's your ex-partner, Dick Mahoney, doing?" asked Markey. "Still representing the boys?"

"You'd know more about that than I would," was Jay's answer.

"You represented Kate Powers, I take it," said Markey. "And now the daughters."

"Right." Jay did not feel he needed to mention that he had called Melissa and Marcy the day before and asked them to get a new lawyer. They were model clients and they had promptly paid their first bill—six thousand dollars and change—but his conspiracy with Linda Marshall could be damaging to Bryce Powers's reputation—now hanging by a thread—and, more significantly, it could jeopardize the assets of the Powers estate, assets that would ultimately belong to the girls. In other words he was now working against the interests of his own clients, a very bad thing for a lawyer to do, hence his quick decision and call yesterday.

"How are they doing, the daughters?" Markey asked.

"Do you know them?"

"No," Markey replied, "but I know of them."

"They're doing okay."

"We've been sent a copy of the lawsuit against them."

"I'm not surprised."

The lawyer representing Plaza I and II had threatened several times to file criminal complaints against Marcy and Melissa—their phony maintenance contracts were in fact vehicles for stealing money from the partners—unless Jay acted to settle the civil case quickly. The girls indeed had no viable defense, and Jay had recommended they settle, but, headstrong, greedy, and thinking themselves clever, they had insisted on letting the case play itself out.

"He just wants you to collect his clients' money for him," Jay said. "I'm sure you've got better things to do."

"Maybe, maybe not."

Jay did not respond. Markey's tone of voice was disdainful. It reminded Jay of Frank Dunn, but without the humanizing touches of alcoholism and illicit sex. He wondered if Markey knew about his affair with Melissa Powers, and was certain, if he did know, of the judgments he would make. Human weakness, according to his friend Francis X. Dunn, was a euphemism for old-fashioned sin. What were Markey's weaknesses? What sins was he concealing beneath the tough-guy, sneering facade he was showing Jay?

"So what is it you wanted to tell me?" Markey asked.

"What's the status of your investigation?" Jay replied.

"What investigation are you talking about?"

"Dan Del Colliano."

"What was his relation to you?"

"We were good friends."

"Did you know he was six months behind in his child support?"

Jay took his time answering. In ten minutes, Markey had made three implied threats: one, by referring to Dick Mahoney, he let it be known that he could reach into Jay's past and stir up trouble if necessary; two, although Jay knew that the Powers girls could have criminal problems, a *federal* prosecution was a surprise. His very unprofessional link to Melissa Powers would be something that the United States Attorney's Office in Newark would not hesitate to use to its advantage if it could; and three, by mentioning Danny's child support problems Markey was saying, in effect, that he could smear Danny publicly if he had to.

"Dan took care of his kids," Jay finally said.

Markey did not reply. He got up and walked to the wall to his right, and looked at a framed picture hanging there: a line drawing of Jay catching a pass, done by an artist for the *Newark Star-Ledger* in 1979, when Jay had been named New Jersey schoolboy football player of the year by the paper.

"We have something in common, Jay," said Markey, turning toward him.

"What's that?" said Jay.

"My daughter died in a plane crash two years ago. She was seventeen. I'd hate for us to be adversaries."

A pause followed this statement, in which Jay could feel the quickening of his heartbeat. Nothing he had ever been able to do or say or think had succeeded in preventing the visual of his parents' last moments from appearing unbidden, and often unprovoked, in his mind. This time of course it had been provoked and, it seemed, provoked deliberately.

"Why should we be adversaries?" Jay asked, looking Markey squarely in the eye, keeping his voice steady.

"What is it you want to tell me?"

"First I need to know the status of the investigation."

"How did you get my name?"

"I got it from Bill Davis."

"I don't know a Bill Davis."

"I talked to the guy. He described you. He says you were in his apartment."

"I read that in the paper, but it's not true. If you want, we can call Davis now, and he can confirm that he was mistaken."

"Look, Agent Markey," said Jay, "I'm sure you have your reasons for denying your involvement, but I'm not asking for any information that might be confidential. I just want to know if your office is investigating Danny's murder. I think I'm entitled to know that."

"First I have to have your information."

Jay said nothing.

"It's not a good idea for a private citizen to pursue a murder investigation," Markey continued.

"Is that my civics lesson for today?"

"It could lead to a federal prosecution."

"That's refreshing," said Jay. "An explicit threat."

Before leaving, Markey presented Jay with a search warrant for the *Powers v. Powers* file, which Jay handed to him without a fuss. He had a copy of the entire file at home, and Kate Powers's letters he would give to Markey when he felt like it, if ever.

17.
3:30 PM, December 9, 2004, Newark

When Markey left, Cheryl buzzed Jay to tell him that a Fran Kaplan had called—identifying herself as Melissa and Marcy Powers's new lawyer—and asked that Jay call her. Jay looked Kaplan up in his Lawyer's Diary, a directory listing all of the attorneys practicing in New Jersey, and saw that she was with Chandler and Roth, one of the state's handful of three-hundred-plus-lawyer megafirms. He went through the switchboard, her secretary, and her paralegal before being allowed to speak to her.

"Mr. Cassio," Kaplan said, "thank you for returning my call. I was retained this morning by Marcy and Melissa Powers."

"Good. I'm sure they'll be in good hands. You want my file, I take it?"

"Yes. Can I send somebody to pick it up this afternoon?"

"Tomorrow morning would be better. I need to copy it, and do a final bill."

"Fine. Can I ask a couple of questions?"

"Sure."

"Can you tell me your reasons for not wanting to handle the case any longer?"

Kaplan's tone had been cool but civil, but now Jay

detected a change in her attitude, as if she expected a confrontation.

"A good friend of mine was killed," Jay said, "while working for a woman who claimed to be connected to Bryce Powers."

"Right, I read about that in the paper. How is that a conflict for you?"

"I explained all this to Melissa and Marcy."

"They're confused, so I'd appreciate it if you'd explain it to me."

"The conflict was emotional, not legal. There were too many reminders of my friend's murder."

"You represented Kate Powers in the divorce?"

"I did."

"Did Marcy and Melissa come up?'

"Their phony contracts with Plaza I and Plaza II came up."

"Phony contracts? They tell me they operated legitimate cleaning service companies."

Jay did not respond. Having been educated, by Jay, about the extreme weakness of their case, Melissa and Marcy had apparently lied to their new attorney about their nonexistent role in the "cleaning service companies" set up by Bryce as covers for paying their personal living expenses. Kaplan would, he was certain, learn about the true character of her clients in due course.

"I have to tell you," said Kaplan, "Marcy and Melissa feel abandoned and betrayed. They don't understand your reasons for dropping the case, and neither do I, frankly, given the fact that your friend died three months ago. Marcy thinks it has something to do with your relationship with her younger sister. They're thinking of filing an ethics complaint against you."

"You sound," Jay said, "like you've made a huge commitment to two people you just met this morning, but you wouldn't be the first one to buy their lies. They package them well. In a month or two you'll know what I mean. They'll probably file an ethics complaint against *you* if you lose the case. Is there anything else?"

"One more thing."

"What's that?"

"Melissa tells me her mother wrote you some letters. Is that true?"

"Yes."

"Then I'd like copies of them."

"They're not relevant to the claims against the girls."

"I'd like to make my own judgment on that."

"I can't give you copies without the permission of Jack Phillips."

"Who's Jack Phillips?"

"The conservator of the Powers estate. The letters weren't sent to me personally. They were sent to me as part of a lawsuit. The file I kept in that lawsuit would have belonged to Kate Powers. Now that she's dead, it would be part of her estate, which is under the control of Jack Phillips."

"I talked to John Parker today. He knows nothing about these letters."

"Why should he?"

"Chemical Bank is the executor of the estate."

"Talk to Judge Moran about that. He appointed Phillips."

Jay hung up, and almost immediately Cheryl buzzed to tell him that Linda Marshall was waiting for him on hold.

"Hi," he said after picking up the phone.

"How are you?" Linda asked.

"I'm fine."

"Anybody pissed at you?"

"Al Garland, Melissa and Marcy Powers and their new lawyer, and Agent Markey, who just executed a search warrant for the Powers divorce file."

"Anybody else?"

"That's it for today. What's up?"

"The paper got a call from the Justice Department today. We need to talk."

"As in the *United States* Justice Department?"

"Yes. Can you meet me at the Spanish Tavern at six?"

"Sure."

"I'll see you then."

18.
6:00 PM, December 9, 2004, Newark

Newark tried to dress itself up for the holidays, but it did not have the money for good clothes or accessories; the generic, politically correct decorations along Broad Street only served to deepen Jay's dark mood as he drove through spitting snow and rain to his meeting with Linda Marshall. The Ironbound section of the city, home to the Spanish Tavern and many other Hispanic and Portuguese restaurants and bars, was a ray of hope. Bound by railroads on four sides, no public housing was built in this tightly packed neighborhood, and thus it had gotten sick in the seventies and eighties but did not die, and was now beginning to recover on its own. The Tavern had started out as a railroad-car–shaped bar, and then expanded to include twenty or so tables and a kitchen that served good, hot Spanish and Portuguese food until the early hours of the morning. Despite the weather, or maybe because of it, the place was quietly busy, with blue-collar men mingling with professional types having a drink at the bar after work and families having dinner.

Jay made his way through the bar and spotted Linda at a table along the back wall of the dining room. He stopped for a second before going over to her. She was a good-looking woman, a few years younger than him, with a head of lustrous chestnut hair, and frank, luminous brown eyes. Her body had thickened a bit over the years, but he could see that under her tailored business suit she was all woman. He could not remember exactly when he had stopped thinking that he could find such a woman—pretty, intelligent, with a good heart—for himself, but he had, and the thought did not lighten his mood.

"You're late," Linda said after Jay had taken off his coat and scarf and sat down across from her.

"It's bad out there," Jay replied.

"Did you come right from the office?"

"No, I had to run an errand first."

"I ordered you a Glenlivet on the rocks. I just got here myself."

"Perfect," Jay said.

"I read the letters," said Linda. "They're pretty juicy."

"She was stoned, don't forget."

"If one tenth of it is true, then I can see why Bryce Powers would find himself murdered one day."

"Are they in a safe place?" Jay asked. "The letters?"

"Yes."

Their drinks arrived—club soda for Linda—and they both sipped.

"So? The Justice Department," Jay said, putting his glass down on the table in front of him.

"Right. The publisher of the paper—he's the owner, Sid Ironson—got a call from the number two man at the Justice Department, a guy named Ben Aranow. Aranow asked him not to run any more stories about the Powers case without talking to him first. He said it's a matter of national security, but wouldn't elaborate."

"National security?"

"Yes."

"What did Ironson say?"

"He said he'd think about it, if and when the next story came up."

"Does he know about the letters?"

"No. I've told no one, but there's more. After I called you, the paper was served with a subpoena for my notes and background material relating to my story. Our lawyers are working on it right now."

"As we speak."

"At this very moment."

"What's the paper's position?"

"We're giving them nothing."

"Good. But you might have to go to jail for a bit."

"I might be better off in jail."

"Why?"

"Aranow says that anyone who is thought to have information about the Powers case, even a reporter, is in serious danger. Does anyone know I have the letters?"

"No, just me."

"Who knows about them, besides you and me?"

"Bob Flynn, Frank Dunn, Melissa and Marcy, their lawyer, and a lawyer named John Parker."

"Who's he?'

"Bryce Powers named Chemical Bank the executor of his will. Parker represents the bank in the suits by the Mesa group and the Plaza I and II groups."

"Who told him?"

"The girls' new lawyer, Fran Kaplan."

"What about Markey. I thought you said he has your file?"

"I forgot to put the letters back into it when I took them out to make copies for you."

"An oversight."

"Markey would call it obstruction of justice. Do you want to give me your copies back?"

"Hell, no. But the sooner I can use them the better. There's some serious shit happening here. And dangerous. What are you waiting for?"

"I would have given them to Markey, but he was a jerkoff, and Al Garland has turned gutless suddenly. Nobody in law enforcement seems to give a shit about Danny. Frank Dunn's contact in Florida says the case down there is 'open but inactive,' whatever that means. I feel like the letters are the only card I have to play, my only leverage."

"Card in what game? Leverage for what?"

"I want somebody to focus on *Danny*, on finding the scumbags that tortured and killed him, and to acknowledge the obvious fact that his death and the Powers deaths are connected. The Powers sisters feel betrayed, the bank has to protect its interests, some partners lost money, the lawyers are all posturing, meanwhile Danny is dead, and he died badly, Linda, and the fucking guy from the FBI acts like he was shit, telling me he owes child support, the fucking asshole."

Jay stopped and took a breath. He looked at Linda, who had placed her hands palm down on the white tablecloth. He saw empathy in her eyes, and something else, he could not be sure what. Could it be regret? He had wanted to ask her out when they first met eight years ago, but she was engaged. Had she wanted him to? You wouldn't have done it, anyway, he said to himself.

"You didn't mention my quest for a Pulitzer," Linda said, smiling.

"I know you loved Danny," Jay answered, looking down at Linda's hands, and then back up to her eyes. "And you're trying to help."

"The mysterious Donna Kelly sounds like she's still

alive," said Linda. "A really ballsy reporter would try to find *her. That* would be a hell of a story."

Jay caught the waiter's eye and motioned for another round. Through the window at the front of the dining room he could see snow still falling. Around him, the people in the cozy room were chatting and gesturing as they ate their dinners. For a few moments his defiance of Chris Markey had given him a sense of purpose—of being alive—that he had not felt since Danny's death. But before meeting Linda he had driven to the suburban home of Danny's ex-wife, Barbara, to give her the eleven thousand dollars in cash that he found in Danny's office, and to give his dead friend's two boys the Christmas presents that he got them every year. Barbara had refused the cash, calling it blood money, and, though she accepted the gifts, she asked Jay not to bring them in the future. Married to a cosmetic surgeon, driving a Mercedes, chairing the membership committee at her golf club, Barbara had come a long way from the streets of Newark where she and Danny met when they were thirteen. Standing on the porch of her swanky house, listening to her rant, seeing the coldness in her eyes, Jay's sense of purpose evaporated into the chill night air.

"Jay," said Linda.

"Yes?"

"Where were you?"

"I was thinking about Danny. He liked this place."

"Are we in danger, Jay?"

"*You're* not. You just wrote a story, naming me as your source. Aranow's just trying to scare the paper into censoring itself."

"Are *you* scared?" Linda asked.

"I suppose," Jay answered, "if I started looking for Donna Kelly, or Herman Santaria, I might be."

"Who's Herman Santaria?"

Jay told her about Santaria, the subpoena he had served on him, and the aggressive reaction it had generated.

"Can I use that?" Linda asked.

"No."

"Why not?"

"Santaria knows about me, but he thinks I'm a dumb lawyer. If it got in the paper he'd obviously know I was trying to connect him to the Powers case. Frank Dunn says I'd get a bullet in my head."

"What if I didn't use your name?"

"Well, if Aranow's telling the truth, then *you* could be in danger. Whoever's behind all this might come after you, to find out exactly how you got your information about Santaria. Besides, how would you confirm it?"

"You could give me the papers with Santaria's name on them."

"From the divorce file?"

"Yes."

"I'll tell you what. Let me have one of your business cards."

Linda extracted a card from her purse and handed it to Jay. Turning it over, he wrote on the back, "Linda, Take no prisoners. Jay." He showed her what he had written and, putting the card in his wallet, said, "I'll send you the Santaria documents tomorrow. You can use them and Kate Powers's letters when you learn that I'm dead, or when you get this card in the mail, whichever comes first."

"You're scaring me, Jay."

"I'm sorry, but the only time I've felt alive in the last three onths was when I banged heads with Agent Markey, and when John Parker called to threaten me on behalf of Santaria. Markey could have had the common decency to acknowledge that he was investigating Danny's murder. I might as well do it myself. If I get in his way, or fuck things up, he'll have only himself to blame."

"What are you going to do?"

"I think I'll have a talk with Bill Davis again. I think Markey tried to intimidate him into changing his story. I'll ask him if that's the case. I mean, does Markey think we're all stupid? If Davis will talk to me, and I think he will, I'll ask him some more questions about the Mexicans. Maybe that will lead to something."

"I'll come with you."

"No way. If I learn anything I'll give it to you. You can add it to your trove of information, to be used as we've agreed."

19.
4:00 PM, December 12, 2004, Newark

On Sunday afternoon Jay drove to Newark to see Bill Davis. He did not call him in advance. If Davis had been persuaded by Chris Markey to retract his story, there must have been a compelling reason, and he might refuse to meet, or avoid Jay's calls. The storm that had started during Markey's visit to Jay's office had sputtered on and off over the last two days, but was now gathering force, and snow was falling heavily as he drove along Route 280—one of the many major highways that crisscrossed northern New Jersey's suburban sprawl—into the city.

He'd spent the bulk of his time over the past two days organizing, in his mind and on paper, the facts, events, and personalities that had been swirling in his head since the night he learned of Danny's murder. He did no legal work in those two days, but neither did he drink. Clearheaded for the first time in weeks, he was certain that the seeds of Dan's death were planted thirty years ago while Bryce and Kate Powers were living in Mexico, and that Bryce and Kate had surely reaped from the same sowing.

Hoping that Davis would go on record with the true story, Jay had brought a small cassette recorder with him—the one he used at his office to dictate letters to

Cheryl—and he checked to make sure it was still in the front pocket of his coat as he neared the Colonnade Towers. There was a *Sorry, Full* sign across the entrance to the underground parking garage. As he drove slowly past it he could see, through the swirling snow, a crowd of people milling about the atrium lobby that connected the two buildings. The spaces on the street were also all taken, but Jay remembered that at the side of Building B there was a service entrance and a small blacktopped area designated for delivery vehicles. Danny, who encountered no rule that he was not happy to break, had pointed this area out to Jay as a good place to park, especially at night, if the underground garage was full. Jay parked there, and after trying the door of the service entrance and finding it locked, he trudged through the snow to the main entrance, over which was hung a sign, rimmed in flashing colored lights, announcing "Tree Lighting Tonight 5 p.m."

In the center of the lobby there was a tall Christmas tree—maybe twenty feet high—decorated to the hilt and strung with as yet unlit multicolored lights. It was four fifty-five. The crowd of a hundred or so people, mostly parents with their kids and a sprinkling of grandparents, was waiting for the big event. Jay made his way through the chatting adults and the scampering kids to the Building A elevator, where, once inside and riding up, he heard the same piped-in Christmas carols that were playing in the lobby. With Danny gone, and his two boys out of the picture, Jay had been trying not to think about Christmas, but what was the use? Too many reminders.

On the tenth floor, Jay found Davis's apartment, 10D, and rang the bell situated on the left doorjamb, hearing its muted ring inside. The long hallway, subtly lit by tasteful brass sconces, seemed hushed after the noisy activity of the lobby, where, Jay thought, Bill Davis could very well be, sipping eggnog with his friends and neighbors, waiting for the tree lighting to take place. After a minute or so, he tried again, and then knocked sharply, saying, "Bill, it's Jay Cassio. Are you there?" Again there was only quiet, and Jay, disappointed, took one of his business cards out of his wallet, found a pen in an inside coat pocket, wrote on the back of the card "Bill, Please call me. It's important," and slipped the card under the door.

At the elevator, Jay pushed the down button and was bracing himself for the seasonal Muzak, when he heard a door opening in the direction of Davis's apartment. Turning, he saw a young Hispanic man, in his mid-twenties, with thick, shiny black hair and a heavy beard, step out of 10D. He was carrying a gun with a silencer attached to the end of its barrel. He stared at Jay and, no more than thirty feet away, Jay stared at him. Then, as Jay heard the elevator doors opening and the sounds of "Silent Night" coming from the car, the man raised his arm and aimed his pistol at Jay's head. As he was pulling on the trigger, another young Hispanic man, a taller, near-clone of the first, stepped out of the apartment into the shooter's line of fire, causing him to crouch and move to the right before firing. As this was happening, Jay was stepping into the elevator, pushing the *L* button, and wondering if the doors would close in time to save his life, or if he would die in Newark, where he was born.

In the lobby the holiday crowd, now even bigger, was gathered around the tree, now beautifully lit, belting out carols while the Muzak continued to play in the background. Jay quickly walked into the crowd, thinking he could make his way to the front entrance and thence out into the night; but before he could get there, he saw the stairwell door open and his pursuers enter the lobby, where he was easy to spot, standing six-foot-three, and white, among a sea of mostly smaller people, all of them black.

The young Latinos headed around the crowd to their right, toward the front doors, to block Jay's escape. Jay watched them commit themselves, and then moved quickly in the opposite direction, toward the service entrance at the side of Building B, where his car, and escape, awaited. The service door opened easily from the inside, and as he was pulling it closed behind him, he saw the two Latinos entangled in a group of children at the hot chocolate table. He got a good look at them, and they him. The last thing he saw was the sly smile on the face of the shooter.

Jay's Saab was equal to Route 280's slick, snow-covered roadbed, with its sweeping curves and steep climbs and descents, as was Jay, the storm and the dangerous road no match for the adrenaline pumping godlike strength and clarity through his veins and into his mind. Not until he was home and had taken off his coat did exhaustion begin to set in, and did his brain register the pain in his upper left arm, which was soaked with blood through his wool sweater and the shirt he wore under it. Peeling off his clothes in his kitchen, he saw that the wound was a two-inch furrow, a half inch deep, and that the flow of blood was slowing to a seeping trickle.

Sweating and a little nauseated, he poured himself a juice glass full of bourbon and drank half of it straight off. Then he found a small towel, soaked it with hydrogen peroxide, and wrapped it around the wound. Naked from the waist up, he brought the bourbon bottle, the half full glass, and his cigarettes into the living room, where he sat on the couch. He finished the glass of bourbon and poured himself another. He did not have the strength to light a cigarette, nor to reflect much on his near-death experience. Just before he fell asleep, he remembered the sardonic smile on the shooter's face as he made his escape. *We will meet again gringo*, it said. *Have no doubt.*

20.
June, 2003,
Mexico City

The suitcase was made of a dark brown, heavy-duty synthetic material with a faux leather look to it. It had chrome fasteners and a belt of chrome around its perimeter. It was on the coffee table when Isabel entered Herman's living room and, although she and Herman and Edgar and Jose Feria were sitting around this table, the suitcase had not come up in their conversation. Isabel assumed it contained cash—American dollars—which she had been transporting for Herman to places in and out of Mexico for the past two years.

"Do you know Juan Paredes?" Herman asked Isabel.

"No."

"You never met him, not even once? He considered himself quite attractive to woman."

"I would tell you if I did."

"He's dead," Herman said. "His head is in the suitcase."

Isabel gave Herman one of her nothing looks, and then glanced over at Jose, who was smiling. She had heard that Jose beheaded his victims, but had been reluctant to believe it, even of him. She looked back at Herman, remaining silent, her face a blank.

"Would you like to see it?"

"No."

"We'll show you, anyway." Herman nodded at Jose, who deftly flipped up the suitcase's clasps and lifted it open. There, lying on a creamy white towel, was indeed a human head, the face pallid and ghostly, the long, dark hair greasy, the raw, jagged flesh of the neck, where Jose's machete had done its work, ringed with dried blood. Jose reached in, took his trophy by the hair, and lifted it, dangling it at eye level before Isabel, who looked from it to the still smiling Jose, not sure which face was the more ghastly.

"Take it away," Herman said, "and say good-bye to Isabel. You won't be seeing her for a while." The facetiousness of this comment was lost on Edgar and Jose, but not on Isabel. They never said hello or good-bye, and everything in between they kept to the absolutely practical. She watched as Jose carefully—tenderly— replaced the head, closed the suitcase, and rose with Edgar. Ignoring her, Herman's panthers, as he had taken to calling them, nodded to their master and left.

"Macho Juan was stealing from us," Herman said when the Ferias were gone. "You will take his place."

Isabel knew who Paredes was: a former high school teacher in Guadalajara who spoke unaccented English, recruited by Herman to run a money laundering operation in the States.

"Where will I live?"

"In West Palm Beach, in a condo owned by Senor Bryce Powers."

"Who is Senor Bryce Powers?"

"A businessman with bank accounts in many cities. Our cash is placed in those accounts and then wired to private banks. Powers gets a fee for each transaction."

"How much cash?"

"Many millions. And business is getting better. You will be busy."

"You trust me so much?" Isabel's affect had remained flat, but she let a slight smile flicker across her face as she said this. It was a deceitful smile, one that she knew Herman would take as a sign of timidity and even affection. It was one among many in the repertoire she used to seduce men so that Herman could photograph them and bend them to his will.

"You could have stolen and run off any time in these past two years. We know each other a long time, Isabel. I have kept my word, have I not?"

Isabel had lived with Herman for five years before moving into a one-bedroom apartment in his building. She drove a Mercedes convertible and had had private tutors in English, world literature, French, and art history. But she was watched at all times and she knew it, her only freedom the freedom to think as she pleased and assess her prison, which she did constantly. The phone in her apartment, she knew, was bugged, the tapes delivered daily to Herman by the woman who cleaned for both of them.

"Yes," she replied, lying again, knowing that Herman's word was worthless, and that, had she tried to run, he would have known about it and run her to ground almost instantly. And then killed her.

"Then you surely know that if you steal from me, you will not get away with it. My young panthers will track you down, and they will do horrible things to you before they slice off your beautiful head. I do not believe you will steal from me. You are too intelligent. I only tell you this because you raise the question of trust. And because now we are talking about large sums of money. *My* money."

"How long will I be in the States?"

"I'm not sure. A year, two years. We think Powers may be stealing as well. Everyone lies—the dealers, the collectors, the middlemen. Some of them are not our people. We launder for several other organizations from time to time, for very fat fees. You will keep a close watch on Powers."

"How close?"

"As close as possible. Sleep with him if you have to. He is coming to the end of his usefulness, anyway, but if he is stealing I of course want to know, and we would want to recover our money. He was a hundred and fifty thousand short last month. I don't think Paredes had that kind of balls."

"It could have been the dealers or the collectors."

"We have killed our dealers in New York and New Jersey. Their replacements will not steal—for a while—so we will see. With the Medellin and the Felix people it is not so simple. We cannot kill them without clear proof. Your job will be to tell us if Powers is stealing. We will handle the others."

"Does Powers handle cash?"

"Yes. Occasionally deliveries are made directly to him. With large sums it is easier, and safer. He would then send Paredes out to make numerous deposits."

"If he's smart, he's taking from the Medellin and Felix people."

"Of course."

"When do I leave?"

"Tomorrow. Powers will meet you in West Palm Beach. You will have a lot to talk about. We have already started contacting the dealers, so you will have no trouble there. You will contact me through our lawyers in Houston. Go and start packing. We will go over the details tonight at dinner."

Isabel got up. She was wearing a long, white cotton skirt, with the miniature faces of Incan gods printed discreetly on it, white sandals, a navy blue jersey top, and a white cashmere sweater tied around her shoulders. Her necklace was of the finest cultured pearls. The faint smell of Mexico City's polluted air reached her nostrils from the open French doors that gave onto the apartment's wraparound balcony. She had slept late that morning, then gone to her spa after breakfast. She stood now, letting Herman, a connoisseur, appreciate her beauty for a second before turning to leave. "Sit," he said.

Isabel sat. "Yes?" she said.

"Your pay will be doubled. And when you return—if all goes well—your life will be different. No more sucking strange dicks simply because I say so. Perhaps it is time for you to settle down with one man. Do you understand?"

"Yes, Herman, I do. Thank you."

• • •

Isabel left, and Herman took his drink out to the balcony, where he stood and gazed out at the endless expanse of Mexico City. The seat of his kingdom. Isabel, twenty-six, was not yet in her prime as a woman, but she, too, was coming to the end of her usefulness. It saddened him that she had to die. No Arabian thoroughbred, no mythical goddess, no flawless, perfectly cut diamond, nothing that is defined strictly by its physical beauty could compare to her. She had suffered, and it did not escape Herman, who, at the age of sixty-four, had seen all there was to see of life, that Isabel's pain had deepened and burnished her beauty. But Rafael was in line to be president, and Lazaro was about to be appointed attorney general; and Herman's tentacles, legal and illegal, reached everywhere. They would control the entire country, and could do anything they wished to do. It would be dangerous to keep Isabel, who knew much too much about Herman's business and his connections with Rafael and others, around. He would do a good thing: He would end her suffering. And perhaps use her to help him eliminate Senor Powers, who had assuredly suffered as well, but who, unlike Isabel, had brought all of his pain upon his own head.

21.
11:00 AM, December 13, 2004, Montclair

"If the police don't have your card, that means the killers do," said Frank Dunn.

Jay did not answer. Frank watched as he consumed the bacon, eggs, home fries, and toast that he had made for both of them. They were sitting at Jay's kitchen table. Outside, the snow had finally stopped and the world was silent. Bill Davis's body, shot once in the forehead and once in the heart, at close range, had been found earlier that morning by his daughter, who had come to pick him up for church. During the tree lighting ceremony last night several people had seen two swarthy Latino men, in their mid-twenties, chasing a tall, good-looking white man with long, wavy brown hair, in his late-thirties-to-early-forties, through the lobby. This Frank had learned from Linda Marshall, who, tipped off by one of her many police contacts, had arrived at the Colonnade Towers while the crime scene team was still in Davis's apartment.

"Do you think Garland's holding the card, playing games?" Jay asked, pushing his empty plate away.

Frank had found Jay in his living room, drinking coffee, reading the *Star-Ledger*, a blood-soaked towel clumsily knotted around the top of his left arm. The detective thoroughly cleaned Jay's flesh wound, put a makeshift butterfly bandage on it, then made breakfast while Jay recounted the events of the evening before.

"No," Frank replied. "I talked to the uniformed guys that responded. There was no business card under the door."

"Well," said Jay, "I'm going to Florida tomorrow, anyway."

"That might not be a bad idea, actually."

Linda had spotted a man crossing the lobby who matched Jay's description of Chris Markey. When she tried to interview him she was abruptly blocked by his two assistants. A few minutes later Ralph Greco appeared to tell her that there would be no press interviews of any kind and that she had to leave the building so that his people could secure it and do their work. When Jay's phone went unanswered, she'd called Frank.

"I'll need Angelo Perna's number."

"Angelo Perna?"

"Yes, Angelo Perna."

Frank, sipping his coffee, remained silent. That Jay had been in a free fall was obvious, but free falls were not always bad. They could clear the head in an amazing way, as long as you didn't hit the ground.

"I'm going to talk to the clerk at the hotel, too," said Jay.

"And what else?"

"Visit the office at Royal Palm Plantation in West Palm. That's the property that Donna Kelly was supposed to be running for Bryce. It's the only Powers property in Florida, in any event."

"Just drop everything?"

"I could use a vacation."

"So you're looking at this like it's a two-week cruise

where the passengers get to solve a murder as a fun activity?"

"Of course not."

"It could take time," Frank said. "What about your practice?"

"I'm worthless at the office. I've been giving Donnie more and more work. He can pretty much run it while I'm gone."

Frank lit a cigarette and looked out of the bay window in Jay's kitchen to the white-clad woods behind the house. Donnie, he knew, was Don Jacobs, an aggressive young lawyer who had been sharing office space with Jay for the past year, and who Jay gave work to from time to time.

"I spoke to Barbara this week," said Jay when Frank did not answer. "I went to her house, actually."

Frank smoked and looked at his young friend.

"She won't let me see the boys," Jay continued, "and won't take the cash Danny left them."

"The eleven grand?"

"Right."

"What did you do with it?"

"I bought annuities in the boys' names."

"How old are they now?"

"Twelve and fourteen."

"The husband's a little twerp."

"Right."

"I'll come with you," Frank said. "When are you leaving?"

"To Florida?"

"Yes."

"Tomorrow at two, on American."

"You'll have to stay with me tonight, at Lorrie's. She has a pullout couch."

"Fine. What about your job?"

"I'll call in sick, then I'll send my resignation in from down there."

Jay said nothing. He looked squarely at Frank, who, conscious that he had just made, on the spur of the moment, one of the biggest decisions of his life, and of the chaos in his soul that had brought him to it, returned his young friend's stare. He's a smart kid, he thought, keeping his mouth shut.

"What about Dick Mahoney?" Jay asked, breaking the stare and the silence. "Did you talk to him?"

"He came up empty."

"So it's not organized crime."

"Probably not. He did tell me one thing. He reads the papers, I guess."

"What?"

"The attorney general of Mexico is named Lazaro Santaria. He has a brother named Herman Santaria."

Jay packed, and they headed to Lorrie Cohen's apartment in nearby Clifton. Frank often saw Lorrie on Sundays, using work, or breakfasts with Jay and Danny—which he sometimes actually made—as excuses for getting out of the house. Not that he needed any. His wife, Margaret, had multiple sclerosis, and often couldn't get out of bed. Her sister, Rose, who lived with them and took care of Margaret full time, was always happy to see him leave. She didn't even listen to his excuses, he knew. He also knew, as a cop for almost forty years, that to hunt, and be hunted, were distractions almost otherworldly in their intensity. The thing was, was it Jay that needed the distraction, or was it him?

22.
8:00 AM, December 14, 2004, Bloomfield

Early the next morning Jay borrowed Dunn's car and drove to Glendale Cemetery in Bloomfield to visit Danny's grave. Near the cemetery was a nursery that was selling Christmas trees, and there Jay stopped and bought a grave blanket—dark evergreen boughs laced with holly and tied together with a red velvet ribbon—which he carried with him as he walked along rows of headstones looking for Danny's. When he found it he was out of breath. The air was bitter cold, the snow deep, and there were no landmarks on the barren hillside to guide him to the spot where his friend lay. Breathing deeply he stood motionless for a moment before reading the inscription on Dan's headstone and then kneeling to place the wreath on the grave.

Jay's parents' airplane had taken a long ten minutes to fall thirty thousand feet. Dan, too, had suffered before he died. And Kate Powers? Bewildered by the turn her life had taken, miserably unhappy—a client whose trust he had betrayed by sleeping with her twenty-two-year-old daughter—had she known she was about to be beheaded? What was Jay's suffering, his loneliness, compared to all of that?

No doubt Al Garland and Chris Markey had their reasons for lying to him and to the public about their noninvolvement in the Powers and the Del Colliano murder cases, and no doubt they would be angered by what he was about to do, and would try to stop him; and no doubt the two young men who had killed Bill Davis and almost certainly Danny and Kate Powers would now want to find and kill Jay. No doubt: a nice, simple, uncomplicated state of mind.

Looking down at Dan's inscription again: *Daniel Michael Del Colliano, Born 1962–Died 2004, Son, Father, Friend,* Jay said, "I waited too long, Dan. I'm sorry. If I was the one killed like that, you'd have started the next day. I don't know what I was thinking, but I'm starting now."

23.
2:00 PM, December 14, 2004, Newark

Chris Markey's career in the FBI was not typical. Born in South Boston in 1948 to working class parents, he realized in high school that the barricaded Southie culture was not for him. The day after graduation, he enlisted in the Air Force, and by 1969, while his contemporaries were getting high and protesting the war, he was flying covert operations for the CIA in Cambodia and Laos. In the mid-seventies a program was instituted to recruit military intelligence and CIA people with international experience into the FBI. Markey made the switch and embarked on a career of special projects involving Latin American countries. In the eighties, the Agency's focus in those countries, especially Columbia, Panama, and Mexico, shifted from political corruption and sabotage, to the explosively growing drug trade.

After twenty years in the trenches, Markey was under no illusions that the war on drugs would be won. The American people did not have the will. He would leave it to the sociologists to figure out why. His job was to enter the fray on orders from above. When faced with a choice between the follow-the-rules mind-set of the FBI and the no-rules philosophy of the CIA—except deniability—he chose the CIA's way.

The bad guys did not grapple with moral dilemmas. To them the end always justified the means. Unfortunately for Markey, the core principal of the Irish Catholic ethic in which he had been raised was that the end *never* justified the means, and when his young daughter died he saw it as divine retribution for a long list of mortal sins.

His current battle was the biggest of his career, with orders coming from the very top. He had had to apply the maximum pressure—a call from the United States Attorney General to New Jersey's attorney general—to get the local prosecutor, Al Garland, to subjugate himself and his staff to the authority of Markey's task force in the Powers murder investigation. And he had had to instigate a major court battle—guaranteed to generate a ton of unwanted publicity—with the *Star-Ledger*, over the reporter, Linda Marshall's notes and sources, pitting the first amendment against necessarily unspecified "national security" interests. And these were only procedural skirmishes.

In the real arena, the one that civilians knew nothing about, where life and death were on the line all the time, Markey knew, despite his newly awakened conscience, that he would continue to use whatever means were necessary to achieve his objective. He knew who killed Dan Del Colliano and Bill Davis, and probably Kate Powers as well. The people they worked for had ordered murder, maiming, and torture as a matter of course over many years. If he ever got the Feria brothers into custody, he would not hesitate to do the same to secure their cooperation.

Given this state of affairs, he would certainly brook *no* interference from Jay Cassio. If the wiseass young lawyer's anger over his friend's murder led to the demise of his practice and of his own health, that was his business; but if it spurred him to inject himself into Markey's investigation, as

Markey feared he had already done, then Cassio would be in for a great deal of trouble.

These were Markey's thoughts as he entered Room 412 in the Peter W. Rodino Federal Building in Newark at two p.m. on the Monday after Bill Davis's murder. Already in the room, seated around an oak conference table, were Markey's two top assistants, Ted Stevens and Jack Voynik, and Phil Gatti, a DEA agent who had spent five years undercover, working the streets and back roads of Mexico's drug scene from Tijuana to Mexico City to Guadalajara. Markey walked to the head of the table and placed the clipboard he was carrying in front of him. He looked around, nodding to the members of his team, before speaking.

"Forensics?" he asked, addressing his question to Stevens.

"No prints, except Davis's," Stevens replied. "The bullets taken from the body match the one in the hallway. Time of death, around five p.m. Nothing under the nails, no sign of a struggle, no toxins."

"The airports?"

"Nothing," Voynik said.

"I can't believe they had the balls to come back," said Gatti.

"Let's talk about the witnesses," said Markey.

"Out of the people in the lobby—a hundred or so—three definitely ID the Ferias," said Stevens.

"I didn't see their names in any of the papers, did you?" said Markey.

"No," Stevens replied. "We don't think they're known."

"Have they been spoken to?"

"Yes. They won't be talking to any reporters."

"Who's the cop that spoke to the reporter Marshall?"

"A kid named George Rodriguez. He came forward this morning. He's been suspended."

"What about Cassio?"

"He was identified by four people."

"He's being brought in as we speak," said Markey. "I hope."

"He wasn't at his house or his office," Voynick replied. "His secretary says she hasn't heard from him and doesn't know where he is."

"The Feria boys may have stayed around to do him," said Gatti. "My guess is he surprised them upstairs, they took a pop at him and missed, and he escaped in the crowd."

"So let's find him," said Markey, "and bring him in. We'll talk to him and let him go, and then follow him for a few days. We may get lucky."

"How would the Ferias know who Cassio is?" Gatti asked.

"They wouldn't," Markey answered. "But maybe we'll publish his picture in the paper: 'Possible Witness to Newark Murder.' That should give them a leg up. This kid wants to help find his friend's killers? Here's his chance."

Markey made one last check mark on his clipboard. He did not have to look up to know that his three subordinates were staring at him. What he was proposing was against all the rules, and probably a crime itself. Gatti, the new man, would have to get over his discomfort, which Markey could feel across the room, or quit the team. Recruited six months earlier, he had had sufficient acumen to obtain photographs of two young punks as they were getting into a limousine in front of a high-class apartment building in Mexico City, knowing that one of Markey's targets kept an apartment there; and he had the street contacts to be able to identify them as Jose and Edgardo Feria, killers for hire who collected heads as trophies.

Markey looked into Gatti's eyes for a second and then

said, "But if he does draw the Ferias out, remember, I don't want them killed. Make sure everyone involved knows that. We can sacrifice Cassio, but not the Ferias. This Donna Kelly woman is either dead or in deep hiding. Without her, the Ferias are our only shot at the guys running the show."

24.
5:00 PM, December 15, 2004, Miami

On the evening of December 14, Angelo Perna and his brother Sam, in separate cars, picked up Jay Cassio and Frank Dunn at Miami International Airport, returning in one car to El Pulpo, Sam's restaurant in Little Havana, leaving the other for the Jersey guys to use. The next day, Angelo caught the last three races at Hialeah with Miami PD homicide detective Gary Shaw, his friend of many years. Afterward, over drinks at the Paddock, a nearby bar, Angelo asked Shaw for an update on the Del Colliano case, first telling him that his detective buddy, Frank Dunn, and a lawyer, Jay Cassio, both good friends of the victim, were in Florida and were hoping to be filled in on the case.

"Why can't the Jersey people call Miami Beach?" Shaw asked.

"There's no case in Jersey. The Powers thing was closed out as murder-suicide."

"Why are these two guys here?"

"I don't know," Angelo answered. "Fish, swim, play the horses."

"Will you be helping them with all that?"

"Yes. I'll be like a tour guide."

"Fuck."

Angelo remained silent, eyeing his friend, whose dark brown face was lined with thirty years of a cop's worries. Shaw's pale eyes, set in this face like amber or opal jewels, were half-lidded, as always, vaguely contemptuous, wary of the human frailty he saw all around him.

"Does Dunn know what he's doing?" Shaw asked.

"Yes," Angelo answered. "He's a good cop."

"What about the lawyer?"

"Dunn says he's smart, and a good kid, but of course he doesn't know shit."

Angelo had been smiling during most of this conversation, grunting after each sip of beer, as was his habit, but he rearranged his face after this last statement. The first time he asked Shaw for information about the Del Colliano murder he didn't mention the close connection between the Jersey private eye and his friend Frank Dunn, who he had gone through the police academy with in New York in 1968. Now he had no choice. Dunn would be off the reservation in Florida, illegally flashing his Jersey ID on someone else's turf. He and Shaw both figured Del Colliano's murder to be drug related, connected to one of the Mexican cartels that were running wild along the border and doing increasingly lucrative business in South Florida. These cartels had an army of killers at their disposal. So Shaw needed to know.

"Is there something you're not telling me?" Shaw asked.

Shaw, Angelo knew, was planning on retiring at the end of the following year. The last thing he needed was any kind of a jam at this point in his life. Dunn or Cassio, or worse, a civilian, getting hurt or killed, with a trail leading back to Shaw, could cause him a lot of heartache.

"There was another murder in Jersey last week," Angelo replied. "Dunn and Cassio believe the victim had ID'd two Mexican punks who they think killed Del Colliano and the rich guy and his wife. They say it's obvious, yet the Powers case is closed. That's why they're interested in the status of the case down here."

"Where are they now?" Shaw asked.

The check had arrived. Picking it up, Angelo said, "This is on me. You picked nothing but losers today." He took a twenty dollar bill out of his wallet and put in on the table.

"I guess you're not telling me where they are," said Shaw.

"I don't know," Angelo replied. "I just have a cell number."

"Is someone in law enforcement looking for them, Ange?"

"They haven't broken any laws," Angelo answered.

"That you know of."

"Correct."

"How close are you to Dunn?"

"We're close. Like you and me."

"I'll call you," Shaw said. "Tell your friends to be careful. We don't want any more Jersey guys killed down here. It's bad for the tourist industry."

25.
5:00 PM, December 16, 2004, Miami

Larry Warner, the detective who handled the Del Colliano case, had since had open-heart surgery and retired to New Mexico. Gary Shaw did not consider that he knew or trusted anyone else at the Miami Beach PD well enough to simply call and ask for the status of a case, especially now that the two Jersey guys would be in the area doing their own investigating. He would need an excuse, and, luckily, he was handed one on his drive home after his drink with Angelo. Over his police radio came word that one of his squad's informants, a heroin addict named Princess Di—he was a transvestite as well—had been found dead in the street that afternoon in the Overtown section of Miami. The uniformed cop who was dispatched to the scene, recognizing the Princess and knowing his role, notified Shaw's squad desk after getting him into an ambulance. One of Shaw's detectives later went to the morgue to identify the body, and it was his call back to the desk, confirming that the deceased was in fact the Princess, that Shaw overheard.

That same detective had pulled Princess Di in, on a pretense, two days earlier, to question him about a triple homicide that had occurred in Shaw's district the week before. While the Princess was at headquarters, Shaw had spent a few minutes alone with him. Jumpy, needing a fix, the addict claimed to know nothing about the triple killing, which was thought to be drug related. Shaw had known the Princess for ten years, had observed him as he pathetically changed wigs each time the real Princess Di changed her hairstyle. He had hoped that if he sat alone with him, he could get something coherent from him, but that did not happen.

When he arrived at his office the next morning, Shaw put a call into Miami Beach, and asked to speak to the detective handling the Del Colliano homicide. A few minutes passed before he was connected to a Detective Ron Hernandez.

"Lieutenant Shaw?" said Hernandez, "what can I do for you?"

"Actually," said Shaw, "I have something for you. How's Larry Warner doing, by the way?"

"He's well, pretty much recovered."

"Does he call you guys?"

"Once in a while I have to call him."

"Tell him I said hello. We went through rookie training together about a hundred years ago."

"I will."

"I'll tell you why I called," Shaw said. "I was interrogating a snitch a few days ago, an addict. He mentioned something about 'the Italian dude from Jersey, with all the cash, who was offed on the Beach.' It didn't ring a bell at the time, but then I remembered the case from talking to Larry a couple of times, so I thought I'd pass it on. What's up with the case?"

"What's the snitch's name?"

"He goes by the name Princess Di. He's a transvestite."

"Does he have an address?"

"Not really, but he's always around."

"Hold on. Let me get the jacket."

A minute or two passed, and then Hernandez returned to the phone.

"Lieutenant Shaw?"

"Yes."

"It says here, 'Case taken over by FBI. Jurisdiction: Title 14. No further activity without authority of Special Agent Chris Markey, Newark Field Office, phone: 201-533-1333. Capt. Jankowski, 10/5/04.'"

"Are any of your people detailed?"

"It doesn't say."

"There's no task force?"

"It doesn't look like it."

"Okay, I thought I'd pass this on."

"Thanks. I'll call Markey. Can you pick up the snitch if he wants us to talk to him?"

"Sure. Like I said, he's always around."

Shaw hung up and went to work reviewing the *State v. Taylor* file, a case that was currently being tried in the Dade County Circuit Court, and that would require his testimony, he was told, that afternoon. The case involved the killing, by contract, of a nine-year-old boy who had witnessed a murder. The assistant prosecutor who was trying the case had prepped him thoroughly over the past two weeks, but Shaw wanted to leave nothing to chance. While he was reading, one of his detectives, a woman named Naomi Teller, popped in to tell him that Princess Di had been found dead the day before, that it looked like an overdose, or bad dope, with no signs of violence. "We'll talk about it at the squad meeting," he said, returning to his file.

At around eleven o'clock, his phone rang, and Shaw was told by the desk clerk that an Agent Phil Gatti of the DEA was on the line.

"Agent Gatti," he said after picking up his phone. "Gary Shaw here."

"Lieutenant Shaw, Phil Gatti. How are you?"

"Good. I'm good. What can I do for you?"

"It's about this informant of yours, Princess Di?"

"Right. I spoke to Detective Hernandez this morning."

"Right. I just got off the phone with Chris Markey. We're on an FBI/DEA task force that he's in charge of. He's in Houston. He's booked on a flight that gets him into Miami tonight at seven. He'd like to meet with you, and the informant, tonight, if possible."

"The informant's dead. I just found out a few minutes ago."

"Christ. What happened?"

"OD. No violence."

"Well, Markey may still want to talk to you. One of us will get back to you."

Shaw did testify that afternoon, and it did not go well. The case against the shooter was over. He had received a life sentence with no possibility of parole. But he was not talking. As a result, the case against the defendant then on trial, who was in jail, awaiting trial on the original murder charge when the boy was killed, was difficult to prove. It hinged on a statement from a rival gang member, whose trial testimony that morning was weak. Shaw had taken a meticulous statement from this witness after interviewing him over the course of several days. He was also in jail at the time, and no promises were made. Something must have spooked him, because on the witness stand, he went about 90 percent into the tank. Shaw was called by the state to, in effect, impeach its own witness. Given the rival gang member's imprecision on the stand, the defendant's lawyer was hard on Shaw, accusing him throughout his cross-examination of coercing the witness into making a false statement.

Disgusted, praying that the judge would not throw the case out, Shaw returned to the Homicide Bureau to find a message that FBI Agent Chris Markey had called and asked to be called back at his hotel in Houston. Shaw was spent, but he called Markey.

"Agent Markey?"

"Yes."

"Gary Shaw, Miami PD."

"Hello, Lieutenant. Thanks for getting back to me so quickly. How are you?"

"I've been better. We have a guy on trial for ordering the killing of a nine-year-old kid—he witnessed a shooting—and it looks like the bad guy may walk."

"Jesus."

"Right."

"Is Jack Kendall still the head of homicide?"

"Yes. Do you know him?"

"We were on a task force a few years ago. Give him my regards."

"I will."

"Tell me about Princess Di."

"A heroin addict, very bad, especially in the last year or two. No help anymore, really. He mentioned something that I connected to the killing of the Jersey PI in Miami Beach."

"What did he say exactly?"

"I was asking him about a triple murder here. He said he knew nothing. He's sweating and swooning. He pops up and says, 'the Italian dude from Jersey, with all the cash, you want them?' I pressed him, but he's a total mess, getting delirious. I didn't know what he was talking about. We released him.

Then I remembered talking to Larry Warner when the case went down. So I called Miami Beach."

"Was there any mention of the cash in the newspapers?"

"I have no idea."

"I don't think it was revealed."

Shaw said nothing, surprised at Markey's intensity, and wondering where this was going.

"What was Princess Di's real name?"

"We think he was born Alan Douglas, in New York City."

"Did he have family, friends?"

"He was a junkie. They don't have friends, just people they get high with. I don't know of any family."

"Where did he live?"

"Sometimes he slept in the back of a beauty parlor in Overtown. The owner's also a queen."

"What's the address of the beauty parlor?"

"It's called Dixie's Do's. It's on Thirty-sixth Avenue."

"What do you know about Little Havana?"

"The usual."

"Have you ever put anyone undercover there?" Markey asked.

"Yes. When I was working drugs."

"How did it go?"

"We did well. But drug buyers and sellers are the same everywhere. It's the rest of the community that's hard to crack."

"Do you have somebody we can put in there now?"

"On what?"

"This Del Colliano thing."

"You'll have to talk to Kendall about that."

"Of course. Do you have any contacts in the community?"

"No, I don't. Who are you looking for?"
"The woman. The Latin beauty."
"You think she's in Little Havana?"
"There's a good chance she is."
"Well, if Kendall wants me to help, I'm here."
"Thanks. I'll call Jack."
"You're welcome."
"Good luck with your trial."
"Thanks. We'll need it."

26.
5:00 PM, December 16, 2004, Miami Beach

While Gary Shaw was talking to Agent Markey, Jay and Dunn were pulling into the parking lot of the South Miami Beach Motor Hotel. They had stopped by earlier that day, but the clerk who had checked Danny in was not there, and they were told she would not be on duty until five p.m. They had lunch in the cramped coffee shop, and then took a few minutes to look around. The guest quarters consisted of some six two-story concrete "villas" with names like Bougainvillea and Gardenia, although there was no evidence of any such flowers in sight. The oversized pool, devoid of swimmers, stood baking in the late day tropical sun. There were long, jagged cracks in its concrete apron, which was also empty and silent.

The desk clerk who greeted Jay and Dunn when they returned at five was a big-boned mulatto woman, around thirty, her skin creamy smooth, with green eyes and freckles and a surprising, beaming smile that turned her plain face pretty and sexy. They introduced themselves and explained their business, Dunn showing her his Essex County Prosecutor's badge and ID, and telling her they were trying to tie up loose ends in the case. She confirmed that she was at the front desk the night Danny checked in and, eying Jay from head to toe, said she'd be happy to talk, inviting them to sit in the "lounge," a fifteen-foot-by-fifteen-foot space with plastic furniture to the right of the front desk. Her name was Rhonda.

"You look like that rock guy," Rhonda said to Jay once they were seated. "What's his name?"

"I don't know," said Jay, smiling despite himself.

"The one who's buried in Paris."

"Jim Morrison," said Dunn.

"That's it!" said Rhonda. "I just saw a TV show on him. Man, he was *cute*."

"I can't believe you know who Jim Morrison is," Jay said to Dunn.

"Love Me Two Times," said Dunn.

"You got that right," said Rhonda.

Jay laughed out loud, as much at the exchange between Rhonda and Dunn as at the detective's deadpan delivery, belied by the twinkle dancing for a split second in his pale blue, bloodshot eyes.

"I remember the guy," said Rhonda, smiling her big smile at Jay and nodding. "What about him?"

"Was the FBI here as well?" Dunn asked.

"Yes, blue suit."

"Anybody else?"

"No. Until now."

"Did you see the body?" Dunn asked.

"No. Just Lourdes. No way I need to see a dead body."

"Did Dan say anything when he checked in?" Jay asked.

"Is Dan the dead guy?"

"Yes."

"No. He was quiet, serious, you know?"

"Nothing?"

"Just 'Hello, I need a room. On the second floor. In the back.' I put him in G208."

"What do you think happened?" Dunn asked.

"*Shit*," said Rhonda, "drugs, robbers, jealous husband . . ."

"Was there a woman?"

"Not that I saw."

"Did Dan look like anybody famous?" Jay asked.

Rhonda smiled again as she thought about this, then said, "No. Maybe a Latin lover type."

"Can you describe him?" Jay asked.

"Tall, black hair, mustache, nice silk shirt."

"Were you shown mug shots?"

"The FBI guy did."

"Not the Miami detectives?"

"No."

"Did you recognize anybody?"

"No, but they were bad pictures."

"Bad pictures?"

"They were fuzzy."

"You mean grainy?" Jay asked, breaking into Dunn's staccato string of questions, "like with a telephoto lens?"

"That's it," said Rhonda, "like they were at an airport, or getting out of a car, you know? Not like mug shots like you see on TV."

"Were you questioned at headquarters?" Dunn began again.

"They said they would bring me down, then they never came back."

"Who, Miami?"

"Yes."

"Does Lourdes still work here?"

"No, she went back to Guatemala around Thanksgiving. Good luck finding her."

"What kind of car was the guy driving?"
"I didn't see it."
"Did he put it down on the registration card?"
"No. He just scribbled his name."

There was a pause, a short moment of introspection for all three.

"How long was Lourdes working here?" Jay asked.
"About six months."
"What time did she come on duty?"
"Nine a.m."
"Did the FBI guy leave his card?" Frank asked.
"No."
"Do you remember his name?"
"No."
"What did he look like?"
"He was a strict-looking guy, gray hair, around fifty."
"Anything in particular you remember him saying, or asking?"
"No, the same as you guys. He showed me the pictures."
"How many pictures?" Jay asked.
"Two."
"What size?"
"Big. Eight-by-ten?"
"Were they of the same guy?"
"It was two guys, Spanish, maybe Mexican-looking. I thought one could be the guy, but I wasn't sure. I didn't want to make a mistake."

Another pause followed this exchange, in which Rhonda looked from Jay to Dunn and back to Jay, ready for the next question. Jay could tell from her face, composed but expectant, that this was more interesting to her by far than checking horny teenagers, budget-obsessed tourists, and tired salesmen into the South Miami Beach Motor Hotel. But the interview had reached the top of its arc, and was over. When she realized this, she said to Jay, "I'm sorry I wasn't any help."

"No, you were helpful," he said. "We appreciate you taking the time to talk to us."

"Was Dan your friend?" Rhonda asked.

Jay looked at Rhonda, finding himself hoping he would get one more of her face-changing smiles before he and Dunn left. He had made a mistake by referring to Dan as anything other than "the victim" or "the dead guy." Or had he? There was a point in the conversation when Rhonda seemed more interested in helping. He shrugged inwardly. It didn't matter.

"Yes," he said. "He was a good friend."

"That's too bad," she said. "That's tough."

They were both, he knew, thinking of the way Danny had died.

"You know," said Rhonda, "while you're in town, you could call me. Maybe I can get that laugh out of you again. You *are* a handsome devil."

"Thank you, Rhonda," Jay replied, smiling, "maybe I will," knowing he wouldn't, unless it had something to do with Danny.

27.
6:00 PM, December 16, 2004, Miami

Jay and Dunn were staying at the Silver Sands Hotel in North Miami Beach—ten stories of white brick, with a pool in back, surrounded by imported palm trees and beds of brightly-colored flowers. From their fifth floor balconies they could see across A1A to the ocean, a dazzling, foamy green, quite different from the steely blue Atlantic along the Jersey coast. They had picked the place because it was close—but not too close—to where Danny was killed, in South Beach, with its all-night noise and its crowds of multicultural and multi-gendered partiers. After their talk with Rhonda, they returned to the Silver Sands, where Jay changed into a bathing suit, took one of the room towels, and walked across the street to the beach. He swam for a few minutes, and then lay on the towel on the warm sand as gulls circled and dove, feeding in the surf. He and Dunn had spent three days at an isolated fishing camp on Big Pine Key, where the wound on Jay's arm, bloody but superficial, had healed, and where they were apprised, via calls to Linda Marshall, of the lay of the land in Jersey.

Jay had been at Ocean Beach in San Francisco the day his parents' plane went down. They had gone first to Seattle to visit cousins who had moved away years before. His mother, anxious to see her only child after a five month interval, wanting to surprise him, had talked his father into cutting their Seattle visit short by two days. Carmela, forty-nine, was completing her seventh year teaching senior English and Latin at a private high school in Montclair. That year her students had read *A Death in the Family* and *So Long, See You Tomorrow*, lessons, she told Jay, in the sadness that permeates and shapes all of our lives.

A.J., fifty-three, could hardly believe that he had put in nineteen years at the A&P, where he was now the head baker. Though he rarely showed it, the sadness that Carmela was referring to haunted his memories of Newark's First Ward, where he had left behind the dignity of running his own business and his own life, losses as profound and life changing as those suffered by James Agee's fictional family and William Maxwell's heartbroken narrator.

Jay heard about the crash on his car radio as he drove home from the beach, thanking God it was not his parents' plane that had gone down. In the chaos that followed over the next few days, Danny appeared. He helped Jay pack his things. He talked him into attending a memorial service on Mount Tam, where people said they saw the plane fall into the sea. He bought airline tickets and took Jay home. And now he was dead, too.

Jay had never fired a gun in his life, not even held one, but while on Big Pine Key, Frank Dunn took him to a godforsaken mangrove swamp, where he fired Dunn's police-issue .38 revolver many times. Lying on the beach, he recalled the rush of adrenaline before, and the euphoric calm after each shot he fired at the bottles and cans Dunn had patiently teed up on a decrepit tree trunk. Dunn, grim faced, showed him the proper stance and grip; told him to squeeze off the round rather than jerking the trigger, to absorb the kick with his full body. Firing the gun had centered him, confirmed for him the necessity, the inevitability, of what he was doing.

When he returned to the hotel, he found Dunn sitting at one of the outdoor tables near the pool bar, drinking what looked like a gin and tonic. He was wearing the same drab suit and tie he had worn on the plane and for the interview with the hotel clerk, and would probably wear the entire time he was in Florida. His only concession to the tropical weather was an odd-looking woven hat that he wore to protect his balding head from the sun. Jay joined him and ordered a scotch to bring back to his room to drink while he was shaving and showering. They were meeting Angelo Perna at eight o'clock at El Pulpo.

"Nice swim?" Dunn asked.

"Yes. It was good."

"Linda called."

"Did you speak to her?"

"I did."

"What's up?"

"Your picture was in the *Times* and the *Daily News* this week. The FBI wants to talk to you about Bill Davis's murder."

"So there's a manhunt on?"

"It's not funny, Jay. There's more."

"What?"

"Cheryl called her. Markey's people are all over her. They've threatened to arrest her as a material witness if she doesn't tell them where you are."

Jay shook his head. He had called Cheryl from Big Pine Key to tell her that he would be away indefinitely and to give all client matters to Don Jacobs, but he hadn't told her where he was or what his plans were.

"Cheryl's gotten a lawyer," Dunn said, "and offered to take a lie detector test."

"Unbelievable."

"She's a tough kid."

"Anything else?"

"There's a hearing scheduled for Monday on the subpoena for Linda's notes. The paper's lawyers say they've never seen the US Attorney's Office so worked up over a case like this. There's a good chance she'll go to jail for contempt."

Jay said nothing. He knew that Linda's notes contained nothing more than what was revealed in her article, that it was Kate Powers's letters that she was prepared to go to jail over. She was tough, but jail? With two young kids? Jay did not trust Chris Markey, and was not about to cooperate in his investigation, but he could get him off of Cheryl's back, and maybe Linda's. When he got back to his room, before getting in the shower, he called the FBI's office in Newark and left a message for Agent Markey to call him at the Silver Sands Hotel in North Miami Beach.

28.
8:00 PM, December 16, 2004, Miami

El Pulpo was an unpretentious place, with a worn mahogany bar, comfortable leather banquettes in the front, and a dining room and kitchen in the back. It was located on 17th Avenue, at the western edge of Little Havana, in a residential neighborhood of tightly-packed bungalows, duplexes, and two-family houses with small patches of lawn or dirt yard in front. When Jay and Dunn arrived, there were four or five kids, boys and girls aged eight or nine, catching fireflies in the street and putting them in a glass jar. The *E* of the neon sign above the entrance consisted of three of the eight legs of a stylized octopus, which flashed red, while the remaining letters flashed yellow. White and silver Christmas wreaths hung on the fixed glass windows that flanked the front door.

Inside, they were greeted by Maria Perna. Petite, gracious, her long, black, gray-streaked hair pulled back and tied with a plum-colored ribbon to match her sleeveless silk blouse, Angelo's Cuban-American wife was El Pulpo's hostess. Her ankle length black skirt and high-heeled sandals made her seem taller than her actual height, which appeared to Jay to be just over five feet. She gripped both of Dunn's hands in hers, and kissed him on the cheek. She did the same to Jay, and then brought them to Angelo's office, a banquette in a corner of the front room. She promised to return later, when they were done with their business. Dunn and Angelo shook hands, and Dunn introduced Jay. A waitress took their drink order.

"So, how are you?" Angelo said to Dunn.

"I'm good. You?"

"I'm good."

"That's a hell of a wife you have there."

"Thanks," Angelo replied. "I'm a lucky guy."

"How's Sam?" Dunn asked. "Is he here?"

"He's good. He's not working tonight."

"How old is he now?"

"He'll be sixty."

"Your kid brother sixty? Unbelievable."

Jay watched the two old friends smile at each other. He had heard Dunn's stories of the days when they were rookie cops in New York. They were sixty-two now. A lifetime had passed. Angelo looked content, younger than his years. Dunn looked tired and older. He had ordered bourbon, and Jay wondered if Angelo knew his friend had been sober for many years, and that it was the torture and murder of Dan Del Colliano that had started him drinking again.

The waitress came with their drinks, and while she was setting them down, Angelo said to Jay, "So, you lost a good friend?"

Jay nodded.

"I was in the Army with a Del Colliano," Angelo said. "In Nam."

The waitress, to Jay's right, seemed to stop in mid-motion as she was reaching with his drink, then it fell from her hand onto the table with a bang, ice and scotch making its way to the edge before she recovered and placed a napkin quickly down. Jay had seen this happen peripherally, but he looked full at her as she cleaned the table, and saw that she was gaunt, but very beautiful, young, maybe twenty-five or twenty-six, with short-cropped dark hair, full lips, and fine, deep blue eyes.

"I'm sorry," she said, wiping the last of the spilled ice onto her serving tray, "the glass was wet. I don't think I got any on you. I'll get you another drink." She was embarrassed, but calm, and her accent was *what*? Jay could not place it.

"There's no damage done," Jay said, "don't worry about it." Her breast had brushed against his shoulder, and he had caught the scent of her perfume when she reached quickly to stop the scotch from spilling onto his lap, and he found himself watching her as she walked back to the bar to get him a replacement drink.

Jay, collecting himself, turned to Angelo and said, "Yes. He was a good friend. We grew up together."

"Where was that?"

"In Newark."

"You're Italian?"

"Yes. My grandparents, three of them, are from Benevento, near Naples."

"My people are from Avellino, the next town over."

Danny's grandparents had emigrated to the United States from the town of Avellino in 1911, but Jay did not mention this to Angelo, thinking instead of the trip to Italy he and Dan had discussed for years, which they had never taken.

"We appreciate your helping us with this," he said, instead.

"It's no problem, except there's one thing we should talk about."

"I'm listening."

"You don't know anything about my contacts in the

Miami Police Department," Angelo said. "I haven't given you a name, and I won't. If anybody ever asks, you don't know where I get my information. I need your word on this."

"You have it."

The waitress returned with Jay's drink and menus.

"What's good?" Dunn asked Angelo.

"Sam bought the place last year, and he's turned it into the only Cuban-Italian restaurant in Florida. I like it all, so you can't go by me. Try the *bistec empanizada*. It's great."

Now that Jay had his drink, the other two men picked up theirs and, reaching to touch glasses, Angelo said, "To your friend."

They sipped their drinks, and then Dunn said, "Anything new?"

"I just talked to my guy today. He'll get back to me. Tell me what's going on."

Dunn told him about Jay's encounter with the two young Mexicans the night that Bill Davis was killed, then recounted what they had learned from the clerk at the South Miami Beach Motor Hotel: that it was not Danny she checked in, but one of the presumed killers, and that the FBI apparently had pictures of them even before Danny was killed. Last, he mentioned Agent Markey's visit to Jay's office the week before, his seizure of the Powers divorce file, and his recent intimidation of Jay's secretary.

"The FBI wants to talk to you, Jay," said Angelo. "You can't duck them forever."

"He's taken care of that," said Dunn.

"I called Markey's office before we left the hotel," said Jay, "and told his secretary where I was staying."

"Good," said Angelo. "You might as well get it over with. Take this"—he handed Jay his business card—"You can reach me at this number twenty-four hours. If you get arrested, I'll get you a lawyer and arrange bail. What's this guy Markey like?"

"He's an asshole," said Jay.

"He's obsessed," said Dunn. "He's got the New Jersey authorities under his thumb, he's brought suit for a reporter's notes, and he's threatening to put Jay's secretary, who's totally innocent, in jail."

"He must have a monster case on his hands," said Angelo.

"No doubt," said Dunn.

"Of course if these two Mexicans are looking for you,"—Angelo addressed this to Jay—"and I think we should assume they are, you've got a lot bigger problem than Agent Markey."

"I'm aware of that," Jay said, "but how would they know I'm in Florida? No one knows I'm here except Linda Marshall—she's the reporter that Markey is also trying to put in jail—and I don't see why they'd think to approach her to find me."

"Agent Markey now knows," said Angelo, "but let's assume for now we can trust the FBI. What's your take on all this, Frank?"

"They all sound like contract hits to me," Dunn replied, "drug related. But Markey can't be interested in the shooters themselves."

"I agree," Angelo said, "which means he must think he has a shot at somebody much higher up the food chain."

"Somebody here in the States."

"Right."

On the plane ride to Florida, Dunn had recounted this theory to Jay, telling him that no South American or Mexican drug lord, no matter how strong the evidence against him, had ever been extradited to stand trial in the United States.

"Let's assume," said Angelo, "that this Bryce Powers guy was cleaning drug money for one of the cartels, as a broker—that's what they're doing nowadays. He steals some, gets caught, and they kill him and behead his wife as a diversion or to get Powers to talk."

"Right," said Dunn. "They want their money back, and they want to know who's helping him."

"He gives them Donna Kelly," said Angelo. "They find her a few days later here in Florida, with Del Colliano. They kill Del Colliano and get their money back, but the broad gets away."

"They go up to Jersey," said Dunn, "to see if they can find a trace of her in Dan's apartment. They run into Bill Davis. Then they read in the paper that Davis has ID'd them to the FBI. They go back, kill Davis, and run into Jay, but *he* gets away."

"For Markey," said Angelo, "the link to whoever he's looking to nail is either the broad or the two Mexicans. Right now, you can be sure he's hunting them both."

"He probably won't appreciate our help," said Jay

Jay saw Dunn looking at him, to see, he assumed, if there was any sign that he fully understood the danger inherent in his pursuing either Donna Kelly or the Mexican killers on his own. *Being arrested for obstructing justice*, Dunn had said to him on the plane, *would be a pleasure compared to what the cartel's hit men would do to you if you fell into their hands. And who's to say that Miss Kelly wasn't in league with them and just as nasty a character?*

"Doing what, exactly?" Angelo asked.

"Tracking down Donna Kelly," Jay answered. "We can save the Mexicans for later."

"And do what with her when we find her?" Dunn asked.

"That's easy," Jay answered. "If she's innocent in Danny's

death, we'll give her to Markey. If she had a hand in it, we'll use her to draw out the Mexicans."

Dunn and Angelo looked at each other.

"I think he's serious," said Angelo.

Dunn, looking at Jay, shaking his head almost imperceptibly, said nothing.

"Look," said Jay. "You guys don't have to help me. You've done enough already. But I'm not stopping. Do you think Markey gives a shit about *Danny*? He's probably glad he got killed. It gets him closer to his big arrest. They crushed his balls, the motherfuckers, think about it."

The banquette they were sitting at was circular, with a circular table in front of it, the three men sitting in a triangle facing one another. Dunn and Angelo leaned back, away from Jay's heat. They each held his glance for a second, then Angelo motioned to the waitress for another round of drinks.

29.
5:00 PM, June 14, 2003, Palm Beach

"How do I advise you of the deposits?"

"You fax me the receipts immediately."

"Who takes care of the wire transfers?"

"I do. I fax you the confirmations. We meet once a month to exchange originals."

"What about the cash you receive directly?"

"I deposit it, and transfer it overseas, faxing you copies of the paperwork. Originals you get when we meet."

"I thought Paredes made those deposits?"

"He did, but he was stealing, so I'll take care of them from now on."

They were sitting at a sidewalk table at Olive's on Worth Avenue in Palm Beach on a warm, sunny day. Isabel had arrived late that morning from Mexico City, and taxied to Bryce's condo, where she found the door unlocked and a note from Powers telling her to meet him at Olive's at five. Next to the note were the keys to a Saab 9000 that was "hers to use" while she lived in the condo. She unpacked and took a long bath, and then went into Palm Beach, where she strolled, not buying, but observing the fashion scene and soaking up the luxury of Worth Avenue, among the *grandes dames* of the world's shopping streets.

She and Bryce had spent the last hour discussing the

details of Isabel's job, Isabel sipping Pellegrino water while Bryce finished off two Jack Daniel's on the rocks. On the table to her right was a folder containing a list of the banks used by Bryce Powers & Company around the country and a dozen or so deposit slips, neatly organized, for each of the company's accounts in each of those banks. Bryce's private fax and cell phone numbers were written on the inside of the folder's front cover. Platinum American Express and Visa cards in Isabel's name were clipped to the outside of the folder.

"What about the ten thousand dollar limit?" Isabel asked, referring to the federal law requiring banks to report all cash deposits of ten thousand dollars or more to the IRS.

"Try not to go over it, but if you have to—on a modest basis—go ahead. We make numerous legal deposits each month over ten thousand dollars. Twenty to twenty-five thousand is okay. If there's too much cash, which will happen often, put it aside and give it to me at our monthly meetings. I'll deposit it in special accounts where I have a relationship with my banker."

Isabel was wearing a pale yellow, sleeveless linen dress, with fine multicolored beading along the top of the square-cut bodice, and sandals of the same pale yellow. The color of the dress and its simple cut created the perfect setting for her beautifully turned arms and legs, richly tanned and glowing in Worth Avenue's late afternoon sunlight. At her neck was a necklace of Bakelite beads, a brilliant red to match her finger and toenails. Her earrings were two-karat rubies on posts, a gift from Herman. On her right wrist was a thick bracelet of the same fine beadwork as on her dress.

She had put on makeup—the little she used—and, relaxed and refreshed after her bath, she was not surprised to see the impression she had made on Bryce Powers when they met, and since then. What surprised her was the impression he had made on her. He was not the serpent, like Herman, or the pig, like Rafael, that she expected, but a man of intelligence and modesty, a combination of qualities rarely found in the men she met in her line of work. And he was good-looking, his dirty blond hair cut short, his gaze direct, his finely cast face, though lined with care and clearly carrying a heavy interior burden, still bearing the stamp—faded but visible—of a youthful beauty not entirely lost.

"Those sums I will of course report to Rafael," said Isabel, reigning in her wandering thoughts.

"Of course," Bryce answered. "I'm sure he has a reporting system up and down the line."

"Not with the client cartels."

"No, but stealing that money would create *two* deadly enemies. It would have to be a one-time thing—you'd have to run immediately—but there's never enough at one time to make it worthwhile."

"How would *you* steal?" Isabel asked. "You know the game as well as anyone."

"I'd need a partner," Bryce answered. "*You* for example. We'd chip away and blame the delivery people."

Bryce smiled as he said this—his first full smile in the hour-plus they had been talking—a smile charming and surprisingly boyish, the sun appearing for a moment on a cloudy day. Isabel, disarmed, smiled in return, and, because her smile was spontaneous, that is, genuine, she could see that Bryce was equally disarmed, delighted to see this beautiful and somber young woman—so willing and able to involve herself in the deadly work of a drug cartel—let her guard down even for a moment. They held each other's gaze, and then two shadows fell across the table. Looking up, Isabel saw two starkly pretty young women standing over them, their smiles anything but genuine.

"Hi, Dad," said Marcy.

"Father," said Melissa.

As Bryce rose and received kisses on his cheek, Isabel saw the quick flash of a mocking look in the girls' eyes as they exchanged glances, and Bryce's face change, the sun having returned behind thick clouds. Still standing, Bryce introduced his daughters to Isabel, his "associate," and then he returned to his seat. Melissa and Marcy sat at the two empty chairs at the table, arranging their Saks and Versace shopping bags around them like ladies-in-waiting.

"Would you like a drink?" Bryce asked.

"No, we can only stay a minute," Marcy answered. "We have to drop these things off, then get ready for dinner."

"Where are you staying?"

"At the condo."

"Isabel will be staying there for a while."

"Were those your things we found?" asked Melissa, turning to face Isabel, her eyes bright but her smile false. "Beautiful things," she said when Isabel did not answer. "We saw them when we dropped our bags off."

"You'll have to go back and get them," said Bryce.

"You mean she can't move out for the weekend?" said Marcy, referring to Isabel without looking at her or acknowledging her presence.

"No. She's living there."

"Where will we stay?"

"Check in to the Breakers. It's on me. Leave your keys on the kitchen counter."

Isabel watched Marcy and Melissa take this in, seeing through the detached air they affected. They had lost a small turf battle, and were trying to conceal their resentment. Gazing at them with seeming disinterest, as a lioness might gaze at two hyenas who had wandered into her territory,

Isabel saw what she might have been had she been the pampered child of rich parents and, for the first time since her brief affair with Patricio Castronovo, she was not absolutely certain of the hopelessness of her life.

"The Breakers is so *passé*, Father," said Marcy, keeping it light. *Isabel*, her eyes said, *whoever you are, I'll deal with you another time.*

"I have an account there," Bryce answered. "Ask for the company suite. Have fun."

Melissa had already risen, and now Marcy got up as well. They gathered their bags, went in turn to kiss their father good-bye, and left, neither of them looking, let alone addressing, Isabel. When they were gone, Isabel picked a cigarette out of her silver case and leaned toward Bryce while he lit it for her. She took a deep drag and, sitting back, blew the smoke out in a gentle stream from her nostrils and partially open mouth.

"Sorry about that," said Bryce.

"De nada."

"I'm divorcing their mother."

Isabel said nothing.

"I divorced them a long time ago. I just pay their bills. For now."

"You don't have to apologize for them."

"I do, and for myself. I'm sorry this is how we had to meet. We might have enjoyed each other under different circumstances. I know you have to spy on me. It could have been me, and not Paredes, who was stealing."

Isabel did not answer immediately. He had it exactly right. She would be spying on him, and sleeping with him would be a way of getting closer to her subject. With these thoughts her old hopelessness returned, like a shroud on her shoulders; but it did not fit as comfortably as before, which frightened—and exhilarated—her.

"But you are still alive," she said.

"I'm valuable, for the time being. But they'll want me dead soon, whether I'm stealing or not."

"Why?'

"Because Rafael will soon be president. I can ruin him—all of them. So you see, I might as well steal. Perhaps I can take a great deal of their money, ruin them, and then die."

"*Suicidio.*"

"Perhaps."

If they are going to kill him, anyway, thought Isabel, then why am I here? Staring at Bryce Powers, she saw the answer in his deep, hazel eyes. Herman, her keeper, had decided that she would give one more performance before *she* died. Despite the wisdom she had gained from all her suffering, she had never realized until this moment that such a death was inevitable for her. The last drop of pain had fallen upon her heart.

"Permit me a question, Senor Powers."

"Bryce would be fine."

"Bryce."

"Go ahead."

"If I was your partner, and we stole money little by little, when would we have enough, and how would we get away?"

Isabel followed Bryce Powers's eyes as he looked at her face, and then at as much of her body as he could see before the table blocked his view.

"We're talking hypothetically, of course," he said.

"Of course."

"Let's have dinner; we'll talk it over."

"*Bueno.*"

"*Bueno.*"

30.
9:00 AM, December 17, 2004, West Palm Beach

In 1979, Bryce Powers, building on the success of his four Texas properties, bought two hundred acres in West Palm Beach, across the bay from Palm Beach—where condos were not allowed—but which he hoped would lend its cachet to the first project he would develop on his own. It did. The eighty luxury condominiums he built were sold out well before construction was finished. West Palm Beach eventually became laced with freeways and strip malls, but Royal Palm Plantation, with its charming, user-friendly golf course, pool, and Spanish Colonial clubhouse, surrounded by lush, tropical green, remained an enclave of privilege and privacy. Twenty-five years later, Bryce Powers & Company was still managing the property. Bryce owned one of the units personally, using it from time to time as a getaway until the time of his death.

All this Jay had learned via his involvement in the Powers divorce case, and passed along to Frank as they drove north on Route 95 on the morning after their dinner at El Pulpo. They would try to find someone at Royal Palm who knew Powers, while Angelo traveled to Jupiter, also up the coast, to show Danny's picture around. Frank did not have much hope for either endeavor, especially Angelo's, but no good investigator would leave them undone.

They slowed down and stopped at the end of the long, palm-tree–lined entrance drive, and Frank rolled down his window for the guard who came out of the gatehouse to greet them.

"Good morning, sir. Can I help you?"

"Detective Dunn," said Frank, holding up his badge. "New Jersey State Police. We're investigating a homicide involving a Jersey resident. We'd like to speak to the person in charge."

The gatehouse was coated with white stucco and had an orange tile roof. Bougainvillea was growing on trellises on two of its walls. The guard, young, blond, muscular, went into it. He came out a few minutes later and told Frank that Mrs. Bradley, the manager, would see them at her office, located down a curving road just past the clubhouse on the right. As they drove they saw that all the buildings on the property had the same tropical charm as the gatehouse. They found the office and parked in front. Inside, they were greeted by a fortyish, freckled, fair-haired woman who introduced herself as May Bradley, the property manager. She guided them through the reception area, where two secretaries were working, to a small conference room at the back of the building.

"Can I offer you anything, gentlemen?" Bradley said. "Coffee, soda?"

"No, thank you," said Jay.

"I'm good," said Frank.

They were seated at a handsome oak library table that was the centerpiece of the dark-green–carpeted, well appointed room.

"I'll need to see some ID," said Bradley.

"Sure," said Frank, pulling out his badge and Essex

County identification card, and handing them to the property manager, who looked carefully at them before handing them back.

"This is my assistant, Detective Cassio."

"What can I do for you?"

"We're looking for a woman," Frank replied. "About five-seven, long dark hair, mid-twenties, possibly Hispanic."

"Yes, I explained all this to the FBI."

"Was that Special Agent Markey?"

"Yes, in the beginning, then an Agent Ted Stevens was here last week."

"We've spoken to them. Do you mind going over it with us? We need to double check a few details. Do you know this woman?"

"Mr. Powers called me about a year and a half ago and told me that a friend of his daughter's would be using his condo."

"What's his unit number, by the way?"

"Seven Royal Palm Drive."

"Go on."

"He told us her name was Isabel Perez, that she traveled a bit, and would be coming and going. He gave her a set of keys. That's it, basically."

"When was she last seen here?"

"At the end of last summer, maybe early September."

"Has she returned?"

"No. The police have the apartment sealed."

"Did Mr. Powers visit her here?"

"Not that I know of, but Nancy, one of the secretaries out front, says she saw them together on Worth Avenue one time."

"Did Isabel have any friends or boyfriends that visited her?"

"Not that I know of."

"Does the gatehouse log visitors in and out?"

"No."

"Did Markey or Stevens interview any of the guards?"

"I'm not sure. I think Stevens did last week."

"Did she have any friends or relationships on the staff?"

"I'm not sure."

"Not sure?"

"I saw her talking a few times to one of the grounds keepers."

"Who was that?"

"Alvie. Alvaro Diaz."

"Is he still here?"

"No. He retired last year. He was in his late sixties."

"Where did he live?"

"Miami. I told all this to Agent Stevens."

"The thing is," said Frank, "we checked out his address, and no such person had ever lived there. Can you recheck it for us?"

Bradley picked up the phone and asked Nancy to bring her Alvaro Diaz's personnel file

"Has anything unusual happened here in the last few months?" Frank asked when Bradley put the phone down. "Violent crime, reports of trespassers, that kind of thing?"

"We had a burglary here last week."

"A residence?"

"No. Here in the office."

"What did they take?"

"Nothing."

"Nothing?"

"Right."

"What did the police say?"

"They said the thief must have panicked."

"Did an alarm go off?"

"We didn't have an alarm. We've since put one in."

"Did you tell Agent Stevens about the burglary?"

"Yes. He was here the next day, right after the West Palm Police."

"Anything else?"

"No."

Nancy came in with Diaz's file, which she handed to Bradley. When she left, Bradley opened it and said, reading from the file, "Here it is: 11566 12th Avenue, Southwest."

"That's the address we have," said Frank.

"He drove up here every day from Miami?" Jay asked.

"Yes, he said he liked the ride."

"Who was his supervisor?" Dunn asked.

"Frank Barnes. He's on vacation at the moment."

"We may need to speak to him."

"Fine. Just call me. I'll make him available."

"Did you have a relationship with Bryce Powers, outside of business?"

"No."

"One last thing," said Frank. "Can you describe Alvaro Diaz for us, beyond his age."

"He was a sweet old man, small, wiry, a little stooped from gardening for twenty years. Very tanned and leathery from all the sun, beautiful white hair, Cuban. He gave me cigars for my husband at Christmas. I didn't get any this year."

On their way out of the complex, Frank stopped Sam Perna's tanklike Buick Riviera at the gatehouse, and went over to the handsome young guard who had greeted them earlier. Frank offered the man a cigarette, which he declined. The two chatted for a few minutes, Frank smoking, the guard keeping his eye out for incoming traffic, which was nonexistent. They shook hands, and Frank returned to the car.

"What did he say?" Jay asked when they were underway.

"He described her the way everyone has: long, dark hair; blue eyes; a great body. He hit on her a couple of times in the beginning, but she turned him down."

"Anything else?"

"Yes. Two young Mexican guys were here about a week ago. They said that Isabel was their sister, that she was missing, and they were very worried about her. They asked if she was especially close to anybody at the complex. He told them the only person he ever saw her talk to was Alvaro Diaz."

"Was that before or after the break-in?"

"The day before."

Jay pulled the Miami map they had picked up that morning out of the glove compartment, studied it for a minute, and then said, 12th Avenue Southwest runs right through Little Havana. I guess that should be our next stop."

"Let's talk to Angelo first," Frank said. "It's his backyard."

31.
9:30 AM, December 17, 2004, Miami

The morning after his telephone conversation with Markey, while Jay and Frank were interviewing May Bradley, Gary Shaw was called into Jack Kendall's office.

"Good morning, Gary," Kendall said. "Coffee?"

"No, I'm good."

"I hear *El Tigre* turned into a pussy."

"He did. Somebody got to him."

"I talked to Lloyd Dodson just now. He says Lambert won't throw it out. He doesn't have the balls. He says if the jury gets it, they'll do the right thing. Liz will show them the way."

Shaw, contemplating the twists and turns of the Taylor case and of justice in America in general, did not answer immediately. Dodson was the Dade County District Attorney. Bill Lambert, up for reelection later that year, was the trial judge. Liz was Elizabeth Siegal, the Assistant DA trying the case.

"Let's hope so," he said finally.

"I got a call from Chris Markey last night at home," Kendall said.

"Right. I talked to him, too," Shaw replied. "Did he tell you?"

"He did. Too bad about Princess Di. He might have helped."

"Maybe."

"Markey wants us to put somebody under in Little Havana."

"What about the Beach? It's their case."

"They don't have the resources."

"It's not our thing. We'd have to call Special Investigations."

"I talked to Joe Powell. He can give us the Ramirez kid. That deal at the Port is finished."

"Markey really wants us involved?"

"Yes. It's a homicide, and he and I have worked together before. We'll do a task force. Us, SI, and Markey and his people. You'll run Ramirez."

"What's the story?"

"We're looking for Isabel Gutierrez Perez, aka Donna Kelly. She was a courier. Drug cash. She handled about ten million a year, going back to 2001, 2002. It was laundered through a big real estate company in Jersey."

"The murder-suicide."

"Right. But it wasn't. Powers—he's the owner—and Isabel were probably skimming."

"She gets away."

"Right, but not far. The people she was working for killed Powers and his wife, and a Jersey PI, and last week an old guy in Newark who ID'd the shooters, two young Mexicans."

"So they must be looking for her."

"Markey believes they want her very badly, as does he, of course."

"Who are they?"

"People high up in the Mexican government."

"How high up?"

"He didn't say, but it must be high. He was pretty intense on the phone last night. Maybe it's the president, or someone one near him."

"Christ."

"He's been working on this for over a year. He believes if he's traced her to Little Havana, then so have the bad guys. He's flying in this morning. We're meeting him this afternoon, with Powell and Ramirez, at the Miami field office. We'll drive over together."

Kendall, a white man five years younger than Shaw, had been made chief of homicide after a series of successes in highly publicized cases, the most recent being the arrest and conviction of a young white narcotics detective who had killed and robbed a black drug dealer, then dumped his body in the Miami River. Gary Shaw had been among the handful of senior detectives who had been mentioned as possible candidates for the job when it came open. It would have been a nice way to end his career, but Shaw was not too disappointed. The pay wasn't much more, the responsibilities were heavy, and the politics, racial and otherwise, were a pain in the ass.

• • •

At one thirty Shaw and Kendall got into Shaw's unmarked car and headed to the FBI's field office in downtown Miami.

"Anything new?" Shaw asked, once they were underway.

"Markey's in. He called me a few minutes ago. He asked me to send someone to talk to Dixie at Dixie's Do's."

"You're kidding."

"He's being thorough."

"Like Princess Di kept a diary."

Kendall laughed, and then said, "He's a tough guy. I worked with him a couple of years ago on a drug sting. He doesn't like to be disagreed with, and if you cross him he'll make your life miserable. A word to the wise."

"You know me, Jack," said Shaw. "I never buck the system."

Shaw and Kendall were greeted by Jack Voynik, who introduced himself as one of Markey's assistants before leading them into a second-floor conference room. Around the rectangular conference table were six chairs, and on the table in front of each chair was a yellow legal pad, a pencil, and a manila folder.

"There's a briefing memo in the folders," said Voynik. "Chris is downstairs meeting with Officer Ramirez of your department. He'll be up in a few minutes. The memo will bring you up to speed. I'll be back with Chris."

"Briefing memo?" said Shaw after Voynik had shut the door behind him.

"This is how Markey operates," said Kendall. "You'll never see a witness statement or an official report unless he thinks you have to. We might as well read."

Shaw opened his manila folder, read the memo, and learned the following: two members of a DEA/FBI task force had been killed—shot in the heart and beheaded—in Tijuana in early 2003 at an isolated airfield in a sting that went bad. The two Mexican members of the team were not killed, and their stories were not convincing. One of them was found dead in the trunk of his car six months later; the other disappeared at around the same time, and was presumed dead. Both Mexican agents had been interrogated repeatedly by the FBI, with nothing to show for it. The Mexican government was AWOL. Pronouncements of aggressive investigation and imminent arrests from Lazaro Santaria, the attorney general, were painfully transparent public relations bullshit.

Another DEA/FBI task force was put together, headed by Chris Markey. After a year of hard work with little to show for it, Markey's team received a tip from a Houston informant identifying Isabel Perez as a courier of drug cash with significant ties to Herman Santaria, Lazaro's multimillionaire brother. Apparently someone in the informant's family had been killed—beheaded—on orders from Santaria, a few months earlier.

This was last summer. Markey's people watched as Isabel, her home base Bryce Powers's condo in West Palm Beach, picked up cash at various locations around the country, each in the vicinity of a Powers property, and deposited it in a local bank. In August, she and Powers spent a weekend together at a luxury resort in the Colorado Rockies. Phone taps yielded nothing. Markey had obtained a search warrant, and was about to execute it, when Bryce and his wife were killed. A team of agents went through Powers's financial records and quickly found wire transfers to overseas banks totaling forty million dollars between 1996 and 1999. These matched up with the deposits Isabel had been making, less a 10 percent broker's fee to Powers.

Powers's records also revealed that Herman Santaria was a co-managing partner in the four properties developed by Powers in Texas in the seventies; that H.S. & Company was formed as a corporation in Texas in 1972 by a Houston law firm; and that its sole shareholder, and recipient of over one million dollars in phony maintenance fees per year, was the same Herman Santaria. An hour before he and Kate were murdered, Powers called Isabel and, with an FBI agent listening in, told her that he was worried about getting killed, and that the "stuff" he had given her was her only protection against the same fate. If she was arrested, she could hand over "de Leon and both Santarias" on a silver platter.

Agents went quickly to the condo at Royal Palm Plantation, but Isabel had fled. A week later, she brazenly turns up in Jersey, and a few days later Dan Del Colliano is dead and Isabel is nowhere to be found. Last week, a civilian named Bill Davis was killed in Newark after it was reported in a New Jersey newspaper that he had seen two young Mexican men in Del Colliano's apartment and identified them to the FBI. The killers—of Bryce and Kate Powers, Del Colliano, and Davis—were believed to be brothers named Edgardo and Jose Feria, Mexicans believed to be in the employ of Herman Santaria. Grainy, eight-by-ten black-and-white photographs of them were also in the manila folder.

Shaw finished reading, stared intently at the photographs for a few seconds, then looked over at Kendall, sitting across the table. Kendall had finished as well.

"I'll settle for nailing these two scumbags," said Shaw, placing the pictures on the table.

"I'm with you," Kendall replied. "Does he really think he can bring down the attorney general of Mexico?"

At that moment, the door swung open and Markey walked in, followed by Voynik, Ted Stevens, and Phil Gatti. Introductions were made, and Markey, sitting at the head of the table, began.

"Have you read the memo?" he asked.

Shaw and Kendall nodded.

"Our immediate targets are the people who killed our agents in Guadalajara last year. We're pretty sure it's the Felix cartel, but they're deep in the hills of the Sierra Madre in Jalisco, and the Mexican government won't act. We now have what we feel is great leverage: We think we can prove that

Herman Santaria, Lazaro Santaria, and Rafael de Leon, the chief domestic advisor to the president of Mexico, are not only protecting drug cartels, but dealing drugs themselves. If we nail them, one of the first things we'll do is get authority to launch a small army on the Felix stronghold in the mountains.

"There are two paths to the Santarias and de Leon. One is via Isabel Perez. Certainly she can give us Herman Santaria, but we think whatever it is Bryce Powers gave her—it's probably documents of some kind—will directly involve Lazaro and Rafael de Leon and, because he's so close to the guy, possibly the president of Mexico. We're pretty sure Isabel's in hiding here in Miami, in Little Havana. We don't want to go in there overtly because those people don't talk to police. They'd probably tip her off, and she'd flee. That's why we've asked for the Miami PD's help. I've talked to Officer Ramirez. He's Cuban, he's smart, and he's got balls. I'd like a cover put together, a good one, and I'd like him in there as soon as possible, tomorrow or Sunday at the latest. Can you do that Lieutenant Shaw?"

"I can do it," Shaw answered, "but I'll need help with documents, people to back up his story, that kind of thing. We can have him coming down from Jersey—there's a big Cuban community in one of those towns near the city."

"Whatever you need," said Markey. "Get together with Voynik. If we get Miss Perez, we've struck gold. Through her, we can bring down the whole fucking banana republic government down there."

"And the other path?" said Jack Kendall.

"The other path," Markey replied, "is through our New Jersey lawyer friend, Jay Cassio."

"Who's he?" Kendall asked.

"He's a friend of Del Colliano. He was representing Kate

Powers in the divorce. He got Bill Davis's name in the paper, which got the guy killed."

"He couldn't have known the guy would be killed," said Shaw.

"Cassio was seen in the building on the night Davis was murdered."

"You don't think he helped kill the guy, do you, Chris?" said Kendall.

"No, I don't. But he's a wise guy. He skipped town right after Davis was killed. When we searched his house, we found two bloody towels. We think one of the Feria boys clipped him. Then I talked to one of the Powers daughters—he was banging her, by the way—and she told me her mother wrote Cassio a bunch of letters accusing her husband of all kinds of bad things. I subpoenaed Cassio's divorce file, and there were no letters in it. I could arrest him for obstruction of justice right now."

"Why don't you?" Shaw asked.

"I've got something better in mind," said Markey. "He's in Miami Beach. I'm going over to talk to him tonight. But I'm not going to arrest him. I'm planting an article in the *Miami Herald* tomorrow, with his picture—'Witness to New Jersey Murder Located in Miami.' We'll put a tail on him starting early in the morning."

"To draw out the Feria brothers?" Kendall asked.

"Yes."

"What if Cassio won't go along with it?" Shaw asked.

"He won't know about it," Markey answered, closing his folder.

32.
5:00 PM, December 17, 2004, Miami

After the team meeting, Gary Shaw, Jack Kendall, and Officer Ramirez had an hour's sit-down with Agent Voynik to talk about what was required in order to put Ramirez safely undercover in Little Havana. They established an identity and a simple history for Ramirez, and agreed to meet again at nine p.m. to pound the story into the young policeman's head and set up communication procedures between him and Shaw. In the interim, Voynik would have his people produce the necessary false papers to back up Ramirez's new identity.

Shaw drove Kendall back to the homicide bureau, and then headed out to Hialeah to try to catch the last race or two. As he drove, Naomi Teller called on his cell phone to tell him that the jury had come back with a guilty verdict in the *State v. Taylor* trial. He made a mental note to call Liz Siegal in the morning to congratulate her. She had already said that she would seek the death penalty, and Shaw had no doubt that Lambert would impose it. Of course it would be fifteen years before William Taylor was executed, fifteen years in which Taylor would have three meals a day, watch a lot of television, and probably have some young punk around to suck him off whenever he felt like it. There was something wrong with that picture, but Shaw was way beyond trying to rearrange it. He was just happy that Taylor had been convicted.

He got to the track twenty minutes before the ninth race went off. There would be a tenth race, too, at five fifteen. Both were trifectas, which accounted for the crowd of addicts milling around the betting concourse and the grandstand, where he liked to sit, near the finish line. The infield and the grounds around the track were green and handsome under a clear, blue sky. He picked up a Racing Form—there were plenty laying around at this time of the day—and sat in a section of seats shaded by the tier of stands above to read it. As he studied the past performances of the eleven horses in the ninth race—a ten thousand dollar claiming race, loaded with the working stiffs of the sport of kings—his meeting that afternoon with Chris Markey, et al, replayed in his mind, sticking each time, like a broken record, at the part where Agent Markey made Shaw, by his silence, a member of a conspiracy to set up Jay Cassio to be executed.

Shaw was not a true gambler. The most he bet was ten dollars, and he never doubled his bets to catch up. If he lost, he lost. What attracted him was the circus maximus atmosphere of the track, the great heart and athleticism of the jockeys and horses, and the satisfaction of successfully handicapping a race. In the twenty minutes before the ninth race, he decided on his bets for it and the tenth: a trifecta in each, the favorite in the ninth, and a fifty-to-one shot in the tenth, across the board. After the ninth race, which the favorite won, he collected his winnings, placed his bets on the tenth, and went to an open-air bar to drink a beer.

The horses for the tenth race were approaching the starting gate, and Shaw decided to watch it on the closed-circuit television at the bar. The jockey on his horse, a Hialeah veteran named Victor Huerta, had already won three races that day, which had been the deciding factor in making the bet. The guy was hot. When the horse, a chestnut gelding named Sonny's Dream, was led into his stall, he stiffened and balked, and the jockey was almost thrown, striking his shoulder hard against a metal cross brace before righting himself. "Christ," Shaw said to himself, "that must have hurt."

Sonny's Dream broke strong, and Shaw was happy to see Huerta rein him in forcefully, his shoulder apparently okay. The horse's problem in its last three races had been early speed, with not enough left at the end. Huerta stayed in the middle of the pack until he reached the far turn, where he made a great move, overtaking the two leaders in the middle of the stretch. Sonny's Dream tired at the end, and was beaten by a nose by the favorite, but he would pay around fifty dollars to place, a nice win for Shaw, who had the horse five times.

Outside the track, on the way to his car, Shaw stopped at a pay phone and called El Pulpo. Angelo was not there, but Maria told him that he was expected soon. Shaw told her that he would stop by.

33.
4:00 PM, December 17, 2004, Miami

Jay and Dunn made it back to their hotel from West Palm at four. Dunn went to his room for a nap, and Jay again went to the beach. This time he swam for thirty minutes, out past the breakers, then parallel to the beach, back and forth in hundred yard reaches. Afterward, exhausted, he fell asleep for an hour on his towel. Back at his room, he showered and put on khaki slacks and a faded denim shirt. He thought briefly of calling his office, but rejected the idea. Cheryl would be gone by now—it was seven p.m.—and, although he had only been away for five days, practicing law seemed like something he had done in another lifetime. He had no desire to hear, and respond to, the usual messages left by clients, adversaries, and judges' chambers, and wondered if he ever would again. He had not shaved since he arrived in Florida, and it felt good not to. He was meeting Dunn in the lobby at seven thirty for the drive to El Pulpo, and decided to have a drink in the adjacent lounge while waiting for him.

The lounge was not busy, and he was served his scotch on the rocks quickly. He took his first, short sip, and was putting his glass down when he saw Agent Markey standing at the arched entrance to the bar. Markey spotted him, walked over, and sat down across from him at the small drinks table he had taken along one side of the room.

"Cassio."

"Agent Markey."

"I'll get to the point."

"You want a drink first? I'm buying."

"No."

Jay said nothing. Markey, in his regulation dark suit, seemed more intense than he had at their last meeting, if that was possible.

"I spoke to Melissa Powers," said Markey. "She said her mother wrote you some letters. There were no letters in your file."

"I forgot all about them. They're in a safe-deposit box. Cheryl can get them tomorrow morning. You can have someone pick them up at my office."

"You must have thought they were important."

"I did."

"Why?"

"Why do you ask?"

"I'm investigating the murder of your friend," Markey replied, "but there's more to it than that."

"There was a lot of babble," Jay said, "but she basically accused Bryce of being in bed with drug kingpins and corrupt officials in Mexico. They lived there for five years."

"Did you keep anything else back?"

"I didn't keep the letters back."

"All of the financial records were intact?"

"Of course."

"How many letters are there?"

"Around fifty."

"You're lucky I don't charge you with obstructing justice."

"You scared the hell out of my secretary, but you don't scare me."

"If you're down here to investigate the Del Colliano killing and I find out about it, then I *will* have you arrested. You and your friend Dunn. I see he's registered here, too."

"He's on vacation."

"It must be a long one. Al Garland told me he got a letter of resignation from Dunn yesterday."

"You spoke with Melissa Powers knowing she was represented by counsel."

"What?"

"Did you read her her rights? She's a target, isn't she?"

"Are you telling me how to do my job?"

"You've heard of the exclusionary rule, I'm sure."

Jay was surprised to see Markey bridling at this remark. What kind of nerve had he touched? He was trying to think of something to say that would touch it again, but before he could come up with anything, Frank Dunn appeared at the table.

"Gentlemen," Dunn said.

"You must be Mr. Dunn," said Markey.

"I am," said Dunn.

"Chris Markey, FBI."

There was no handshake.

Dunn motioned to the waiter as he sat down.

"I was just leaving," said Markey.

"Have a drink," said Dunn, his eyes twinkling.

Markey shook his head, then said to Dunn, "I spoke to Al Garland today. He wants your badge and ID."

"I'll make sure I stop by the post office tomorrow."

"I hope for your sake you haven't been using them down here."

"Are you sure you won't have a drink?" said Dunn. "You look like you could use it."

"Make that call," Markey said to Jay, and he left.

34.
5:00 PM, December 17, 2004, Miami

Angelo was seated at his regular banquette in the corner, a club soda with a wedge of lemon in front of him. Maria kissed him hello and sat down to his left.

"You're early," she said. "And not smiling."

"No."

"Talk to me."

"It turns out the woman we're looking for knew Alvie Diaz."

"Alvie's dead," she said. Alvaro Diaz had died in his sleep in September, Maria recalled.

"I know, but they'll come looking for her. The FBI just got his name last week."

"You mean the Donna Kelly woman."

"Right."

In bed last night Maria had asked Angelo about his business with Frank Dunn and Jay Cassio. Sometimes he would tell her what he was doing in a case, and sometimes not. He told her about the killing of Dan Del Colliano, the alleged murder-suicide of Kate and Bryce Powers, and the promise of help he had made to Dunn back in September. He told her not to worry, but of course she did. Showing a picture around of a person who had been tortured and executed by a drug cartel was a dangerous thing to do. Word could pass from mouth to mouth, and Angelo, an ordinary citizen, would not be hard to find, or to kill.

"What does she look like?" Maria asked. "Tell me again."

"Mid-twenties, long black hair, well developed, as we used to say in Brooklyn."

"Cuban?"

"We don't know, possibly. Probably Hispanic of some kind."

Maria looked around the restaurant. The place was quiet, the tables in the dining room pristinely set after the lunch cleanup. She didn't expect to see anybody and did not. Turning back to Angelo, she said, "Alvie brought me Isabel."

"I know."

They looked at each other.

A few days before he died, Alvaro Diaz, who lived only a block away, had appeared at the restaurant with a pale, thin young woman, who he introduced as Isabel Sanchez. She was a friend, he said, who needed a job and a place to stay. Requests of this kind were routine to Maria, whose work as a volunteer at the Cuban Cultural Center on Eighth Street often brought her face-to-face with immigrants, legal and illegal, desperate for help. Isabel had a strange look in her eyes, and a bad haircut, but Maria had seen much worse. She might have been sick, or pregnant, or running from a husband, or trying to get clean of drugs or alcohol. She wasn't even Cuban. It didn't matter. Alvaro Diaz was a sweet man, and one of Sam Perna's best friends. Sam gave the girl a job as a waitress, and let her live in the small apartment above the restaurant. A week later, he cried like a child and closed El Pulpo for the three days it took to wake and bury Alvie.

"It could be her," Angelo said.

"Alvie wouldn't dump someone bad on us."

"Not knowingly."

"Tell me again what this woman did," said Maria.

"She had a half million dollars in cash in an airport locker in Jersey. She claimed she worked for Powers, that he gave her the money. She hired Del Colliano to bring it to Florida for her. He does. Two days later he's dead. The girl's gone, the money's gone."

"When was this?"

"September."

"How do you know this?"

"Frank and Jay went to Royal Palm today, where Alvie worked. Two Mexicans were there a couple of days ago asking about their sister—Isabel Perez—who lived there but who was missing. They wanted to know who her friends were. Alvie was mentioned. The next day the office was broken into, probably to get Alvie's address."

"I'll go talk to her," said Maria. "She's upstairs right now."

"What time does she start work?"

"Five."

"Wait until she comes in, and then sit with her someplace where I can see you."

"No. I'm going up there now."

"Maria."

"Yes, senor?"

"Take my gun."

"No."

"Well, listen to me, then."

Maria had gotten to her feet, and now sat down again.

"Go ahead," she said.

"The FBI knows about the Alvie connection, too. They're probably working Little Havana right now. These two Mexicans sound like trouble. Then there's Cassio. She might have had a hand in killing his friend. I'm supposed to be helping him. She's running out of options. She'll want to run. Tonight, probably. I don't blame her. Before she goes anyplace, she has to talk to me."

"You can't turn her in, *Angel*."

"I won't if you don't want me to."

"I don't."

"I'll wait right here."

Maria could pronounce Angelo's name as well as any native-born American, but occasionally she shortened it by a syllable, and said it the Spanish way, giving the *g* a rough *h* sound, usually in moments of passion, or tenderness, or, as on this occasion, to underscore a point. Her father, a journalist, had been executed by one of Castro's firing squads after *la revolución*, for questioning the kind of government the so-called rebel hero intended to establish. Then her older brother had been tortured and killed in the bargain. Maria had escaped Cuba soon afterward, but she knew what it was to be hunted, and to hear death in every knock on your door. Isabel Sanchez, or *Perez*, or *Kelly*—whatever her name was—was deeply scarred, but she was no killer. She was the hunted, not the hunter.

• • •

Maria went upstairs, and Angelo sipped his club soda and watched as Sam dried and racked glasses at the bar and the two busboys began stocking the waitress stations in the dining room. Tonight he was not soothed, as he usually was, by the routine predinner activities of the restaurant. If Maria did not return in fifteen minutes, he would go up and get her. Isabel had been a model waitress, quiet, hardworking, uncomplaining. And though good-looking and unattached, she had gracefully but firmly spurned all attempts by the male customers and staff to engage her in the presexual dance. But if, as he suspected, she was the mysterious Donna Kelly, the Latin beauty who had somehow managed to come into possession of five hundred thousand dollars via her relationship with a New Jersey real estate magnate, the siren who had lured Dan Del Colliano to his death, then there was another side to her altogether, and Maria might be in danger. I'll help her, Angelo said to himself, looking at his watch. But the sooner she's out of here, the better.

When he looked up, Angelo saw Victor Ponce, the owner of a nightclub called El Caribe, located around the corner on Eighth Street, enter the bar and head toward his table.

"*Buenas noches*, Victor," said Angelo when Victor arrived at the table.

"*Buenas noches*, Angelo," said Victor. "Can we talk?"

"Of course. What would you like to drink?"

"Nothing, *gracias*, I have to get back."

"What can I do for you, Victor?"

Victor, a hawk-faced, sharp-eyed Cuban in his late fifties, took the chair across from Angelo. He wore a tropical print shirt that hung loosely over a large belly, his fingers flashing with the silver rings he affected, his gray hair swept back into the pompadour he had been wearing ever since Angelo first met him and probably since he was a teenager in Havana.

"There have been two men in the neighborhood," Victor replied, "in the last few days, claiming to be looking for their sister, a beautiful young woman who is missing. Have they been in here?"

"Not that I know of."

"These men were in my place last night. They showed their sister's picture to Manuel and Miguel."

"And?"

"It is Isabel, your new waitress."

Manuel and Miguel were Victor's bouncer and bartender, respectively. Both of them had hit on Isabel when she first started working at El Pulpo.

"Did they send them here?"

"No."

"What did these men look like?"

"I didn't see them, but Manuel thinks they are Mexican, both young—in their twenties—black hair, black clothes. He thinks they're twins."

"Manuel was suspicious."

"Yes. He sees many punks. These were the worst kind."

"Where else have they been?"

"I stopped by Ascension's on the way over here. They had lunch in her place today."

"Did she recognize Isabel?"

"No, but someone will."

"Thank you, Victor. I'll talk to Isabel."

"De nada."

"One more thing. If they stop by your place again, try to keep them there, and call me, *immediatamente, sí?* But be careful."

"Of course. *Buenas noches*, Angelo."

"*Buenas noches*, Victor."

35.
5:30 PM, December 17, 2004, Miami

"It's her," said Maria.

Angelo shook his head, then said, "Will she talk to me?"

"No. She doesn't want to implicate you, or Sam or me."

"She already has."

"She's aware of that. 'Any further,' I should have said."

"What did she say?"

Maria paused to look around. The bar was empty. It was five thirty. The earliest dinner patrons usually arrived around six.

"Not a lot. She knows she's in great danger and wants to run, but she has no car, no passport, and no money."

Angelo took this in, then said, "What about Del Colliano?"

"The same people that killed him are looking for her, to kill her."

"The law?"

"They'll crucify her. It seems she's done a lot of bad things."

"Did she kill Del Colliano, Maria?"

"No. She's very hard, Angelo, cruel even, but I don't think she's killed."

"Did you ask her?"

"No, *Angel*, I didn't."

Angelo knew his wife, knew by the grim set of her usually lovely face that she was thinking of her own bad times, of how much she had had to harden her heart in order to survive, of how often she thought of revenge against Castro and his lackeys for the murder of her father and brother, the humiliation of her family.

"If we help her," he said, "we could be in deep trouble."

"If we give her to the government," Maria replied, "they'll use her, then throw her to the wolves, who will immediately devour her."

"Sam could lose the restaurant. They confiscate everything connected with drugs."

"That sounds much like Cuba."

Angelo did not reply. Two men had come in while he and Maria were talking, and taken seats at the bar. He had been concentrating on Maria when they first entered, but now took a moment to study them as they engaged Sam in conversation. Both were in their mid-twenties, both dark-haired, dark-eyed Latinos, very much fitting Victor Ponce's description of the men looking for Isabel. He turned his attention back to his wife, her last remark re-forming itself in his mind. Maria knew that the American and Cuban political systems had nothing in common, but, though she fiercely loved her new country, she was no friend of government, not after living under Batista and Castro for half of her life.

"She won't get far, unless we help her," he said. "And even then, it's probably just a matter of time. She's in a lot of trouble."

"She says she has leverage that can save her life."

"What kind of leverage?"

"Documents and tapes that would put the Mexican attorney general in jail."

"Christ."

"I believe her."

"Where are they, these papers and tapes?"

"In Mexico."

"Is that what she wants to do? Go to Mexico to get this stuff?"

"Yes."

"Did you tell her about Cassio?"

"Yes. She says he's a fool to try to track down the killers. They will happily torture and kill him as they did his friend."

"Will she talk to him? Tell him what happened?"

"I don't think so. She's very scared. She wants to leave now, this minute."

"That's impossible."

"Yes. She needs our help. She knows that."

"And you want to help her?"

"Yes, I do."

"She has to talk to Cassio," Angelo said. "It's the only way I'll help her. He's entitled to know what happened to his friend. If she won't talk to him, then we can't help her."

Maria locked eyes with Angelo, and he thought for a second she was going to fight on. She had, he knew, loved two men before him, her father and her brother. Last night in bed she told him that Jay Cassio had the same look in his eyes as Tomas, Sr. and Tomas, Jr. did when Fidel's police took them from their home. *Desafío*. Defiance. She would understand.

"I will talk her into it," she said.

Angelo leaned back and sighed. The two Latinos had left, and Sam was looking at him like he wanted to talk. Leaning forward again, he said, "Go up and get her. We'll take her to Libby Morales. Go down the back stairs. I'll meet you in the kitchen. I'll drive you in the van. Get her a passport, birth certificate, driver's license, whatever Libby can do in a few hours."

"Then what?"

"I'll come back here. Borrow Libby's car, or take a cab, and take her home. Wait there. Don't leave the house, or let anyone in. How much cash do you have at home?"

"About a thousand."

"There's fifteen hundred in my money clip in my blue jacket, in my closet. Get that, too."

"What about Cassio?"

"He's coming here later. I'll bring him home with me. He can have his talk with Isabel."

"One more thing, *Angel*."

"What?"

"Gary Shaw's stopping by. He said it was important."

"What time?"

"He said around six. He said not to call him on his cell phone."

Angelo looked at his watch. It was just past five thirty. "I'll be back in time," he said.

"One more thing," Maria said.

"What?"

"*Te amo.*"

"*Te amo*, Maria."

36.
8:00 PM, December 17, 2004, Miami

Libby Morales—the master forger to the Cuban community in Little Havana—was not home when Angelo and Maria arrived at her house. She was, according to her fourteen-year-old daughter, at Conchita's, a beauty parlor on Eighth Street. Maria managed to persuade the girl to go to the shop and bring her mother home. Libby arrived forty-five minutes later with a head full of pink curlers, and got right to work, needing little except Angelo and Maria's word for the dire urgency of the situation. When Angelo got back to El Pulpo, it was close to eight and Gary Shaw was sitting at the bar chatting with Sam. They shook hands and retired to Angelo's office, where they eyed each other for a moment, both well trained at reading the life map that is on all of our faces.

"Sorry I'm late," Angelo said. "I got tied up."
"I was late, too," Shaw said. "Traffic everywhere."
"What's up?"
"William Taylor went down."
"Thank God."
"Right. Now maybe he'll get offed in prison."
"That would be nice."

They both knew that whether Taylor was executed by the public or the private sector, it would not diminish the suffering of the parents of the nine-year-old victim. Sam came over with two Amstel Lights and two tall glasses, placed them on the table, and returned to the bar. They each poured their beer and sipped.

"Where's Maria?" Shaw asked.

"She's not working tonight. Committee meeting."

"Who's watching the door, you?"

Angelo smiled and said, "Sam can do it, and Carla. It looks like we won't be too busy."

"Are your friends in town?"

"They're here. Can you tell me anything?"

"The FBI is investigating Del Colliano's murder, as well as the Jersey killings," Shaw said. "They're obviously connected. They've taken over Jersey completely."

"What about Florida? Is there a task force?"

"Yes."

"Stop me whenever you want."

"Go ahead."

"Who's on the task force?"

"I am."

"When did that happen?"

"Today."

"And the FBI guy, Markey, he's in charge?"

"Right."

"Can you talk?"

"No, I can't. Except for one thing."

"I'm listening."

"You didn't tell me Cassio met the killers."

"I didn't think you needed to know."

"Well, Markey knows. He's setting Cassio up for them, hoping to move in."

"Jesus."

"Right, Markey's obsessed. He's putting an article in the

paper essentially marking Cassio, and if that doesn't work he'll try something else."

"The kid is just as obsessed. He may actually want to go along with it."

"You can't let him do that, Ange. The killers are predators. They've been killing since they were kids. It's all they know. Cassio wouldn't survive. They behead people. It's their trademark."

Angelo had spoken to Sam before taking Maria and Isabel to Libby's, and confirmed that the two men he saw earlier at the bar were the ones looking for Isabel. Sam had recognized the woman in the photograph they showed him as his new waitress, but told them he had never laid eyes on her. Angelo had quickly filled Sam in, and then left for the ride to the master forger's small house on 14th Avenue. He had Isabel lie down in the back of the El Pulpo van, but saw no sign of the Mexicans as he made his way through the back streets of Little Havana. He saw no reason to tell Shaw that the killers were in the neighborhood. Shaw would have to call in a ton of cops, and all hell would break loose, possibly thwarting Isabel's escape and Cassio's chance to talk to her. And likely also to result in the arrest of everyone involved in harboring Isabel, including Sam and Maria, with questions asked later.

"He's due any minute," said Angelo, looking at his watch. "You can stay and talk to him yourself if you want."

"Is this him?" Shaw asked, nodding toward the bar, where Jay and Dunn were shaking hands with Sam. "If it is, it looks like I don't have much of a choice."

"It's him," Angelo replied, getting to his feet to greet Jay and Dunn, and introduce them to Shaw. They all sat, and Sam appeared with beers for Jay and Dunn.

"There's been a development," said Angelo, looking at Shaw.

"Angelo can give you the details," said Shaw, "but we've identified the killers: two brothers, Mexicans, in their mid-twenties. You don't need to know their names. The thing is, Jay, they know you're in Miami, and they want you dead. I suppose you know why. You need to hide, or better yet leave the state—without being followed."

"Miami's a big place," said Jay. "How would they know where to find me?"

"You have to trust me on this, and you have to leave immediately."

Jay leaned back, and looked at Angelo and Dunn.

"It sounds like somebody's setting him up," said Dunn, looking at Shaw. "Is that your take?"

"I can't say any more," Shaw answered. "In fact, I have to get going. Talk to Angelo."

"We're leaving, too," said Angelo, rising along with Shaw. "We might as well get Jay out of his hotel right now. I'll fill him in, Gary. We know the position you're in."

Angelo assumed that the two Latino strangers were continuing to ask questions in the neighborhood, and that it was only a matter of time before someone innocently directed them to El Pulpo. The sooner all of them were out of the restaurant, the better. Jay and Dunn had come to have dinner, and talk about the Isabel Perez-Alvaro Diaz-Little Havana connection, but they quickly stood, not about to object to anything after hearing what Gary Shaw had to say. Shaw went to the bar to attempt to pay for the drinks, but Sam, shaking his head, looked at the Miami detective and said, "Are you kidding?"

Angelo ushered Jay and Dunn out of the restaurant, and Shaw followed. As they emerged onto the sidewalk, the four men were lit briefly by the light that spilled through the front door from inside the bar. They were heading toward the small parking lot on their right when two men stepped out of a car across the street and approached them with guns drawn and pointing in the direction of Jay and Dunn. Shaw shoved Angelo, who was walking directly in front of him, while shouting, "Get down!" and drawing his gun. The two men began firing at Jay, who was in the process of being dragged to the ground by Angelo. Shaw moved quickly toward the cover of a nearby parked car, as the gunmen, whose first shots had missed, took aim again at Jay, who was now on the ground. While Dunn was diving on top of Jay, and Angelo was reaching for the gun in his ankle holster, Shaw raised up and emptied his service revolver at the gunmen, both of whom swung and returned fire before scrambling back into their car. Angelo got off two shots at the car as they sped away, and then turned and saw Shaw on his back on the sidewalk, bleeding from the chest. Angelo reached Shaw quickly, and knelt over his friend to examine his wound, which was high up toward the right shoulder.

"I'm okay, Ange, I'm okay," Shaw said.

"It's only the arm," Angelo replied. "We'll get you to a hospital."

"No, Sam can take care of me. You get out of here."

Sam had come out, taken things in, gone back into the restaurant, and emerged again with ice packed in a clean bar towel, which he was pressing against Shaw's bleeding shoulder. Dunn and Jay, who were unhurt, were leaning over Shaw as well.

"What happened?" Sam asked.

"I stopped by to meet Angelo," Shaw answered. "He wasn't around. I had a drink and left and ran into these bad guys on the way out. That's it, Ange, now go. It's the best way to handle it all around. Sam will back me up. Go."

Angelo looked at Sam, who nodded to him, then got to his feet, and said to Jay and Dunn, "Let's get the fuck out of here."

Angelo's LeBaron and Sam's Buick Riviera, which Jay and Frank were still using, were parked side by side in El Pulpo's parking lot. When they reached the cars, Angelo turned and said to Jay, "There's a lot to talk about, but first go to your hotel and check out, then come to my house: 10315 20th Street, Southwest. I found Isabel Perez. She's there waiting to talk to you. Go."

37.
Midnight, December 18, 2004, Miami

The Friday night traffic on the MacArthur Causeway was bumper to bumper. By the time Jay and Dunn reached the Silver Sands, packed, checked out, and made it back to Angelo and Maria's duplex in Little Havana, it was close to eleven p.m. They were let in by Maria, who, grim-faced, led them through a small living room and dining area, then through French doors onto a screened-in porch, where they found Angelo seated at a redwood picnic table, a scotch and a pack of Marlboro Reds in front of him. Jay and Dunn sat. Insects were banging against the screen behind Angelo. The sharp chirping of cicadas was drifting in from the shrubs bordering the backyard. Angelo pushed his cigarettes toward Jay, who took one and lit it.

"Can I get you something?" said Maria, who had remained standing. "Beer, coffee, a drink?"

"I'll take a beer," said Dunn.

"Nothing," said Jay.

"Is Shaw dead?" Dunn asked. The house was too quiet, the night too still and hot, Angelo and Maria too stricken-looking for there to be anything but bad news.

"No. He's okay," Angelo answered. "I just got back from

the hospital. He was in surgery, but his wife said it wasn't critical. His shoulder's torn up."

"Where's Miss Perez?" Jay asked.

"She's not here," Angelo replied, staring at Maria, who had returned from the kitchen with Frank's bottle of Corona, and was standing in the doorway, holding it.

"She ran," Maria said, stepping forward and placing the beer on the table in front of Frank.

"Fuck," said Jay.

"What happened?" Frank asked, pulling the Corona to him, and lifting it to take a long drink.

"She had a gun. Libby came with the papers—a passport, a driver's license, and credit cards. When she left, Isabel pointed the gun at me. I had already given her the money, twenty-five hundred dollars. She called a cab. When it came, she left. I'm sorry."

"Where was she going?" Jay asked.

"We think Mexico," said Angelo.

"What name was on the passport and license?"

"Isabel Sanchez-Hill of Miami," Maria replied.

"And the credit cards?" asked Frank.

"I don't know. Fictitious names. Libby applies for them, gets them, and sells them. These had fifteen hundred dollar cash advance limits. She was very proud of her work."

"Why Mexico?" Jay asked.

"She said she had documents there, and tapes," Angelo answered, "that would incriminate the Mexican attorney general in the drug trade. She thinks she could bargain them for her life. Those two shooters tonight killed your buddy and were at the restaurant to kill her. They must have recognized you from your picture in the paper in Jersey, which was Agent Markey's idea—using you as a decoy to draw them out. He was planning on doing the same thing here—planting your picture and naming your hotel in the *Herald*. That's what Gary Shaw came by to tell me."

"Where in Mexico?" Jay asked.

"We don't know," Maria answered.

"No idea?"

"No."

"Is she Mexican?"

"Yes. She said she was born there, an orphan."

"Where was she living?"

"Above the restaurant. There's a small apartment."

"Have you looked through it?" Jay asked.

"No. I was waiting for Angelo. He just got back. Jay, I'm very sorry. She said she would talk to you, tell you how your friend died, before she ran. It was such a small request, I believed her."

"It's okay, Maria," said Jay. "A talk is nothing. I would not have settled for a talk."

Dunn stayed with Maria while Angelo drove Jay to El Pulpo. When they got there, there were two couples having a late dinner in the dining room. Sam was playing dominoes with Victor Ponce at the bar. Angelo joined them, first pointing Jay to the back stairway near the kitchen that led to the apartment.

It was not an apartment, Jay found, but rather one room, with a sloped ceiling and a window facing the parking lot. Under one eave was a single bed, neatly made, with a brown jute rug on the floor next to it. Under the opposite eave was a four drawer dresser, with a lamp on top that came on when Jay flipped the switch by the door. There was a small table under the window with a second lamp on it that he also switched on. The hardwood floor was worn bare, and there was nothing on the walls. Outside Jay could hear the clank of garbage cans in the alley behind the kitchen and, faintly, the traffic on Calle Ocho, always busy on a Friday night. Next to the bed was a small closet that was empty, its door standing open.

Isabel Perez's scent was in the room, the aroma of her perfumes, soap, and lotions lingering in the hot night air, as if she had showered, dressed, and gone out only moments ago. Two small jars of face cream and a bottle of cologne stood on a flimsy plastic tray—something swiped from a cheap hotel—next to the lamp on the otherwise naked dresser top. Except for these there was no trace of Isabel in the room, nothing in the dresser drawers, nothing under the rug or the bed, nothing in the bedding, which Jay tore apart. Nothing, except her scent. He flicked off the table lamp, and then, before leaving, picked up the bottle of cologne, twisted off its top, and brought it to his nostrils, the smell, sweet and clean, reminding him sharply of Danny: Danny had smelled this scent, been close to this woman.

He fumbled with the bottle's tiny plastic cap as he tried to replace it, and it fell to the floor and rolled under the dresser. When he bent down to retrieve it, he saw what he thought was a small box in the shadow at the back of the old chest of drawers. This turned out to be a packet of letters in yellowed envelopes bound by a faded red ribbon. On top was a cheap scapular medal—a green line image of the Virgin Mary on a square piece of white cloth tucked into a clear plastic protective cover. He extracted the first letter from its envelope. It was written in a chaste and unadorned script, like the vows taken by its author:

My dearest Isabelita,

As you know, we are not allowed to have money or possessions, but even if we were, the Blessed Mother would be the best gift I could give you. May she be with you always as you enter your new life. Please keep in touch with me. I fear I will be lonely without you, and though I must bear all suffering for Christ, sometimes it is difficult, and your serenity and beauty of heart have brought much joy to my life.

With great affection and hope for your future,
I am, your friend,

>Josefina de los Angeles, O.P.
>August 25, 1991

At the top of the faded, yellowing letter was the name and address of the Convent of Santa Maria in Polanco, Mexico City.

Jay reached for the switch near the door and turned off the light, and as he did, the room now pitch-dark, he felt the muzzle of a gun at the side of his head, and a woman's voice said, "I came back for that."

Jay gathered himself, smelling again the same scent he had just sniffed from the bottle on the dresser, gauging the position of Isabel in the room, and the distance between them, the outline of her body beginning to take shape in the darkness only a foot or two away, slightly behind him and to his left.

"You must be Miss Perez. *Isabelita.*"

Silence.

"You steal from your friends, then you return for *this*," said Jay, snapping open the letter in his left hand, and simultaneously ducking and swinging with his right fist, aiming for Isabel's midsection and hitting her squarely—and very hard—directly in the stomach. As she grunted and bent swiftly forward in reaction to the blow, Jay grabbed her gun arm and twisted it, bringing her to the floor on her stomach, the gun clattering away. Holding her arm twisted behind her, his knee pressed to the small of her back, Jay caught his breath, and again paused to get his bearings. Accustomed now to the darkness, the light from a streetlamp spilling softly in through the window, he spotted the gun on the floor near the bed, and was able to reach it with his free hand.

"Let me up," said Isabel. "I can do you no harm." She was winded, her words coming in swift spurts between deep breaths.

"Where's your passport?"

"In my purse. I dropped it when you struck me."

Jay saw the purse near the door.

"Dan spoke of you," Isabel said.

"Was that before or after he was tortured? Or during?"

"I was not a part of that."

"And you don't steal from your friends," Jay said, his breathing returning to normal, but unable to keep the anger from his voice. "And betray them."

"I can help you get your revenge. I know that is what you want. Please let me up. My arm hurts, and I am sick."

"How?"

Before Isabel could answer, the door swung open and the dresser lamp went on. Angelo was standing in the doorway holding his gun straight out before him.

"Fuck," he said, taking in the scene.

Jay released Isabel, and got to his feet.

"I see you found our friend," said Angelo.

"She found me."

"I'll call the police."

"No, don't," Jay said. "Leave me alone with her for a second, then we'll decide."

"Whose gun is that?"

"Hers."

Isabel had rolled over and, rubbing her right arm—the one that Jay had twisted behind her and jammed almost up to her neck—dragged herself to the bed, where she sat on the floor, her head against the mattress. She was wearing black jeans and espadrilles, and a white blouse, which had gotten dirty and had come out of her pants while Jay was scraping her on the floor. She worked to tuck it back in now, clutching the neckline, where the three top buttons had been torn off.

"Take her purse, Ange," Jay said. "The passport's in it, and the money, too, probably. I won't be long—a few minutes."

"I'll be in the bar," said Angelo. "Don't be long. The police were here talking to Sam. They said they'd be back to talk to the staff." He picked the purse up off of the floor and left.

Jay sat on the floor across from Isabel, his back against the dresser, the gun, a lightweight revolver, in his right hand, which he rested on his drawn-up knees.

"Tell me how you can help me," he said.

"The man I work for, Herman Santaria, is looking for me, to kill me I am sure," Isabel replied. "If I call him, and tell him where I am, he will send his two killers—the ones who killed your friend—to kill me. You can be waiting for them. I will do that for you, but I must be in a position where I can flee immediately upon making the call. Also, I have hard proof that Santaria, his brother Lazaro, and a man named Rafael de Leon—the top aide to the president—have been in the drug and money laundering business for many years. They have committed murders, and worse. I have been thinking that it would be difficult for me to simply hand this proof to the American authorities. Who would believe me, a . . ."

"A what?"

"A nobody. A thief," Isabel answered, running a hand over her short thatch of jet black hair. "If you come with me to Mexico, I will give you the evidence. You can read it—you are a lawyer—and ask me questions about my dealings with Santaria and Bryce Powers. You can bring it back and give it to your FBI, or do what you think best with it. From there also I will call Herman. He is the one who ordered your friend's death. He will be happy to hear that I am in Mexico. The Feria brothers—his killers, his *panthers* he calls them—can kill me with impunity there."

"Where in Mexico?"

"Puerto Angel, a poor town on the southern coast. I put the evidence in a house there that I used to visit as a child."

"What kind of evidence?"

"Tapes of telephone conversations, and documents, many documents."

"Where did you get them?"

"From Bryce Powers."

"You were partners in crime."

"Yes."

"And lovers?"

"Yes."

"How much did you take?"

"Several million, but I don't have it. Bryce took care of the money."

"Why bother with the documents? Why not just run?"

Isabel's perfectly sculpted nostrils had been flaring while she was gasping for air, but now her face was composed, its natural high color, a creamy olive, returning as she recovered from the shock of Jay's blow to her gut. She had folded one half of her broken blouse over the other, leaving it at that, resting her hands on the floor at her sides. She held his gaze as he waited for her to answer, and then said, "I want revenge, like you."

"For what?"

"That is my business."

"Why should I trust you?"

"You shouldn't. I am a bad person. I have lied all my life. But I am your only chance to avenge your friend, who I know you loved. Otherwise why would you be sitting here, talking to me?"

"What happened to Danny?"

"If we go to Mexico, it will be a long journey. I will tell you as we go—what I know, and what I assume to be true. You can carry all of the money, and once we go through customs, you can also have my passport. I am tired of running. It is like a slow death, to always be running and hiding. I need to stop dying. You are my only chance."

38.
4:00 PM, December 18, 2004, Merida, Mexico

The used car salesman looked at the papers a long time, pretending careful scrutiny, but concerned, Isabel knew, only with getting the highest price possible for the Jeep Wrangler she was interested in. Or getting her into bed. Probably both. Isabel Sanchez-Hill, US citizen, resident of Miami. A tourist, in the country for thirty days. The salesman, a paunchy, middle-aged hustler, saw enough tourists, she was sure, to know that she did not look like one. She was dressed simply, in jeans and silver leather sandals, and a simple blouse. But her grooming was impeccable—clean eyebrows, light lipstick, her fingernails shiny drops of crimson—and her bearing was what it always was, proud, unconsciously superior. Neither could she hide her perfect diction, the unaccented speech of the high-class Castilian, instilled in her by Sister Josefina from birth.

"Would you like to take it for a ride, senorita?"

"No," Isabel replied. "That's not necessary."

"Do you know how to handle a stick shift? I will be happy to give you a quick lesson. Perhaps we can stop for a cool drink."

"You're very kind, senor, but I am pressed for time. I will

pay the full price if you can have the paperwork done in ten minutes, no more. Will you take American dollars?"

"Of course, senorita. Please follow me."

Isabel smiled to herself as she drove out of the used car lot. The fat salesman had stuck to his price—two thousand dollars—his lust for money asserting itself once he realized his lust for her was going nowhere. If she had had the time, she could have gotten the car for much less, possibly for nothing, but she was meeting Jay Cassio at the bus terminal in downtown Merida in an hour, maybe two, depending on the bus schedule from Cancun, and she wanted to be there on time so that they could begin their long journey—she calculated it to be seven hundred miles—at once. She stopped at a grocery and a bank, and then, map in hand, made her way through the handsome Yucatán capital until she found the terminal on Calle 69, not far from the Plaza Mayor, the shaded, parklike square that was, by a myriad of names, the heart of all of Mexico's colonial cities.

Inside the station, Isabel found a seat as far away from the milling travelers and scampering children as she could get and still be able to see the glass doors that led to the departure/arrival area. She had slept fitfully on the morning flight from Miami to Merida, and been too busy to think since she landed. Now, sitting on a plastic bench, waiting for Cassio, oblivious to the noise and sweltering heat of the station, the events of the night before organized themselves in her mind: the photo and rapidly concluded discussion in Libby Morales's basement printshop; threatening Maria with the gun; fleeing; returning to El Pulpo; the agreement reached with Cassio; the look on Angelo's face when they told him they were leaving immediately for Mexico; Cassio promising to repay the twenty-five hundred dollars, and Morales's fees, when he returned; her apology—without tears—to Maria when they returned to pick up Cassio's passport; the redness of the face of the Irish detective; the drive to the airport; the sleepless waiting; the exhausting plane ride.

They had agreed that separate flights would be safer, that they should not be seen together until they were away from airports and cities. Isabel was free to run when she landed in Merida. She had her fake papers and twenty-two hundred dollars, but Angelo had watched her board her flight, and watched the plane take off, and one call from him, or Cassio, to any number of people—Agent Markey, the police in Merida, the Mexican Justice Department—and she would be quickly caught, and probably killed. She had lived her life in bondage, her one attempt to escape, with Bryce Powers, ending in disaster. And now once again she was shackled, to Cassio, but what choice did she have? An American prison? She had thought him a fool when Maria first mentioned Del Colliano's lawyer friend, but she was wrong. The look in his eyes as he sat on the floor across from her in her room above El Pulpo was a familiar one. It was the look, a mixture of despair and hatred, that she remembered seeing in her own eyes when she looked in the mirror on a couple of very bad days in the last thirteen years. Days she could have easily killed had she the means.

If Cassio didn't kill the Feria brothers, he would die as a man. Bryce's papers would then not be delivered, but Isabel's desire for revenge grew smaller as her chance for freedom grew larger. She would draw out the Ferias for the handsome, angry lawyer, and be long gone when they arrived. Whatever happened, Isabel would be unshackled, out of bondage, free, for the first time in her life, and she would then do everything in her power to keep it that way.

Spotting Cassio coming through the terminal's glass doors, a battered canvas knapsack slung over one shoulder, dark sunglasses hiding his strikingly beautiful gray eyes, Isabel rose to greet him. Watching him as he walked toward her, not yet noticing her, her heart constricted, for, despite his week's growth of beard and his obvious travel weariness, he was indeed very handsome, as proud and graceful and as sure of himself as a top athlete or a great matador, and Isabel wondered what it would be like to hold him in her arms, to choose him freely as her lover. He saw her, and she put these thoughts aside. In twenty-four hours she would be on her way to Guatemala, and he would be returning to Miami, or dead.

39.
8:00 AM, December 19, 2004, Miami

The bullet that put Gary Shaw on his back shattered his collarbone and lodged behind his right shoulder, requiring immediate and extensive reconstructive surgery by a team of specialists at Miami's Beth Israel Hospital. He was unable to speak intelligently to anyone until Saturday afternoon, when Jack Voynik and Ted Stevens descended on him. Heavily sedated, he managed to tell them that he had gone to meet his friend, Angelo Perna, at El Pulpo for a drink on Friday evening. He was late getting there. When Angelo did not show, he left. On the way to his car he spotted the Feria brothers heading toward the restaurant. He recognized them from the pictures he had seen earlier that day. He confronted them, they drew their guns, he drew his, and shots were exchanged. He went down, and the next thing he knew, Sam Perna was kneeling beside him; then he blacked out.

Shaw's statement meshed with Sam's, and there was no one else in the restaurant or the neighborhood who had heard or seen anything unusual. But Chris Markey was suspicious. That morning, when his men had gone to the Silver Sands to begin their stakeout of Cassio, they learned that he had checked out late the night before. Coincidence, maybe, but if Cassio were warned it had to come from someone on his team, making the local cops—Shaw and Kendall—the likely suspects. Markey ordered his people to find out as much as they could about Angelo and Sam Perna, and to check airport manifests for departures by Cassio and Dunn, and he called a meeting for Sunday morning to plan strategy, which was about to begin. Present in the conference room were Stevens, Voynik, Gatti, Ramirez, and Jack Kendall.

"Let's start with you, Ted," Markey said.

"Cassio left on Aeromexico flight 435 for Cancun on Saturday at nine a.m. Dunn we haven't located yet, but he hasn't left by a commercial flight. We're staking out his house in Jersey. Angelo and Sam Perna grew up in Brooklyn. They both served in the Army. Sam moved down here in 1965 and fought professionally for a few years under the name Kid Brooklyn. He's been bartending ever since. He's single, never been married, lives on one side of a duplex in Little Havana, his brother and his wife on the other. He was arrested twice for assault in the sixties in Miami Beach, but there were no convictions."

"And Angelo?" said Markey.

"He was a cop in New York City until 1974, a detective at the end. He quit and moved down here with his brother. He's had a Florida PI license since 1979, and a carry permit since 1980. No arrests. He married in 1988. The wife is Cuban. She works at the Cuban Cultural Center on Eighth Street, and hostesses at El Pulpo at night. She's clean. It seems that everybody in Little Havana knows Perna and his wife, and vice versa."

"Why did he quit?"

"He turned in some cops who were beating on a black kid with a telephone book. He was hounded out."

"Was the wife working on Friday night?"

"Sam says she took the night off."

"A Friday night?"

"That's what he says."

"Dunn was a New York cop, too."

"Right. Why don't we bring Angelo in? He says he'd be happy to talk to us."

It was no secret that Shaw and Angelo Perna were friends. If Perna and Frank Dunn had a similar relationship, then the dots were easily connected: Shaw to Perna to Dunn/Cassio, making Shaw the traitor. But why would the Feria boys show up at the Pernas' restaurant, unless they expected to find Isabel there?

"Not yet. I have other plans for him," said Markey. "How are you guys doing?" This question he addressed to Kendall and Ramirez.

"We're ready," said Kendall. "Matt's going in as a truck driver from Jersey. He's just been separated from his wife. We have telephone numbers, addresses, an ex-employer—the works—set up to corroborate him if it's needed. He rented a room today. He'll start looking for a job tomorrow, doing anything, bartending or bouncing preferably, working the Eighth Street joints, etc."

"Good. He can start at El Pulpo. The Ferias might have been going in just to ask questions, or they might have tracked Isabel there. I also want him to get a line on Angelo Perna. Was he helping Dunn and Cassio? Did he know Isabel? Was he helping her? Did he know the old guy, Alvaro Diaz? We'll lay off Angelo for now, make him think the heat is off. Then, if we learn that he was helping Cassio, or he was involved in hiding Isabel, we'll get him in, let him lie to us, and then put the screws to him."

"What about Cassio?" said Gatti.

"Are the papers ready?"

"Yes."

"Deliver them to Mexico City personally. Try to get one of your people attached to the case."

"They may realize who he is and eliminate him," said Kendall. "I mean, if Lazaro Santaria is really the top bad guy, he'll know who Cassio is. He'll have an accident or something, or be killed 'while fleeing police officers.'"

"Maybe not," Markey replied. "The bureaucracy there is unbelievably fucked up. They may just pick him up and hand him to us. If they *do* make the connection, then of course we've lost Cassio as a lure for the Feria brothers, but we'd never find him down there ourselves, anyway."

"And the Feria brothers?" said Gatti. "We can't exactly ask Lazaro to pick them up—they're his boys— assuming they're back in Mexico."

"We need to do everything we can to pick up their trail," Markey answered. "They'll lead us right to Isabel. We need people on the ground in Mexico City, undercover. The blood on the street doesn't match Shaw's so it's a safe bet one or both of them was hit. Maybe they went home to lick their wounds. If we spot them there, then we have to stay with them at all costs until they locate the woman. Take care of it, Phil. Don't stint. Any problems with the suits, come to me."

"And Frank Dunn?" said Voynik.

"Find him, but don't confront him. We'll get an order for a phone tap. His connection to Cassio should be enough of a basis. He's a fugitive. I'd like to tap the Pernas' phones, too, but first we need something that connects them to Isabel or Cassio. If they're involved, we'll arrest them all later, but for now I'm hoping they lead us to Cassio or the woman. There's one more thing. I don't want anybody talking to Shaw except me, and I want to know who visits him from the civilian world. Keep the cop by his door, and have him get names and addresses, except for the immediate family."

"What about the press?" said Stevens. "The guy from the *Herald* called twice this morning."

"Call him back," said Markey. "Tell him we've traced Cassio to Cancun, and that we're asking the Mexican government to execute our arrest warrant pursuant to treaty. He was a witness to a murder in New Jersey, and he withheld evidence duly subpoenaed in a second murder investigation. That's enough sex appeal for another story, I would think. Any questions?"

There were no questions. Markey didn't expect any. He cared little for Shaw, but there was nothing like a cop getting shot to motivate other cops, so Shaw, whether he was a traitor or not, had made himself useful.

40.
5:00 PM, December 18, 2004, Merida

"Where are we going?"

"Here," said Isabel, handing Jay a map and pointing to a spot toward the right half of Mexico's twelve-hundred-mile-long southern coast.

"How far is it?"

"Seven hundred miles, maybe seven fifty."

They were sitting in the jeep. Jay, behind the wheel, studied the map, their route marked in red pencil. Around them, people were making their way to and from their cars as the late afternoon sun blazed down on them and shimmered off of the asphalt surface of the terminal parking lot in visible waves. Jay had changed into khaki shorts, a T-shirt, and sandals at the airport in Cancun, and had the feeling that he would be getting a lot of use out of this basic outfit. He had made the mistake of taking a second-class bus from Cancun, spending the two hour ride standing in one hundred-degree heat next to a family of six peasants, the parents sullen, their eyes downcast, two of the children carrying chickens in burlap bags. The canvas sides of the jeep were open, but he was still very hot, his long hair matted to the back of his neck with sweat. He could use a shower, but there was no point in wasting time. This was not a vacation.

"Do you know the roads?" he asked.

"No, but the map says they are major highways."

"What about this stretch here?" Jay said, pointing to an area called the Isthmus of Tehuantepec.

"A wasteland, I am told, but the road looks good."

The quarters were close in the jeep. As Isabel leaned toward him to look at the map, Jay caught the scent of her—sweat and skin lotion—and something else, probably the cologne he had found on her dresser. There was no ignoring her as a woman: her soft, golden olive skin, her breasts pushing against her cotton blouse, the secrets of a lifetime in her blue eyes. Danny had been right about how beautiful she was. For once he wasn't exaggerating. Danny—always ready to fuck first and ask questions later—had probably sat in a car like this with Isabel, smelled her perfume, maybe even licked away the dampness in the hollow of her throat—and been killed before he could ask any questions. Keep that in mind, Jay thought to himself as he started the jeep and headed toward Calle 65, which would take them to Highway 180, and the first leg of their journey. Highway 180 took them inland and south for fifty miles or so before it swung back to the coast where they would have the Bay of Campeche on their right for about two hundred miles. Night fell as they entered this long stretch of blacktopped road, but there was little relief from the heat or the humidity and no appreciable breeze from the bay, which was dotted with oil rigs rising mutely from the shallow water. Flocks of exotic-looking birds flew across the wide expanse of open water, some landing to perch for a while on the rigs before taking off again en masse at the silent command of the flight leader in their midst. The moon, waxing, just past half full, rose over the bay and followed the jeep as it made its way south along the flat, monotonous coastal plain of the eastern Yucatán.

"Are you tired?" Isabel asked, looking at her watch. It was eight p.m. She had tried to sleep, but the jeep's hard, bumpy ride made it difficult. They had both been awake for the better part of thirty-six hours.

"I'm okay."

"I would like to stop to pee."

"Of course." *And it's time to talk,* Jay thought, *before I lose my nerve.*

Jay slowed down and pulled the jeep to the right into the sandy scrub that bordered the highway, beyond which, only a few yards away, lay the stony shore and the calm blackness of the bay. Jay watched Isabel walk toward the beach, then turned on the interior light and looked at the map. They had just passed the town of Sabancuy, and had perhaps two hours of driving ahead of them before they reached Villahermosa, a city of two hundred thousand people, where they planned on spending the night. He then checked the box of supplies that Isabel had bought in Merida: bottled water, chocolate, potato chips, six bottles of beer, insect repellent, paper towels. He grabbed one of the beers, turned off the interior light, and headed to the beach.

When he got there, Isabel was buttoning her jeans at the edge of the water, her back to him. He walked toward her, and when he got closer he saw that she was taking her jeans off, not putting them on. Her panties, blouse, and bra quickly followed and she dove in. Jay drank off half of his longneck bottle of Corona, then took off his clothes and waded into the bay, bringing the beer with him. Holding the bottle aloft, he dunked himself, rising to see Isabel, her naked body shimmering in the moonlit water, swimming slowly across his path. He finished the beer, threw the bottle far out toward the horizon, then dove and swam straight out for maybe three hundred yards before turning and swimming back. When he reached the shore, Isabel, dressed, was sitting on the pebbly beach drinking a beer and smoking. She handed him a beer when he finished dressing, then lit a second cigarette and handed it to him as he settled next to her.

"You are a good swimmer, and strong," she said.

"I almost didn't make it back. I'm beat."

"We're both tired."

Jay flipped over a shell and rested his cigarette on it, then took a long swig of his beer. Behind them a tractor-trailer went screaming by on the highway, and then a bus, and then the night's stillness and silence fell on them again, broken only by the soft rush of the surf.

"Talk to me, Isabel."

"If you're tired, we can talk later, in the car, or when we arrive."

"I'm fine."

"There is no good time for this, I suppose."

"No."

"I liked your friend. He was a funny man, and brave."

Jay said nothing.

"He arrived at the airport in Miami and put the money in a locker there. He took a cab to Miami Beach, where he got a room. This was on a Monday. The next day, I picked him up in front of the Fontainebleau. We drove to Jupiter. We wanted to make sure we weren't being followed before getting the money."

Isabel stopped here, and took a drink of her beer. Jay watched her profile for signs of calculation or spin control as she stared for a long moment at the bay. He had assessed her in this way several times during the long, quiet ride from Merida, but, as now, had come up empty. There was no telling from looking at her proud, beautiful face what she was thinking or feeling.

"Go ahead," he said, breaking the silence.

"I was staying at a hotel in Jupiter. We drove there. I was in fear at all times of being discovered and killed by the Ferias. I knew they had killed Bryce and his wife—Jose likes to take heads as trophies when he can—and were looking for me. Dan was certain that we had not been followed. The next morning he left for the airport to get the money. He assured me that he would not get it if he thought there was any danger. He must have crossed paths with the Ferias. We had agreed that I would change hotels, which I did. The next day I saw in the newspaper that he was killed. I called my friend Alvaro Diaz. I did not want to involve him, I was afraid he would be killed, too, but I was desperate. I stayed with him for three days, and then he took me to Maria."

"Did Dan know the name of your new hotel?"

"No. I was supposed to call him on his cell phone."

"Did you?"

"Yes. Edgardo answered."

"What hotel did he check into in Miami?"

"I don't know. He cabbed to the Fontainebleau."

"You had a car at the time?"

"I left my car at Royal Palm. I took a cab from there to the hotel in Jupiter, where I rented a car, the one that Dan drove to Miami."

"Did you tell Dan what he was getting into?"

"Yes."

"Did you mention the Feria brothers, and Herman Santaria—that they killed Bryce and Kate Powers?"

"Yes."

"When was this?'

"When he arrived in Florida. I offered him more money, told him he could back out."

"What did he say?"

"He laughed. He said I could buy him dinner."

"What happened to the rental car?"

"I don't know, but it doesn't matter. I rented it with false ID."

"Do you know these Feria brothers personally?"

"Yes, I have met them."

"You sound like you're pretty familiar with Santaria's operation."

"I started working for him when I was fourteen years old."

"Doing what?"

Isabel shook her head, just slightly.

"Do you want another beer?" she asked. "I will get it from the car."

"No. I have another question."

"Yes."

"How is it that Danny and the Ferias happened to 'cross paths'? If they were following him, they would have gotten you, too. Or did you set him up?"

"You're sitting here with me right now. Are you afraid for your life?"

"There's a big hole in your story."

"I sent him to Royal Palm, to get my passport. Two passports, actually, one real, the other false. I left the condo very quickly, and took nothing with me except my purse. I was trapped without the passports, especially if we did not recover the cash. They must have been watching the condo."

"You sent him."

"Yes."

"And he followed orders."

"I was paying him."

Jay went to the jeep for two more beers. Danny wouldn't

take more money. A deal was a deal. Which meant they had slept together. For *that* his friend would take extra risk, follow certain orders. *Pussy,* he recalled Frank Dunn saying on the night of the Powers murders, *it makes us weak.*

On the beach, Jay opened the beers and handed one to Isabel as he sat down next to her. She again lit a cigarette for him and handed it to him. They smoked and drank for a minute or two, watching the bay, then Isabel said, "I am sorry about your friend. Truly sorry."

"Did you have dinner with him?"

"Yes."

"Did he hit on you?"

"Yes."

"What did he say?"

"He said I was so beautiful it was killing him. He said if I slept with him it would make him immortal."

"Danny," said Jay, finishing his beer in one long drink, then throwing the bottle into the bay, watching it bob in the moonlight. "*Danny.*"

Then Jay put his head down onto his drawn-up knees, facing away from Isabel, and cried, murmuring Danny's name as he did. Isabel took Jay's head in her hands, laid him on the sand, and held him until he quieted. Soon they were both asleep, too exhausted to change positions or slap at the insects that buzzed around them in the sweltering eighty-five–degree night air.

41.
9:00 AM, December 21, 2004, Mexico City

The section of the Mexican Justice Department that dealt with requests by foreign countries for the issuance of arrest or search warrants in Mexico was the Division of International Warrants and Arrests, or DIWA, and was headed by Lazaro Santaria's nephew, Pedro Alvarado. Handsome, in his mid-thirties, educated at Amherst and the National University Law School in Mexico City, Pedro had known only good in his life. His family's fortunes had risen with those of his uncles Lazaro and Herman, one high-profile, the other decidedly not, but very rich. Uncle Lazaro had climbed steadily to very near the top of the Institutional Revolutionary Party—the PRI—the political party that had held power nationally for over seventy years, before adroitly switching to the new Mexican Action Party—PAM—the year before it took power in 2000. A switch made easy by large donations from Herman, under cover of unregulated political action committees, to PAM. Very large donations. Pedro's work was routine and handled by a jaded but competent staff of lawyers, investigators, and clerical help. One task that Pedro took to himself was the daily review of requests for action by the US government pursuant to treaty, with comments attached from his department heads indicating the suggested response by the Mexican government. To these Pedro added his own comments before handing a copy personally to Lazaro late every afternoon.

When Lazaro received his daily DIWA report for Monday, December 20 and saw Jay Cassio's name on it, he picked up his private line and called his brother Herman and arranged for them to meet for dinner at Las Vacas Gordas, a steak house on nearby Avenida Madera, at nine p.m. that night. The next morning, Herman was having breakfast on the balcony of his twenty-fifth floor penthouse on Avenida Cinqo de Mayo, when his bodyguard brought Edgar and Jose Feria out to join him. The brothers had arrived in Mexico by private jet on Saturday morning, three days prior, and immediately reported the highlights of their recent trip to Miami to Herman. He had not spoken with them since. In recent years he rarely met with them personally, but, given the information he had received from his brother the night before, he thought it necessary to chat face-to-face with his young killers. Below him *La Ciudad de Mexico,* vast and dense, spread to the horizon in all directions, while the morning sun struggled to penetrate the smog that covered the city like a shroud.

"Sit. Would you like coffee?" said Herman, pointing to the silver service and china cups on the table between them. "Help yourself. Leave us, Stefan."

The bodyguard stepped back into the apartment, leaving Herman and the Ferias to their coffee and their dazzling view. Herman eyed the brothers, knowing they were waiting for him to speak first. One of Gary Shaw's bullets had grazed Jose's temple. The wound was not serious but it had bled profusely, and Jose was still wearing a bright white bandage over his partially shaved scalp. This he fingered while his brother poured coffee.

"An inch to the left and you would be dead," said Herman.

"Leaving my brother to avenge me," Jose replied.

"The black was a cop," said Herman, "so it was good that you left quickly."

The brothers, uninterested in the occupation of the people they killed, nodded and waited for their employer to continue. Herman, sixty-two, his body florid and bloated from years of unrestrained indulgence in rich food and the best wine and champagne the world had to offer, marveled at his luck at having two such killing machines at his disposal. His panthers, he had befriended them as cubs, and they had been utterly devoted to him ever since. Stony-eyed, supremely confidant, unhurried—he often thought they would have made excellent bankers—they would calmly set out to assassinate the Pope if he ordered them to.

"You will have to stay out of the States for a while," Herman continued, "but there is work for you here. Senor Cassio landed in Cancun on Saturday. The US Justice Department wants him picked up. We are checking the car rental agencies and the hotels. The Yucatán and Campeche police have a bulletin on him. If they find him we will send you up there to take care of him."

"And the woman?" said Edgardo.

"She has not been seen at the restaurant in Miami. As I have said, she can bring me down, and if that happens my dear brother and Senor de Leon are concerned that *I* will have no choice but to bring *them* down. I tell them not to worry, but they are terrified. There is no trust among us thieves. Therefore we must find Isabel, and take care of her. I have located two of the sisters from her days in the convent. One is in Mexico City, the other is in Guadalahara. They may know where Isabel would go to hide. Do not frighten them. You are looking for your sister, so that she can receive her inheritance from her long lost father."

"We will leave today."

"Yes, pronto. And come back pronto. I want her head to give to Lazaro and Rafael as a Christmas present."

Herman liked to give the impression that he was careless, that he knew only vaguely what was going on in his legal and illegal organizations, and that he did not know precisely how big his empire was or how much money he had. But that was artifice, designed to lull both friend and foe. He had over two hundred million dollars in Russian and Philippine bank accounts, and holdings worth another two hundred million. He liked being in the thick of the fray, not above it; when he was young, he had done his share of violence in order to clear the way for Lazaro and Rafael, and of course himself.

Lazaro would never let him down, and neither would his panthers, but Rafael had shown signs of weakness lately, and fear. He would naturally consider the possibility of the Santaria brothers turning on him. De Leon, a man sixty-five years of age who still liked to fuck fourteen-year-old girls. Perhaps it was time to show him the photographs that Herman had been accumulating over the years, to discourage him from pursuing the foolish idea of a preemptive strike. It would be nice to see the arrogant *mandamas* frozen in amber, to be dealt with at Herman's leisure.

"Here are the names and addresses of the good sisters," Herman continued, sliding a piece of notepaper across the snowy white tablecloth to Edgardo. "Bring me a trophy. When you return there may be more interesting and more difficult game than an innocent young whore."

42.
10:00 AM, December 20, 2004, Puerto Angel, Mexico

"I have never had to be a nurse before," Isabel said.

"You don't have to be one now," Jay replied.

"You were truly sick."

"This rash. I thought I was getting better."

"It is a good sign. It means it is dengue fever, and not something worse."

They had woke on the beach outside Sabancuy at dawn, driven all day, covering some five hundred miles in twelve hours, most of it through the sweltering, sterile scrubland of the Isthmus of Tehuantepec, and arrived exhausted at Puerto Angel, where Jay was almost immediately flattened by a blinding headache and a fever that reached one hundred four degrees in an hour. After a night of this, along with vomiting and severe joint pain, a rash had appeared on his chest and spread to his arms and legs. Until the rash appeared this morning, Isabel thought it very possible that Jay would die. Cholera and typhoid fever were not unknown in Mexico, and although they had been very careful about what they ate and drank, a small amount of the swallowed water of Campeche Bay would be enough to give Jay any number of deadly diseases.

"How do you know about dengue fever?" Jay asked.

"The sisters taught us," Isabel answered. "We were going to be missionaries. It only takes the bite of one mosquito."

They were staying in a house owned by the Mexican Provincialate of the Congregation of Dominican Sisters. The house, a one-story affair made of local stone and timber, was situated on a hill overlooking Puerto Angel Bay, which lay sparkling some three hundred feet below. They were on a veranda shaded by a once-dark blue canvas awning, tattered now, and faded to dishwater gray by years of exposure to the relentless sun of southern Mexico.

With the appearance of the rash, the fever and nausea had subsided, and Jay was able to drag himself to a chaise. He was weak, but with the fever broken, Isabel could see his spirits rise as he sat in the fresh breeze watching the morning sun play on the bay.

"Are the papers here?" he asked.

"Yes, everything is where I left it. Are you hungry?"

"No. Is there water?"

"Yes. I went out this morning. I'll get you some."

Isabel brought the bottled water and handed it to Jay, who sipped it cautiously. He had put on his khaki shorts and a fresh T-shirt while she was gone, and had moved to the veranda by the time she returned. She could see the telltale dengue rash, red and blotchy, on his forearms and extending down his thighs past his knees.

"Thank you," said Jay.

"De nada."

"What day is it?"

"We have only been here one day. You should sleep. When you awake, we will eat, and make our plans."

"I can't eat."

"The fever has broken. You will be hungry. Hector will bring us something. He asks about you."

"Who is Hector?'

"A childhood friend. He is the handyman at Vista del Mar, the restaurant below us on the hill."

"Have I met him?"

"No," said Isabel, smiling.

"You have a beautiful smile."

Isabel did not answer. She had not meant to smile. Smiles are invitations. But perhaps he was not asking for one. He was disoriented, exhausted. Still, his simple compliment gratified her. They had made the long drive from Sabancuy in near silence, a silence Isabel had attributed to hatred on Jay's part.

"Was it a dream?" Jay asked. "Or did you tell me? About Danny."

"I told you, on the beach near Sabancuy. Do you remember?"

"I remember," he answered. "You were going to make him immortal."

Jay laid his head back on the chaise's ratty old pillow. Within a few minutes he was asleep, breathing softly. Isabel, who was sitting next to him on a wicker ottoman, stared at his face for a moment. Then her mind drifted to the night before.

"Who are you?" Jay had asked once, sitting up abruptly in the sweat-soaked bed.

"I am Isabel."

"I'm hot, Isabel."

"You have a fever."

"I'm hot."

She had reached into the bucket of ice that Hector had brought up, and filled a small towel with the rapidly melting chips, pressing it against Jay's chest, pushing him onto his back, then rubbing the wet coldness onto his nipples and stomach and back up to his neck and face. Then down onto his abdomen and thighs and his genitals. Then the chest again, and the neck and face. He slept, but not for long.

Isabel rose, and went to the waist-high stone wall that separated the veranda from a drop of some one hundred feet to a grassy ravine below. She stood and gazed out at the bay and, beyond it, to the vast, green expanse of the Pacific. She had had only two emotionally charged love affairs in her life. One of them had been with Bryce Powers. After he died, and she aborted his child, men were the last thing on her mind. Her plan to flee would go forward. What other options did she have? Staring down at the sad little town of Puerto Angel, she recalled the time she had spent at this house as a girl, going through puberty, the last days of her innocence. And then she let her mind drift to Isla La Roqueta, in 1996, to her other love.

• • •

"First I will show you the house, and then you can land the plane."

"Land the plane? Are you sure?" She was sitting in the passenger seat of Patricio Castronovo's Cessna 150, cruising at fifteen hundred feet on a cloudless fall day on the last leg of the short flight from Mexico City to Castronovo's parents' home on Isla La Roqueta, the lushly forested island that guards Acapulco Bay on the west. She had been dating Patricio, on Herman's orders, for two months. During the short trip in the two-seat, single prop aircraft, Isabel had allowed herself a brief daydream of what it might be like to marry Patricio, have his children, share his ambitions. His last remark had awakened her from this reverie.

For an answer Patricio reached over to caress Isabel's knee

and thigh, and smiled the handsome, self-assured smile that had broken through defenses that at the age of nineteen she took for granted were impermeable but obviously were not.

"If you do that," she said, "I will not be able to concentrate." Her return smile was real, not fake, like the ones in the beginning, when she first started taking flying lessons from him, a contrivance that had worked perfectly until she fell in love.

"You can do it," Patricio said, squeezing her knee a last time, then returning his hand to the yoke and maneuvering the plane into a banking descent before leveling it at five hundred feet.

"It will be to your right," he said, "the yellow house with the swimming pool in the courtyard." They were flying along the island's northern coast, the side that faced the mainland, where moments earlier Isabel had seen old-town Acapulco nestled on a hillside, its zocalo, central fountain, and strolling tourists clearly visible from the plane.

"There," she said. "I see it. It's beautiful." More than beautiful, breathtaking, the pool a sapphire blue, the bougainvillea trained on the courtyard walls a mass of velvety red and purple and green.

"Do you see the landing strip?"

"Yes, I see it. There is no tower. Who runs it?"

"We do, the families on the island. I will take us up."

The day before, in the same plane, Patricio had practiced touch-and-goes for two hours at Puebla Airport to the east of Mexico City, with Isabel in the passenger seat. He had let her handle a few, which were bumpy. His were feathery, dreamy, the *touch* incredibly light, a kiss of the runway, the *go* a commanding, confident surge and then an ascending bank and turn to get into position to do it again. *This is how you make love*, she had said to him and he had smiled.

The next morning, Isabel had awakened early. Leaving Patricio soundly asleep, she made coffee and brought it to the veranda outside his bedroom. The house faced a small bay that gleamed emerald green as it caught the slanting rays of the rising sun. The water was still and calm, the mild morning breeze riffling almost imperceptibly across its sparkling surface. As she sipped her coffee she saw what at first she thought was a fleet of toy boats enter the bay. Standing, puzzled, shading her eyes with her free hand, she saw that the boats were dolphins, dozens of them if not more, swimming lazily, some breaking the surface in twos and threes in small, arcing leaps. Leaving her coffee, she went down to the beach, stripped off her nightgown, and joined them.

How long was she there? She could not tell. Some circled her, drawing nearer with each circuit, some swam to her and brushed her with their long, smooth flanks as they passed, others nudged her hands with their snouts. She dove under and played with them, twisting and turning and stroking them until she had to surface for air. The last time she surfaced, Patricio was standing on the beach holding two cups of coffee and smiling broadly, his teeth white and perfect, his dark eyes happy, like a child's.

She stood naked with him and drank her coffee, which he had reheated for her, then they rushed upstairs to make love.

"They are there most mornings this time of year," he said when they were lying in bed afterward.

"I could not resist," she said. "They were calling me."

"They usually swim away if someone enters. My mother says they choose only the unhappy to swim with."

Isabel could not remember what her answer was, only the dreamy feeling of security she felt in Patricio's arms, in his bed, in his life.

...

Love does not come alone. It brings a host of other feelings with it, feelings that, long neglected, assert themselves with a startlingly persistent energy: demons, it might be said, who will have their day in the sun. Perhaps it is to confront these demons that we fall in love in the first place. Perhaps facing them squarely is the price we pay for love. If so, that price would be heavy for Isabel, who stood now, the sea breeze drying the tears running down her face, aware—more sharply than she had been in many years—of the river of anger and shame and sadness running through her heart.

43.
5:00 PM, December 23, 2004, Miami

It took Matt Ramirez four days undercover in Little Havana to learn that a woman fitting Isabel Perez's description had until quite recently been waitressing at El Pulpo. It took a call from the US Attorney in New Jersey to the US Attorney in Manhattan to New York's chief of police to get the city's human resource people to search their records, but it was eventually learned that Angelo Perna and Frank Dunn were partners in a patrol car in Bensonhurst from 1964 to 1967. Perna was therefore linked to Isabel, Shaw, Cassio, and Dunn. Shaw was sticking to his story, and Dunn was still among the missing.

Phil Gatti's request to have US agents directly involved in the search for Jay Cassio in Mexico had been denied by Attorney General Santaria. Gatti had assigned two Mexican-American DEA agents, without the knowledge or consent of the Mexican government, to look for the Feria brothers in Mexico City. Luckily they had spotted them exiting Herman Santaria's apartment building on Tuesday morning and, according to Gatti, who was monitoring their activities from a hotel room in the capital, the agents had followed the Ferias to residences in Mexico City and Guadalajara that turned out to be communal homes for retired nuns. They had seen no sign of Isabel, and were now trailing the Ferias along Mexico's southern Pacific coast.

Chris Markey was acutely aware that his investigation was stalling. His instincts told him that Lazaro Santaria had spotted the Cassio warrant request and would hunt the young lawyer down and execute him on a back road somewhere, ending Cassio's usefulness as a decoy or anything else. And why were the Ferias in Guadalajara? If they were chasing Isabel, Gatti's agents would have a hard time getting to her before the killers did, and arrests on Mexican soil were out of the question. If they were there on other business, then following them was a waste of time.

Most disturbing of all, a story had appeared in the *Newark Star-Ledger* that questioned the motive behind the article Markey had planted in the *Miami Herald* identifying Cassio and revealing the name of his hotel in Miami Beach; the reporter, Linda Marshall, suggested that an attempt had been made by the FBI to use Cassio as an unwitting decoy in a mysterious investigation involving murders in New Jersey and Florida. Marshall was awaiting a ruling by a federal judge in Newark as to whether or not she should be held in contempt for refusing to reveal her sources in her previous articles on these murders, and was presumed, at this point in her career, to be no friend of big government.

Marshall had even called the *Miami Herald* reporter, who had refused to name *his* source inside the FBI, although it was not hard to infer from her story that it was Markey, whose name she used prominently. But how did she get the idea of a planted story in the first place? Only his team members knew about it, and only Gary Shaw had a link to Cassio. Gary Shaw, Angelo Perna, Frank Dunn, the more these names ran through his mind the more incensed Markey became. He would not be surprised if they knew where Cassio and Isabel were, and if they were behind the story in the Jersey paper.

When he was working for the CIA Markey was able to put an end to this kind of interference with brutal finality, restrained only by the fear of being caught, in which case he would die by the sword as he had lived by it. But now the rule of law restrained him as well, that is, that portion of it that applied America's laws to the government as well as to its citizens. Still, Markey was good at bending the rules, and clever at breaking them when necessary. Shaw was in the hospital, a hero for the time being, and Dunn had gone underground, but Angelo could be dealt with, which is why Markey and his assistant, Ted Stevens, were, at five p.m. on Thursday, six days after the Shaw-Feria shootout, turning into the El Pulpo parking lot on 17th Avenue in Little Havana.

Sam was behind the bar, drying glasses; Maria was in the dining room helping the busboys set tables; Angelo was in his office. Markey stated his business to Sam, who pointed to Angelo, who watched as the agents approached him. Angelo had met Stevens the Saturday before when he stopped by to talk about the Shaw shooting. Stevens introduced Angelo to Markey, who gestured for the FBI agents to sit.

"Were you ever a New York cop?" Angelo asked Markey once they were seated. "You look familiar."

"No," Markey replied, "but we know *you* were, and that you and Frank Dunn are friends."

"Good friends."

"Where is he?"

"He went home to Jersey."

"When was that?"

"Last week."

"How did he get there?"

"I think he took a bus."
"Did you meet Cassio?"
"Yes. Would you guys like something to drink?"
"Why was he here?"
"I guess you don't want a drink."
"Why was he here?"
"He didn't say."
"Where is he now?"
"I don't know."
"What was Shaw doing here Friday night?"
"We're friends. He stops by for a drink sometimes."
"You never saw him that night?"
"No. I went to the hospital, but they wouldn't let me see him. I talked to his wife and daughter and came home."

Markey watched as Angelo broke off eye contact with him and looked over at the bar, probably at his brother, the former boxer.

"You had a waitress named Isabel Perez working here," Markey said.

"Isabel *Sanchez*," Angelo replied, looking back at Markey.

"Where is she now?"

"I don't know. She didn't show up for work on Friday night. We haven't seen her since."

"Where was she living?"

"In the apartment upstairs."

"Upstairs here?"

"Yes."

Markey glanced at Stevens, sitting to his right.

"We'd like to look through the place," he said to Angelo.

"You mean search it."

Perna's contemptuous attitude was a surprise. He apparently thought that being some kind of minor nobility in

Little Havana immunized him from the kind of pressure Markey could bring to bear.

"Yes," he said, remaining outwardly cool, "I mean search it."

"You'll have to ask Sam, it's his place."

Markey nodded to Stevens, who got up and went to the bar to talk to Sam.

"How did Isabel come to you?"

"A friend of hers brought her in, and asked us to help her out. Alvie Diaz."

"Who's conveniently dead."

"He died in his sleep."

"Your wife is the hostess here."

Angelo nodded.

"She didn't work last Friday night."

"No."

"Where was she?"

Sam and Stevens walked past the table on their way to the back stairway that led to the garret apartment above the restaurant.

"She was with me. We had dinner at home."

"Isn't Friday a busy night here?"

Angelo didn't answer immediately. A trained observer, Markey saw the slight flare of Angelo's nostrils, and the flattening of his eyes as he considered his answer.

"Sometimes yes, sometimes no," was that answer.

"I could subpoena the restaurant's records to find out."

"You could do a lot of things."

"I could put you, your brother, and your wife in jail for harboring a fugitive."

"You could try to do that, I suppose."

"I'd like to speak to your wife."

"I think not," said Angelo. "I think we'll hire lawyers, and then your lawyers can speak to our lawyers."

"If you helped this woman, Perna, or your wife did, or your brother, rest assured I won't stop until you're all in jail."

"We'll jump off that bridge when we get to it."

On the drive back to the field office, Markey told Stevens to begin the paperwork needed to obtain a court order for taps on the phones at El Pulpo and the two Perna residences. Back at his office, he picked up his phone and made an appointment, for the next day, to see the United States Attorney for the Southern District of Florida, to discuss impaneling a grand jury to inquire into events at El Pulpo beginning in September and culminating on the evening of Friday, December 17. He had to find Isabel, and one way to do that was through the Pernas. Maria Perna was their soft spot. Angelo would protect her with his life, that was obvious from the way the tenor of the conversation had changed once she was brought up. Markey hoped the taps would yield good stuff. If it looked like they were all going to jail, Maria Perna's caveman husband might make a deal in order to save her, assuming he knew where Isabel was. But even if he didn't, it would be satisfying to bring the asshole to his knees.

44.
9:00 AM, December 22, 2004,
Puerto Angel

The next morning, Jay, sitting on the cottage's veranda, opened an old-fashioned leather satchel with the initials *B.S.P.* engraved in the brass handle. It contained seven folders labeled *Banking, Correspondence, H.S. & Company, Photographs, Cash Payments, Miscellaneous,* and *Banque de Geneve, Etc.* At the bottom was a dime-store composition book filled with dated, handwritten entries, starting in 1970 and ending in 2004. This he took up first. At noon he stopped for lunch—steak and eggs brought by Hector—and two hours of sleep. The sun, the food, and the sleep were good medicine. His rash had not subsided, but at least it had stopped spreading, and the aloe cream that Hector also brought up was cool and soothing. In a day, maybe two, he would be well enough to do what he came to Mexico to do. In the meantime, he would go over what looked to be a treasure trove of documents and other evidence in Bryce Powers's beat-up old briefcase.

Jay had slept most of the previous day and night, and had woken this morning feeling oddly serene, accepting of life's vicissitudes, as if his delirium and night sweats had wrung the anxiety from his soul. His mood changed, however, as he came to the end of Bryce Powers's diary and looked at his photographs.

Sam Perna had given Jay a survival kit: two fifth bottles of Chivas Regal, a carton of Marlboro Reds, a vial of Valium, and a vial of Black Beauties. Jay showered and shaved, and brought a pack of the cigarettes and one of the bottles of scotch out to the veranda. Isabel had gone down to the Vista del Mar to pick up dinner. Among the twenty or so eight-by-ten prints in the *Photographs* folder were two of a young Bryce Powers—in his late twenties or early thirties—having sex with a teenage girl.

Jay put ice, made with bottled water, into a glass, and splashed some scotch into it. The day was lovely. The sun, starting its descent over the mountain behind him, warmed his head and shoulders as he sat in his khaki shorts, old white shirt, and sandals. Sipping his drink and smoking, the notebook and the folder containing the pictures on the table next to him, he pondered the rat's nest he had gotten himself into.

In 1971, two years after he arrived in Mexico City, Powers began bribing a government official named Rafael de Leon, then the minister of Interior Development for the Federal District of Mexico, which consisted of the heart of Mexico City and its surrounding prime real estate. All approvals for development plans, and all building permits, in the *Distrito Federale*, were issued by de Leon's office. Powers, unable to get a shovel in the ground for two years, met de Leon at a party, and soon Gentex was a prime player in the building boom that swept the capital in the early seventies.

De Leon's good friend, Herman Santaria, also in the government at the time, handled the cash transfers, but occasionally, beginning in 1971 Rafael sent his daughter, Christiana, then fifteen, to Bryce's apartment overlooking Alameda Central to pick up money. Bryce and Christiana, mature beyond her years and ravishingly beautiful, became lovers. In early 1977, Christiana was pregnant. She told her mother, who told her father, who ordered her to continue the affair, and to tell him when and where she and Powers would be having their liaisons. Pictures were taken. Powers was confronted with them, and with the hard fact that in Mexico, statutory rape was punishable by twenty unreduceable years in prison.

De Leon told Powers that his ship had come in: he would quit Gentex, leave Mexico, and start his own development company in the States. Rafael and Herman would loan Bryce the money for his first project, which he would then be expected to leverage into many others. The price: one million dollars per year, funneled through H.S. & Company, first as phony consultant's fees and eventually for "maintenance" of properties—plus various future services to be rendered by Bryce. Those services came to include the laundering of cash when Rafael and Herman entered the drug business in the early nineties.

Ten years later, the pressure on Powers was enormous: he was going through a nasty divorce; his Arizona property was failing; he still had to find a million dollars a year for de Leon and Santaria, and the cash he was laundering for them had reached alarming numbers—over ten million in 2003. If the Arizona partners forced an audit, or if the IRS decided to look at his books, he would be ruined. On top of all this, he was in love with Isabel Perez, de Leon's cash courier *du jour*, twenty-seven years younger than him.

Isabel returned with the food, in brown paper bags, which she placed on the table outside. Seeing the bottle of scotch, she went into the kitchen for a glass with ice, came back out, sat down across from Jay, and poured herself a drink. She was wearing white shorts and a navy blue halter top, a simple outfit that accentuated her long legs and her heavy, unmistakably lovely breasts. In the shadow of the faded awning, her teeth were whiter than the foam on the breaking surf below, her eyes bluer than the sky above. Looking at her sipping her scotch, touching the glass gently to her lips, Jay understood why Bryce Powers had contorted his life even more than it already was in order to have her.

"Have you seen this?" he said, handing her the composition book.

"No," she replied, putting her drink down and taking the book. "What is it?"

"Bryce's diary."

Isabel opened the notebook randomly, recognized Powers's precise handwriting, then thumbed through a few more pages before looking up at Jay, her face unreadable.

"How about these?" Jay asked, handing her the photographs of Bryce and the teenager.

Jay watched Isabel closely as she looked at the pictures, and saw the ceramic mask of composure that she usually wore slip for a second, to reveal the confusion and pain that anyone would feel on seeing a former lover in such a situation. It was the reaction he had been hoping for: hurt for hurt, pain for pain.

"This is Bryce," she said, "as you know. And Christiana Santaria, Lazaro's wife, Rafael's daughter."

"De Leon."

"Yes."

Picking up the diary, Isabel thumbed casually to the last entry, which Jay knew was dated May of 2004. She put the book down, and looked at Jay, the look in her beautiful eyes speaking to him of both pride and deep, resigned sadness.

"He mentions his love for you," said Jay.

"I don't doubt it. He compulsively recorded the events of his life."

"Was it Bryce's idea to steal from Santaria?"

"Yes."

"When did he start?"

"A few months before meeting me."

"How much did he take?"

"Two or three million. I'm not sure."

"Where is it?"

"I don't know. Probably in a bank in Switzerland."

"Did you love him?"

"For a moment, I did, yes."

"How old are you?"

"Twenty-seven."

"That girl in the picture looks a lot like you."

"I wasn't born yet."

Jay poured them each more scotch, lit a cigarette for himself, and handed Isabel one. The sun had set, and they were sitting in the quick, dreamy twilight of the tropics. Jay leaned over the small wooden coffee table that separated them to light Isabel's cigarette. He watched as the smoke from her first drag drifted across her face, which had recomposed itself into its usual unreadable mask.

"Did you do the same thing for Herman that de Leon's daughter did?"

"I'm not playing this game anymore."

"What game?"

"Whatever game it is you're trying to play."

"Did you tell Danny that de Leon had his fifteen-year-old daughter fuck Powers so he could blackmail him?"

"I never knew that."

"The thing is, you knew the cesspool these people lived in, and you lured Dan into it."

"You dishonor your friend. I told him enough for him to assess the danger. He made the decision of a man, and consequently he died like a man."

• • •

Jay rose and walked to the stone wall. The moon, getting on to full, was shining bright as it hung above the sea in the night sky. Watching him standing there, his back to her, his long hair lifted at its edges by the night wind, Isabel felt something stir in her heart, something she had suppressed since the night on the beach in Sabancuy. She rose as well, took a step toward him, and then stopped, thinking of her dark secret, immobilized by its terrible weight.

45.
8:00 AM, December 23, 2004, Puerto Angel

"What time did you get up?" Isabel asked.

"Seven," Jay replied.

"I thought you had left."

"Left? You mean run off with Bryce's papers?"

"Yes."

"We're not done here."

"*Bueno.* How do you feel?"

"Better."

They were sitting on the veranda, drinking coffee. It was eight a.m. Isabel was wearing a denim shirt and her white cotton shorts. Her hair, growing in, but still cropped to above her ears, was damp and glistening from her shower. She wore no makeup, and knew that she could be taken, from the neck up, for a pretty teenage boy—but only from the neck up. Jay was wearing his shorts and no shirt. His rash was almost gone, and it was hot.

They had been in Mexico five days. Frank Dunn had insisted on knowing where Isabel was taking Jay—"at least we can come down to pick up your body," he had said—but Isabel had refused, knowing that the torture tactics employed by Herman and the Feria brothers had a 100 percent success rate. Jay was to place a call to Victor Ponce at El Caribe—

they agreed that it was likely that Angelo's phones would be tapped once Markey learned that Jay, Dunn, and Isabel had vanished on the same night that Gary Shaw was gunned down in front of El Pulpo—if he needed help.

Except for Isabel's short walks to the Vista del Mar to pick up food, they had not left their hillside retreat. Jay's strength had not fully returned, but they could not stay much longer. Jay was the only American within a hundred miles, and Isabel did not exactly blend in with the natives, mostly impoverished Mixtec Indians. They were bound to attract attention, and there was always the possibility that a Dominican Sister would show up, requiring Isabel to do some fast talking.

"I'll rest one more day," said Jay. "I'll read the documents, listen to the tapes. Tomorrow you will call Herman."

"And then what?"

"I don't know. You can take the jeep after you make the call. I'll figure something out."

"Would you like me to stay to help you kill the Feria brothers?"

"No."

"Why not?"

"That wasn't our deal."

"Can I ask you a question?"

"Sure."

"Why are you not married?"

Isabel watched as Jay's beautiful gray eyes turned inward, surprised at his reticence. He drummed his fingers on the wooden arms of his patio chair, as if giving the question more weight than she intended. Much more.

"I was married once," he said, finally. "For a short time."

"What happened."

"My parents died in a plane crash."

Isabel said nothing, not realizing, until this moment, that Jay had been a puzzle from the start. And here was a key piece of that puzzle floating in the air toward her, its contours handles she might grab and hold on to.

"When?" she asked, finally.

"Fifteen years ago."

"And you left your wife?"

"No."

"She left *you*? Are there children?"

Jay did not answer immediately, but neither did he look inward or drum his fingers. When he turned to face her, Isabel saw the pain in his eyes, and regretted asking her initial question.

"I was dating her. When my parents died I married her because I was afraid of being alone. She wanted children. I immediately had a vasectomy."

"That must have hurt her very much."

"It did. She left."

"Did you love her?"

"No."

"Now you have lost your friend."

"Yes."

"Were there other women?"

"Yes, a few."

"Did you love any of them?"

"No."

The whole conversation had taken on a life of its own, the reins, Isabel realized with a start, held by her heart, not her head. There was a precipice ahead, but she knew somehow that it was too late. She would not be able to wrestle the reins back in time. Perhaps she did not want to.

"What about you?" Jay asked. "Have you loved anyone, besides Bryce Powers?"

"I loved a young man once, a politician."

"What happened?"

"The Ferias killed him. On Herman's orders."

Now it was Jay's turn to stare hard at Isabel. Yes, she said to herself, there it is, a small piece of *my* puzzle.

"Is that why you want to stay and help me kill them?"

"No. It's Herman I want to kill."

"Is there any way we can get him here?"

"No. He will stay in Mexico City and send his panthers."

"Can I ask you a question?"

"Yes."

"What is it you did for Herman Santaria starting at the age of fourteen?"

Isabel gripped the arms of her chair for a second, then let go and reached into the neck of her shirt, where she found the Mary scapular that Sister Josefina had given her when she left the convent in Polanco. She had kept it with Sister's letters all these years, but had started wearing it when she promised to help Jay and they fled to Puerto Angel. Fingering it, she remembered Sister's words. *It is not magic. It is a sign of your commitment, of your faith. Do not lose either, no matter what the future brings.*

"I will tell you tonight," she said. "We will drink your scotch, and I will answer your question."

46.
8:00 PM, December 23, 2004, Puerto Angel

"Until I was fourteen, I lived in an orphanage in Mexico City, in Polanco, run by the Dominican Sisters. They also ran a home for unwed mothers, and a clinic where they gave birth, where I was born. I was lucky. I had a relative, *Tio Hermano*, who visited me occasionally, and brought small gifts. When I was fourteen, he took me away, and trained me to be a whore."

It was eight p.m. They had eaten dinner, and were sitting on the veranda on old wooden chairs facing each other. The scotch and a pack of cigarettes were on the small table between them. The night was very warm, and humid, and the full moon shone from behind a checkerboard of gathering clouds.

"Herman never touched me; Rafael did. He fucked me several times in the beginning. He was the first, actually. He was the governor of the State of Mexico at the time. Herman was out of government by then; he was doing other things. They were both rich, but greedy for more."

Watching her face in the intermittent moonlight as she spoke, Jay thought something had changed, but he could not say what. Did she look younger? Or older? Sadder? Happier? What? He had a scotch over ice in his hand. The glass, a fading Mickey Mouse juice glass, was sweating profusely in the humid night air. He put it down, and then reached over and touched the back of Isabel's hand, and said, "Isabel, you don't have to tell me any more."

"I thought you wanted to know?" Isabel replied. "To see me hurt as part of your revenge for Danny." With her mask removed, her eyes, staring straight at him, were, despite the hardness of her voice, even more beautiful, or perhaps beautiful for the first time.

Jay remained silent.

"I'm sorry," said Isabel, "that wasn't fair. There's not much more."

"How old was Rafael at the time?"

"Fifty. Around there."

"And you were fourteen."

"Yes."

"Go on."

"In the beginning, they used me as a reward, or to set men up—police chiefs, prosecutors, judges—so they could have protection for their activities. Sometimes they took pictures, to blackmail men into cooperating, or backing off. For ten years, I was their prize whore. I had to pretend it was fun. Sometimes it was, if I could get to know a man a little bit, but that was rare. I must have fucked a hundred men whose faces I can't remember, whose touch repulsed me."

Jay finished his drink and poured himself another. He had spent close to two hours that afternoon listening to conversations involving Powers, Herman Santaria, and occasionally Rafael de Leon, recorded surreptitiously by Powers between 1970 and 2004. The voices of the Mexicans—confident, mocking, contemptuous—were still echoing in his head.

"Last summer," Isabel continued, "they sent me to the

States to work in their money laundering operation. The man that had been doing it previously had been stealing from them. The Ferias killed him. They showed me his head, which they were carrying around in a suitcase."

"So you became the new courier."

"Yes. And I seduced Bryce, which was Herman's suggestion. He thought Bryce was stealing. He wanted me to confirm it, and to get close to him, to make it easy to kill him, if that became necessary."

"But you fell in love with him."

"Yes."

"And you helped him steal, and were planning to run away when he was killed."

"Yes."

"Is that it?"

"No. There is one more thing."

A wind had come up, which Jay hadn't noticed until the sound of the house's side door slamming shut startled them. Large drops of rain were beginning to fall on the awning above their heads, and on the flagstone floor of the veranda. Jay looked around. They would be dry for the time being.

"What is it?" he said.

"Bryce Powers was my father. Rafael is my grandfather."

At first Jay was not sure he had heard right. Then he saw Isabel's face, and he knew what the change he had puzzled over earlier was. She was a girl again, fourteen, confessing to sins she could hardly believe she had committed, stunned by their scope.

"Are you okay?" he asked.

Isabel had leaned back in her chair, and was shaking her head, breathing softly, her eyes vacant. Jay poured her a drink, which she took from his hand, and sipped. The rain was beating down now, but they were oblivious.

"Talk to me," he said.

"This house washed away," Isabel said, "in the first year it was built. The local people rebuilt it for the Sisters. That was a hundred years ago."

She looked around at the falling rain.

"I thought I would be a missionary, a teacher, a nurse . . . a wife, a mother . . . Until Herman took me away to a better life. My sin, I think, is that I convinced myself that it *was* a better life."

"How could that be a sin?"

"I was proud, my heart was cold."

Jay said nothing. He had indeed wanted to see Isabel suffer, but now, having gotten what he wanted, he was learning, perhaps for the first time in his life, how bitter was the taste of self-recrimination.

"Herman flew to Miami in August, last year," Isabel continued. "He came to my apartment—Bryce's condo. There was money missing, he said. Who was taking it? The local collectors? Me? Bryce Powers? He asked me if I was happy in my love affair with Bryce. He showed me my birth certificate, naming Christiana de Leon as the mother, and Bryce Powers as the father. He showed me the pictures of Bryce and Christiana. He pointed out how much I looked like my parents. He said that Bryce knew I was his daughter. He wanted me to set Bryce up to be killed, but first he wanted his money back. I was to convince Bryce to give it to me, or let me know where it was."

"Maybe he was lying, trying to trick you with phony papers."

"I have a birthmark on my right side, a light patch of skin in the shape of a crescent moon. Bryce had the same birthmark."

The rain was coming through the battered awning in

spots, and the wind, stronger now, was driving it sideways at them. The two candles Jay had lit and placed on the coffee table were out. The storm had blotted out the moonlight. The darkness around them was complete. Jay poured them both more scotch, thanking God for Sam's survival kit.

"*Did* Bryce know?" Isabel said. "I don't think so," she answered herself. "I met him in Aspen the following weekend and confronted him. He cried, and said he had no idea. I think his life was over then, and he knew it. When we were leaving, he said it would soon be time to use the stuff in the suitcase. He said if he called and said that his life was in danger, I should run, drop everything and run. A week later, he called, and I ran. And here I am."

Here we both are, Jay thought. Out loud, he said, "Isabel."

"Yes," she replied.

"Forgive me."

"Forgive *you*?"

"Yes."

"For what?"

"For wanting to hurt you."

"You are forgiven."

"But who will forgive me?" Isabel said.

That question hung in the wet night air.

For an answer Jay knelt in front of Isabel's chair and put his arms around her. He could feel her hot tears mingling with the cold raindrops on his neck and face. Fifteen years he had wasted in self-absorption and self-pity. Fifteen years.

47.
9:00 AM, December 24, 2004, Puerto Angel

Jay stood at the stone wall, looking down at the bay and the two small beaches that straddled the mouth of the Arroyo River. Local children were playing on one of them, while nearby a group of men were hauling in a net by a long rope that was the thickness of a man's arm. The storm had thrashed itself out in the night, and in doing so washed away the torpid heat that had been pressing down on Mexico's southeastern Pacific coast for the last week. The morning sun brought with it the promise of a hot but brilliantly clear day.

Up early, Jay had spent an hour drinking coffee and reading the last of Bryce Powers's paperwork, which contained, among other things, notes of all of the bribes paid to de Leon in the seventies, and which meticulously tracked all of the drug cash that had passed through his company's accounts over the past ten years. In addition, Powers had somehow managed to acquire copies of the contracts between Herman and Rafael and the various overseas banks, which named them, along with Lazaro Santaria, as the owners of the accounts where much of the cash ended up. If he had the contents of Bryce's old leather suitcase, Chris Markey would not need Isabel to put Herman, Rafael, and Lazaro in jail for many years.

There was another contract in the *Banque de Geneve* folder, an original that Jay had pulled out and put in his knapsack. Now, hearing the cottage's back door open, he turned and saw Isabel coming out, carrying a tray of buttered bread and another pot of coffee.

"*Buenos días,*" she said, as she set the tray on the wall.

"*Buenos días.* You look beautiful."

"Thank you."

"Did you sleep well?"

"Yes, the Valium worked. And you?"

"Yes, I was up early, but I slept."

"How long have you been awake?"

"An hour or so."

"Reading?"

"Yes."

"Will Rafael go to jail?"

"Yes. And Herman and Lazaro."

Isabel looked down at the sea, shimmering in the morning sunlight, then across at Jay.

"I am sorry about last night," she said.

"Sorry?"

"It is an awful thing to know."

She poured coffee for both of them, but they did not pick up their cups. They were sitting on the stone wall, the breakfast tray between them. Jay reached across and took her hand.

"What is the name 'Jay'?" Isabel asked. "Is that your proper name?"

"Do you know the story of the golden fleece?"

"Yes."

"My mother foresaw great things for me."

"Did she tell you that?"

"Many times."

"Do you miss her?"

"Yes, I miss her, and my father. They spoiled me." But expected me to grow into a man, thought Jay. It's a good thing they're not around to see what I've made of my life.

"You deserve to be spoiled."

Jay said nothing.

"I don't want to call Herman," Isabel said.

"You gave me your word."

"We can leave together, drive into Guatemala, or fly someplace safe. I have lost my desire for revenge."

"I haven't."

"If I call," Isabel said, "I will stay with you. You cannot force me to leave."

Jay reflected on this. The logistics of killing the Feria brothers were not complicated. He had Frank Dunn's service revolver, the one he had practiced with on Big Pine Key. The road up the hill was visible for its entire length from the veranda. The cottage was inaccessible from behind, where a thick, rock-strewn forest covered the mountain as it ascended in abrupt stages another two hundred feet or so to its crest. He would watch them approach, then step behind the cottage. When they emerged from their car, he would step out and shoot them both. If something went wrong—and he did not doubt that it could—he would try to kill himself before the Ferias could torture him as they had Danny. There were forty ten-milligram tablets of Valium left. He could keep half with him, and Isabel half with her. There were worse ways to die.

"If you stay," he said, "one of us would have to keep watch at all times."

"Yes."

"I have Sam's amphetamines to keep us up, if necessary."
"*Bueno.*"
"Let's go make the call, then I would like to swim before we settle to our watch."

48.
12:00 PM, December 24, 2004, Miami

"Chris, Phil Gatti."

"Phil. Talk to me."

"My guys missed their call in."

"By how much?"

"They're twenty-four hours overdue."

Markey looked at his watch. It was noon on Friday.

"Where were they?"

"Zipolite."

"Where the hell is that?"

"It's a little town on the coast. Hippies and surfers live there on the beach. It's a shit hole."

"Where are you?"

"I'm in Puerto Escondido, about fifty miles away. I thought I'd better get there."

"To do what?"

"The Ferias stopped in two houses owned by the Dominican Sisters. Maybe they've got a place around Zipolite, or the next town, Puerto Angel. I'll ask around."

"You're on your own, Phil."

"I'm not complaining."

"I'm worried about your people. If they're dead, I may

have to do something about our friends personally. I've had enough."

"If I find the Ferias, Chris, I'm taking them out."

"Like I said, you're on your own. Do whatever you have to do."

Markey was at his desk in downtown Miami. He hung up and swiveled his chair around to look out the window behind him, where he had a view, across Biscayne Bay, to South Beach, the flanks of its row of high-rise hotels glowing a golden yellow in the late afternoon sun. The US Attorney had agreed to impanel a grand jury, and would start taking testimony in a few days. The Pernas and Gary Shaw would be the first witnesses, but unless they folded, or turned on one another, both of which were highly improbable, not much would result from it except to set them all up for later perjury charges, assuming the phone taps—in place the last two days—yielded a smoking gun or two. So far they had yielded nothing. He had come very close to arresting both Isabel Perez and the Feria brothers, but they had slipped away, and it was looking more and more like a year's work had come to naught.

The FBI agent swung back to face his desk, picked up the phone, and dialed Ted Stevens's extension, to ask him to get Lazaro Santaria's official schedule and itinerary for the next two weeks. Then he put a call in to Don Sullivan, a friend from his CIA days, now working as a consultant to the Colombian military. Markey, divorced for fifteen years, had spent many Christmases alone since his daughter died; this one would be no different, except that, if things worked out the way he planned, it would probably be his last as an employee of the United States government.

49.
12:00 PM, December 24, 2004, Puerto Angel

Instead of going to the beach to swim, Jay and Isabel took a path that led from the back of the cottage, winding and ascending for about a half mile through broad-leafed tropical thorn trees, to a place where the Arroyo River was naturally dammed. There, a small waterfall splashed into a calm, clear pool that shone brightly in the midday sun—a lovely, quiet spot that remained, Isabel said, upon reaching it, much the same as it was when she last saw it as a girl. They splashed and swam for a few minutes, and then sat on a flat rock at the pool's edge in the sun. Jay had on his khaki shorts and Isabel a T-shirt over her underwear.

"Are you afraid?" Jay asked.

"Yes. I could hear Herman's mind spinning as we talked."

"He will fear a trap."

"Yes. But there is no doubt he will send the Ferias."

Jay had been afraid that Herman would send someone else to deal with Isabel, or ignore her, but Isabel had reassured him. As planned, she had asked Herman for his forgiveness, and his help. Most important, she had told him about Bryce Powers's papers. Isabel knew Herman. He looked for simple solutions first. Killing Isabel and retrieving the papers was the perfect assignment for his panthers, involving, as it did, stealth, bloodshed, the possibility of torture, and a triumphant return to their master.

"It would be nice if he came, too."

"That will never happen."

"I still think you should leave," said Jay. "You can take the bus to Puerto Escondido, or Hector can drive you in the restaurant's truck."

"No. I have lived in fear all of my life. It must stop. We will take our pills if we have to. I will meet you in heaven."

The pool was about forty feet at its widest, enough for Jay, a swimmer all of his life, to do rhythmic laps of some ten strokes each. He swam for fifteen minutes, while Isabel watched. Afterward, drying off with the towel they brought, he was tired, but happy to know that he had regained much if not all of his strength.

"Jay," said Isabel.

"Yes?"

"Let me help you."

Taking one end of the towel, she began to dry his chest and stomach, then, wrapping it around his neck, she drew him to her. They kissed, both still wet, the sun caressing them as they caressed each other. Shocked by his need for her and by the sudden rock-hardness of his erection, Jay tore off his shorts, threw the towel down, and lay on it on his back, oblivious of the smooth, hard stone beneath him. Isabel quickly stripped and then straddled him. They were looking into each other's eyes when they came. Afterward, they stayed locked together for a few moments, chest to chest, the spray from the waterfall reaching them, cooling their sticky bodies.

"I was pregnant by Bryce," Isabel said, keeping her face in Jay's neck, speaking softly into his ear. "I had an abortion in Miami. I wish you had not been fixed. Your child, I would have kept."

• • •

At the cottage, Jay showered and packed. All of his things—a few shirts, an extra pair of shorts, his shave kit—fit into his knapsack along with Bryce Powers's satchel full of folders and tapes. Afterward, he checked the action of Dunn's gun and put it into the cargo pocket of his shorts. To get to Puerto Angel, the Ferias would have to take a two-hour flight from Mexico City to Puerto Escondido, then drive fifty miles along the coast. After calling Herman at nine, Isabel had called the airport in Puerto Escondido and was told that the earliest flight arrived daily from Mexico City at four. It was now noon. The earliest the brothers could be expected to appear would be around six.

While Isabel showered, Jay sat with a Modelo under the awning and stared down at the village, whose multi-colored buildings—most of them shacks—looked deceptively pleasant from three hundred feet up, especially with the shimmering blue-green bay as a backdrop. Some of the town's structures, like the cottage, and the Vista del Mar below it, were tacked onto the side of the hill that ascended from the unpaved and muddy main street, and that formed a natural amphitheater around the bay. Several dirt roads intersected with the main street and ascended the hill. The first of these led up to the restaurant and ended at the cottage. Jay had an unobstructed view of this intersection. Any vehicles—or pedestrians—who turned upward from it would be clearly visible. Isabel appeared with a beer and sat across from Jay under the awning, out of the unforgiving tropical heat.

Below they could see Hector walking slowly up the dirt road toward the cottage, carrying their lunch in two white paper bags. Isabel had told Jay that when she saw Hector earlier, she mentioned that she and Jay might have to leave soon, and quickly. She also said that she would pick up their lunch, but that Hector had insisted on bringing it. When he reached the cottage, he knocked, as was his custom, on the side wall, before turning the corner of the small building and entering the veranda.

"Isabel."

"Hector."

"Senor."

"Hector."

"All is well?"

"Yes, Hector, my friend," said Isabel. "Thank you."

Jay got up and went into the house, where he retrieved an envelope with a thousand pesos in it, money he had put aside for Hector. When he returned, Hector, who had put the food and beer on the table, was standing, talking to Isabel, an ancient pride in his bearing, and in his chiseled, weathered face, despite his dusty work clothes and makeshift, peasant's sandals.

"Please take this," Jay said, handing the envelope to Hector. "We are grateful to you for climbing the hill so many times."

"No, senor," said Hector, "it is my pleasure to assist Isabel and her friend."

"Please, Hector," said Isabel, "we would like you to buy something for Luisa and the girls. Please."

Hector took the envelope, nodding, then resuming his erect stance before them.

"Hector was telling me that there is a roadblock," Isabel said to Jay. "At Pochutla."

"Did you come through it?" Jay asked.

"No, senor. Miss Clara told me. She went early to Puerto Escondido. When she returned, it was there."

Miss Clara was Clara Cardenas, the owner of the Vista del Mar.

"Did she say which police?"

"Federales."

"Who are they looking for?"

"I do not know, senor."

"Have you seen this before?"

"This is the first I have heard of."

"Is it the only way out of here?"

"Yes, senor."

Jay looked at Isabel, then back at Hector, standing, motionless, in the shade of the awning, his coal black eyes indecipherable.

"Is there a way around the roadblock?" Jay asked.

"Not from the town, senor, but from here, yes, there is."

"Here?"

"Yes, senor. If you start to go to the waterfall, you will see the old riverbed going to the right. It is rocky, but your jeep will drive on that."

"Yes, I remember," said Isabel. "We used it to get through the woods to your house."

"Yes," said Hector, smiling. "My children use it now to go to the waterfall."

"Where does it come out?" Jay asked.

"On the highway, two or three kilometers to the east of the roadblock."

"Is there a road to the north, Hector? I didn't see one on the map."

"Over the mountains, senor?"

"Yes."

"Yes. Across the highway the riverbed continues as a dirt road."

"Have you driven it?"

"I sometimes go with my brothers to visit our cousins in Miahuatlán. The road is narrow, senor, and the mountains are high. It is better in the dry season, which is now. In the wet, it falls apart, and there is no repair."

"Is there an airfield in the mountains?"

"There is one in Ejutla de Crespo."

"How far is that?"

"Eighty kilometers."

"Can we get gas, if we need it?"

"There is no gas until Oaxaca. I will give you gas to carry, five gallons."

"Can you bring it now?"

"Yes, senor. I will return with it in a few minutes."

"*Gracias*, Hector."

"*De nada*, senor."

When Hector left, Jay opened the bag of food on the table. Inside on top he found an envelope and a small box wrapped in silver paper and tied with a red ribbon. The envelope contained a Christmas card addressed to "Isabel and Senor Jay" with a picture of the Virgin of Guadalupe on the front and the words "Feliz Navidad, Hector," written inside in careful script. Jay brought the gift to Isabel to open, which she did. Inside were two hand-carved wooden angels, painted black, each about three inches high, each with wings spread wide. The angels had the flat eyes of a statue, but eyes that nevertheless seemed to look upward in anticipation of the delights of being aloft.

50.
Midnight, December 25, 2004, Puerto Angel

While they were eating their lunch, a black SUV appeared on the ocean road, coming from the direction of Zipolite to the west. Jay and Isabel watched it slow down as it passed their intersection before continuing on into the village. Twenty minutes later it drove by again on its way out of town, this time not slowing, but looking sinister and out of place as it bumped and rocked over ruts and through pools of standing water steaming in the sun. It was much too early for the Ferias to arrive, but the car, with its big wheels, black tinted windows, and command of the road, had *hit men* written all over it.

While they were cleaning up, Hector returned with a red, five-gallon can of gasoline, which Jay put into the boot of the jeep. At six o'clock, the sun low in the western sky, a helicopter came whirring out of the hills behind them, flying directly over the cottage, then turning right at the shoreline, maintaining about a hundred feet of altitude. Isabel, sleeping on the chaise, was wakened by the angry noise of the helicopter's engine and rotors, and sat up to watch, with Jay, as it disappeared into the setting sun. They exchanged glances.

"We could leave now, Jay."

"No."

At midnight, the SUV, clearly visible in the light of the full moon, returned and stopped at the foot of the hill. A minute or two later an open-bed truck pulled up behind it. In the bed of the truck, on benches facing each other, were a dozen soldiers, carrying rifles, wearing black baseball caps, their faces darkened with smudge. Two men, dressed in black, emerged from the SUV, and an officer climbed down from the passenger side of the truck's cab. They conferred, and returned to their vehicles, which began slowly to drive up the dirt road toward the cottage, the troop vehicle swinging around the SUV to lead the way.

"They're not going to dinner at the Vista del Mar," said Jay.

"No," Isabel answered. "What shall we do?"

"Run," said Jay. "Get in the car."

Jay grabbed both bags and threw them in the backseat while Isabel got in the passenger side. Looking down, Jay saw the truck approaching the switchback near the entrance to the Vista del Mar, whose terrace was strung with blinking, multicolored Christmas lights. Jay took the gasoline can from the boot of the jeep and brought it on a run into the cottage, where he spilled its contents rapidly over the furniture and floor. He then threw the can down, lit a full book of matches, and threw it onto an old cotton rug that was hungrily soaking up the dark, acrid-smelling liquid. It caught immediately, and as Jay ran out the side door he could feel the heat pushing him into the night. He started the jeep and pointed it toward the narrow opening in the woods that led to the riverbed. Looking back, he saw the troops leaping from the truck as it rolled to a stop at the top of the drive, and then throwing themselves to the ground as the entire cottage burst with a fierce sucking noise into flames. Ten minutes later, Jay turned the jeep's headlights off and nosed it onto the rough shoulder of Highway 200. To the left was the roadblock, to the right, about fifty miles away, lay the town of Huatulco, a minor tourist destination with an airport.

"They will be watching the airport," said Isabel, reading Jay's mind.

"Yes," he said, "and probably patrolling this road once they figure out how we got away."

"We could head into the mountains. Hector told us the road continues."

"No," said Jay. "Not yet. Were those the Ferias?"

"I think so."

"If it was, then they were nearby when you called Herman."

"They may have spoken to the nuns in Polanco. I didn't think of that. Herman still gives them money."

"Lazaro and Rafael have the entire federal military at their disposal," Jay said. "Herman must have called them."

"Hector lives about a mile that way," said Isabel, pointing down the highway to her right.

"We have no choice."

"Yes . . . *mi amado*?"

"Yes?"

"Are you depressed?"

"Yes," said Jay. "If the Ferias had approached first, I would have shot them, then tried to light the fire."

"There was no time. The soldiers would have killed us."

"I know, but I may never get that chance again."

"You will. They will come looking for us, and this time they will not know we are waiting for them."

With the headlights still off, hugging the tree line, they made it to Hector's whitewashed cinder block house, down a dirt road in a rocky clearing at the foot of the mountains. Jay waited in the jeep, while Isabel went to the front door, knocked, and then stepped back into the dirt yard. A minute or two later, Hector emerged. He and Isabel talked, then together they approached the jeep.

"I will take you to a place where you can park the jeep," said Hector.

In the house a light came on, and Jay could see a woman standing at the front window, watching them. Behind the house, the forest rose mutely with the mountain, its treetops, bathed in moonlight, turning from black to silver, black to silver, as the night breeze rustled through them.

Hector got into the backseat of the jeep, and directed Jay to a path that climbed about a hundred feet to a small clearing, encircled by trees, in the center of which stood an ancient stone well and a rusted pump, its curved iron handle laying next to it on the ground. They parked at the tree line, under a thick canopy of branches. They walked back to the house, now dark again, in silence. Once inside, Hector lit a candle, placed it on a small table, then went to the rear room—there were only two small rooms to the place—and returned with a blanket, which he placed on the floor under the unglazed window at which his wife had been standing when they first arrived. The candle cast flickering shadows on the room's low ceiling, and by its mellow light they could see a small Christmas tree in the corner, decorated with paper cutout snowflakes. Under the tree, in tiny wooden rocking chairs, were two handmade dolls in bright holiday dresses, their ceramic faces fixed in happy smiles.

"Tomorrow," said Hector. "I will take my family early to my brother's house in the village. You are welcome to stay here while we are gone. There is food, and water in the cistern, which you must boil before you drink. I will bring you bottled water when I return tomorrow evening."

"We will probably stay here tomorrow," said Jay, "and

leave at night. Can we drive on the mountain road without headlights?"

"It is dangerous," Hector answered, "but if the night is clear, the moon will help you. I will try to explain the turns to you."

"Thank you, Hector, *again*."

"*De nada*, senor. *Buenas noches*."

"*Buenas noches*, Hector."

51.
6:00 PM, December 25, 2004, Puerto Angel

The next morning Hector and his family were gone when they woke. While Isabel made coffee in an old aluminum pot, on a wood burning stove that was still glowing from the family's breakfast, Jay stood at the house's one front window, the one they had slept under, where he could see directly down the dirt road to the highway. They had woken to the distant, droning buzz of a helicopter, and now he heard it again, flying low and slow somewhere close by. They spent the day taking turns sitting at the window, watching the dirt road and listening for sounds of truck engines on the highway.

The house baked in the sun and, unlike the cottage, where the sea breeze blew all day, the air was still, the world motionless in the ninety-degree heat. The house, a twenty-foot-by-twenty-foot square, had no plumbing and no electricity. In the far right corner was a door that led out to a stone cistern. Fat, and as tall as a man, it sat on cement blocks, connected at the top to a series of tile gutters and troughs from the house's tin roof. Taken as a whole, Hector's crude water collection system had the look of an avant-garde sculpture, patched together from things found on the ground. Around four o'clock, the troop truck, empty, went by, followed a few minutes later by the helicopter, this time sounding like it was traveling much faster.

"I think they're searching homesteads along the highway," said Jay.

"What if they don't come today?" Isabel asked. "We cannot stay here long. We will put Hector in great danger."

"We'll leave tonight, whatever happens."

"And the Ferias?"

"We'll go into the mountains, and figure something out. Chris Markey wanted to use me as a decoy. Maybe I'll call him and make a deal."

"That would take time."

"We'll find a place to hide. Unless you want to leave."

"I will not leave you."

At six, Jay brought two clay jugs out to the cistern to collect water. The pump was old, and he had to work the clanking handle vigorously for several minutes to produce a trickle. He filled one jug, and, as he was placing the second one under the spigot, he heard a car door slam shut, and then another. Reaching for his gun, he stepped behind the cistern, gathering himself, listening, hearing the front door open and shut and then voices, one of them Isabel's, inside.

Crouching, he edged away from the cistern until he had a view of the front yard, expecting to see Hector's patchwork pickup. Instead he saw the black SUV. He flipped the safety off the gun and, flattening himself along the side of the house, he made his way slowly toward the back door. He was only a few feet away when it crashed open, and Isabel came spilling out, stumbling on the gravel under her feet, and pitching headfirst into the cistern. On her heels came the shorter Feria brother, wearing a white shirt and black slacks, his black hair thick and slicked back, aiming a pistol as he calmly walked toward Isabel.

Jay, only ten feet away, aimed carefully and shot Jose, the bullet catching him high and right and torquing his body to the left as he fell. When he hit the ground, he dropped his gun, and Isabel, bleeding profusely from the forehead, scrambled to pick it up. Kneeling, she pointed it at Jay, screaming something in Spanish, and Jay thought surely he had been betrayed and was going to die. Instinctively he dove to the ground; at the same time Isabel fired two shots toward the side of the house, over Jay's prone body. Turning onto his side to look behind him, holding his gun straight out, Jay saw the taller brother standing in the long shadow cast by the cistern, a bright crimson stain blossoming on the front of his white shirt where one of Isabel's shots had hit him. Jay watched as the elder Feria, in slow motion it seemed, fell face forward into the gravel; then he quickly got to his feet and pried Edgardo's gun from the blunt, manicured fingers of his right hand.

"I thought you were aiming at me," said Jay to Isabel.

"No, *mi amado*."

Jay walked over to Jose, who was lying on his back at Isabel's feet. The younger Feria was alive, breathing raspily through his mouth, his black eyes open and staring with hatred at Jay. Jay's shot had gone through Jose's body, coming out above his heart, where a trickle of blood was beginning to darken his snowy white shirt.

"*Buenos días*, Jose," said Isabel, keeping the gun—Jose's nine-millimeter automatic pistol—pointed at him.

"This one's alive, too," said Jay, who had rolled Edgardo onto his back.

Isabel's bullet had hit Edgardo squarely in the chest, and his shirt front was covered entirely in blood. His eyes, as dark and reptilian as his brother's, were open, but were losing their focus.

"Do they speak English?" Jay asked.

"Yes. Herman required them to learn."

"I'm going to kill them."

"Jay."

"Yes?"

"I will help you."

"No."

"Edgardo," said Jay, kneeling on the ground next to the body. "I am going to kill you. I am taking your life for the life of my friend, who you killed in Miami, first crushing his manhood. Do you remember him?"

Without waiting for an answer, Jay placed the barrel of his gun against Edgardo's crotch and pulled the trigger. The elder brother's body jumped as if jolted by electricity. Then Jay put the gun's muzzle into Edgardo's mouth, saying, "*Hasta la vista,* Edgardo," before pulling the trigger, spilling the Mexican's brains and fractured skull pieces onto the ground beneath what was once his head.

"Step back," Jay said to Isabel as he approached Jose, kneeling before him in the same intimate position in which he had faced and killed Edgardo.

Later, Jay would think of the religious nature of what had transpired in the shadow of the ancient cistern—the kneeling, the purification in blood, the joining forever of his life with the lives and deaths of the Feria brothers. Now though, he was focussed on one thing and one thing only.

"*Buenos días,*" he said, leaning close, his voice low, looking into Jose's eyes, half closed, but still angry and alert.

"You killed my friend, Jose, and crushed his *cojones,* and now I will do the same to you. You can hear me, I see. Can you speak?"

For an answer Jose opened his mouth and lifted his chest, but could make no sound other than the death rattle in his throat. He glared at Jay, but the fire in his eyes quickly turned to terror as Jay placed the barrel of the gun to his penis and slowly squeezed the trigger. Then he pointed the gun at the bridge of Jose's nose, an inch away, looked with hatred, and peace, into the Mexican's eyes, and fired.

"*Hasta la vista* to both of you motherfuckers," Jay said, getting up and flipping the safety back on on his gun.

52.
7:00 PM, December 25, 2004,
Puerto Angel

In the house, Jay first reloaded his revolver, then cleaned and bandaged Isabel's wound, which was nasty, but not too deep. "Don't fall asleep," he said, and then went out to assess the death scene in the backyard. Acting quickly, but deliberately, he removed thirty-five hundred dollars in cash from money clips in the Feria brothers' pockets, along with the keys to the SUV, which he drove around to the back. He then lifted the Mexicans into the big car's spacious rear compartment. He was about to toss their automatic pistols in after them, but decided at the last second to hold on to them. He splashed water on the blood stains already drying in the last heat of the day, then, using a hoe he found near the back door, he did his best to rake the gravel and the hard-packed, dusty earth of the yard into a semblance of its former self. The SUV he parked next to the jeep under the trees in the old well clearing.

Back in the house, he stoked the stove to a full blaze, then stripped and threw his blood-stained T-shirt and shorts into the fire, first using the clean parts of the shirt to wipe off the blood that had soaked through onto his chest from grappling with the dead bodies. Isabel watched as he then took a clean shirt from his knapsack, soaked it with water, and wiped the last of the blood from his hands and arms; his muscles supple, his body tall and beautiful as he stood before her in the small room now infused with pale twilight. He dressed in his extra khaki shorts and his last T-shirt, then poured coffee—heating on the stove top—for himself and Isabel.

"They thought you were alone," Jay said.

"Yes, they wanted the papers. I told them they were hidden out back. Jay?"

"Yes."

"How are you?"

"I've never felt better."

Looking at him seated across from her on a crude kitchen chair, his long, dark hair—still damp with perspiration—swept back from his face, his brow clear, his eyes calm and penetrating, Isabel had no doubt he was telling the truth.

"What will we do?"

"If Hector doesn't come soon, we'll leave, try to find that airfield in the mountains. Here, take this," he continued, handing Isabel one of the Ferias' automatics. "Put it in your purse."

As Isabel was putting the gun away, they heard the sound of a car coming down the dirt road from the highway. Going to the window, reaching for his gun, Jay saw Hector's pickup pull up and park out front; then Hector emerging, alone, carrying a large, brown paper bag.

"Isabel," Hector said, once inside, surveying the scene, seeing Isabel's bandaged head, the blazing fire in the stove. "Senor."

"Hector," said Isabel.

"Hector," said Jay.

"Are you well, Isabel?" Hector asked.

"Yes, Hector. I fell. *Desmañado*, no?"

"No," Hector replied, allowing a slight smile to cross his face, placing the bag on the floor. "I have brought you water, and food."

"Thank you," said Jay. "We will bring it with us. We must leave immediately. Is the roadblock still up?"

"Yes. And soldiers have been in the village as well."

"We have a second car now, which we have to remove from here, and get rid of. Can you help us? Is there someplace nearby we can put this car?"

"Are you going into the mountains?"

"Yes."

"I will go with you, and show you a place to put the car."

"Just tell me Hector. I will find it."

"No. It is easier if I show you, and I will tell you about the mountain road . . . senor."

"Yes."

"The house of the sisters has burned down, and the Vista del Mar."

Jay turned to look at Isabel, and then back to Hector, his dark eyes flat, his face the inscrutable mask that all peasants show to the civilized world.

"I am sorry, Hector," he said. "Tell Miss Clara that we will send money."

They formed a three-car caravan, their headlights off, Hector in the lead in his truck, followed by Isabel in the jeep, and Jay in the SUV, creeping along the shoulder of the highway, and then turning right onto the dry, pebbly riverbed, which ascended gradually for about a mile before coming to an abrupt end in a small canyon that must have once been a waterfall. At the mouth of the canyon, Hector turned left and headed across an accumulation of pebbles and broken stones that ran along the foot of a hill for another half mile. Even in the moonlight, this path, such as it was, would have been difficult to locate, and follow, and Jay was happy that he had not flatly refused Hector's offer, as he had been thinking of doing.

At the end of this long scree, they came onto a dirt road that continued to hug the side of the hill as it brought them steadily higher. After negotiating a sharp curve to the right, Hector pulled over, and Isabel and Jay did the same. They emerged from their vehicles, and Hector led them across the roadbed to the edge of the cliff, crudely marked off with rocks of various sizes. Straight down was a drop of some two hundred feet to a ravine covered with a thick growth of brush and small trees, probably nurtured by a stream that trickled on the canyon floor. In the distance was the coast, marked dramatically by Zipolite's wide white beach. The surf crashing wildly, bathed in moonlight, dotted with campfires, it was a sight to take your breath away, even if you were about to dump a car loaded with two dead bodies and run for your life.

Within minutes, the SUV was at the bottom of the ravine, under the trees. Before shoving it over the edge, Jay had put down the two front windows, so that whatever creatures lived in the area could feast for a day or two. Jay shook Hector's hand, and Isabel hugged him and whispered something in his ear, and then he was gone, his taillights disappearing around the curve. The sound of the truck's engine receded until Jay and Isabel were left, in silence, to contemplate the fifty mile ride ahead of them on an uncharted road through the Sierra Madre mountains, which towered all around them in forbidding darkness.

53.
8:00 AM, December 26, 2004, Ejutla de Crespo

"Isabel."

"Yes."

"Did you sleep?"

"Yes."

"Your head looks good."

"It is fine."

"I found a pilot."

Isabel smiled. "I knew you would. Where are we going?"

"Belize City. Have you been there?"

"Never."

They were parked in a thick strip of woods, on a small rise. Through the trees in front of them they could see a grassy runway, burned to a crisp brown by the sun, and beyond it, to their left, an ancient corrugated steel hangar, with *Decker Aviation—Flying Lessons* stenciled in peeling white paint on its roof, the *i* in *Flying* a small airplane doing a backloop. Two single-engine props were parked in front. The one on the right, with the words, *DECKER AVIATION* stenciled on its fuselage, was out of commission. The one on the left, devoid of markings, would take them to Belize City.

The tiny airfield was ringed by thick woods extending for several miles in all directions. Through the woods ran the

Rio Verde, a trickle now in the dry season. On the banks of the river sat the dusty town of Ejutla de Crespo. The snow-capped peaks of the Sierra Madre del Sur encircled the entire valley. In rural Mexico, Jay was learning, you saw beauty in the distance. Close at hand, you saw dirt and misery.

Jay reached around and pulled his knapsack from the back of the jeep. From it he retrieved a manila folder that he had found inside Bryce Powers's *Banque de Geneve* file. Handing it to Isabel, he said, "This is for you."

"What is it?"

"It's a contract for an account in your name at the Bank of Geneva. Bryce opened it for you, using a power of attorney. Did you ever sign papers for him?"

"Yes. Several times."

Jay was still holding the folder.

"Take it," he said. "In case we get separated. There's two million dollars in it, and change."

Silence. And then Isabel said, "We will share it."

"No. It killed my friend."

"It is my due as a whore who fucked her father."

"He didn't know, Isabel. He was just a man trying to escape from a nightmare."

"I seduced him."

"But then you loved him. At least he was loved by someone before he died. His wife was an alcoholic, his daughters are piranhas. Herman and Rafael owned his soul. You gave him his life back for a few months. There is no blame for either of you."

Jay, who was in the driver's seat of the jeep, put the folder in Isabel's lap, leaned his head back against the headrest, and closed his eyes. The road through the mountains had been barely wide enough for the jeep. Every switchback promised to plummet them into the black abyss that for fifty miles was only a foot or two away. At one point, stopped by a rockfall, Jay, surrounded by utter darkness except for the glare of the jeep's headlights, had moved some thirty boulders, ranging from fifty to a hundred pounds, out of the way, leaving his hands raw and bleeding and his entire body aching. He had taken one of Sam's amphetamine tablets before embarking from Hector's house, and another when they arrived at the edge of the airfield at dawn. He had been awake for forty-eight hours.

"When do we leave?" Isabel asked.

"Decker said to come down when we see him start the engine of the plane on the left."

"What is he doing here?"

"He's American, a shitbum. Probably flies drugs in and out."

"How much did he want?"

"Four thousand. I gave him two and told him I'd give him the other two when we were in the air."

"Why Belize City?"

"It's reachable on a tank of gas and it's not Mexico."

"Do you trust him?"

"We have no choice."

54.
9:30 AM, December 26, Southwestern Mexico

"What are you doing?" Isabel asked. She had been resting her head against the passenger window, her eyes closed, thinking about Herman Santaria, wondering if there was any way he could track her to Belize.

"Change of plans."

Jake Decker was gazing out of the window on his side as he said this, maneuvering the plane into a steep bank. This abrupt turn was what had jarred Isabel from her reverie. Jay was asleep, curled up in the small compartment behind the cockpit. As the plane straightened and began to descend, Isabel could see an airfield cut out of the top of a scrub-dotted mesa, with a winding road leading up to it from the barren desert floor a hundred feet below. At the end of the dusty runway stood four men, each with machine guns slung over their shoulders. Behind them was a black SUV and an open truck with soldiers seated in it and another soldier standing watching the plane descend. Decker was staring straight ahead now, smiling, a thin stream of spittle oozing from the corner of his mouth onto the red and gray stubble of beard that covered his jaw and chin.

"We just took off," Isabel said.

The men at the end of the runway had moved to the

side. One of them was hailing the plane, swinging his right arm in long arcs.

Isabel had her woven wool shoulder bag on her lap. She reached into it and pulled out the automatic pistol, a Glock 19, that Jay had given her after hiding the bodies of the Feria brothers. *It doesn't have a safety* he had said, *be careful when you handle it.* Safety or no safety, she put the barrel against Decker's right temple and said, "Take us back up or I will kill you." When he did not react, she pressed the steel barrel very hard into Decker's skull and put pressure on the trigger. "It shoots twenty rounds in a second," she said, improvising. "We will die together. But your brains will be all over Mexico."

The plane was in its final descent, about fifty feet from the ground. Decker pulled back on the yoke and the plane leveled and then began to climb. Jay was still sleeping, out cold. Below, the four men on the runway had unslung their machine guns and were taking aim. The soldiers were jumping out of the truck. Bullets screamed by as Decker continued to gain altitude. Isabel heard a popping sound at the back of the plane. Turning, she saw Jay wide awake and pointing the other Feria gun at the back of Decker's head.

"That's the fuel tank," Decker said. "We have to go back and land. There's no other place." He was sweating profusely, his Boston Red Sox cap soaked to a rich, wet black.

Isabel looked at the fuel gauge and saw that it was holding steady at almost full. "Keep going," she said.

"Those were federal troops," Decker said. "They're all over the place looking for you."

"How do you know?" Jay asked.

"I spoke to the sheriff in Ejutla. He must have telephoned."

"You sold us out," said Jay.

"You were bringing us to our deaths," said Isabel.

The plane had leveled at a thousand feet, and they were about fifteen miles from the runway on the mesa heading west. Below, Isabel could see they were crossing over a dry riverbed and a two-lane, blacktopped highway that ran parallel to each other about a mile apart through scrub-covered low hills.

"Land in the riverbed," said Isabel, pressing the pistol against the sweat-slickened side of Decker's head.

"Are you crazy?" said Decker. "I'm heading back." He began to bank the plane. Isabel flattened the Glock in the palm of her hand and struck Decker with it on the side of his head with a force she did not know she possessed, bouncing his head off of his window and knocking him out cold. Level, she thought immediately, looking for the attitude indicator and finding it in the top center of the instrument panel. Level the aircraft. Using the yoke in front of her, she corrected the bank that Decker had initiated and leveled the plane. Keep it straight and level, she said to herself. Take a deep breath. These were the first two things Patricio had told her to do in the event she ever had to land a plane in an emergency. The third was to engage the autopilot, which she did. The fourth was to radio for help, which was out of the question. In fact, it would not be long before the Mexican Air Force was out in strength looking for them.

"Are you flying the plane?" Jay asked.

"I am," Isabel answered, her eyes straight ahead, scanning the horizon and the instrument panel, especially the fuel gauge, which was not falling.

"You're Superman," said Jay.

"I took lessons when I was nineteen."

"Did you get as far as landing?"

"Once."

"Can you? From there, I mean?"

"Yes. The plane has dual controls. And our friend is not waking up soon. Keep your gun on him just in case."

Jay nudged Decker's head with the barrel of his Glock, bumping it against the window again. The welt raised by Isabel's blow was swelling along the scruffy ex-pat pilot's forehead and starting to turn his right eye into a small eggplant. The other eye was closed and his head bobbed occasionally when the autopilot made a small correction.

"Can we fly to Texas?" Jay asked.

"No, not enough fuel."

"What are you thinking?"

"The riverbed. It's bumpy, but there's a chance we won't be seen."

"Can I help?"

"Can you pray?"

"To whom?"

"The Virgin of Guadalupe. She is the protectress of the Americas."

"Not just Mexico?"

"No."

"Are you serious?"

"Yes, it will be a comfort."

"Okay, here goes. Hail Mary, full of grace . . ."

Isabel maneuvered the plane over the riverbed. She could see a trickle of water in some parts of it, with small boulders on either side. She looked at the altimeter: one thousand feet. Ahead was a stretch where the trickle was wider but with no boulders, unless of course they were concealed by the water. Beyond this, the bed narrowed and then made a series of turns around and through some low hills. She made a 360-degree turn, giving herself plenty of altitude to gradually descend to the boulderless stretch, lining up the nose with the small and relatively straight stream of blackish-looking water. Jay had finished his prayer.

"Here goes," Isabel said. "Keep praying." *Reduce airspeed. Keep it in the green.* She could hear Patricio's voice—calm, professional, filled with confidence in her—as if he were behind her, not Jay. *Nose down.* The plane began its descent. *Trim.* She found the trim wheel and rotated it until the plane, pitching as it descended, steadied. Now came the hard part, slowing the plane down without losing lift. *Reduce power, use the throttle. Small adjustments. Deploy flaps.* Before she knew it, the altimeter read one hundred feet. The airspeed indicator read ninety knots. *Too fast. Throttle all the way back to idle.* They would hit hard. *Flare the plane, nose up smoothly, bleed off airspeed,* said Patricio, which she did. A half second later they were jarred by the *whump* and *thud* of the rear wheels hitting the ground. *Nose down*—she did it—feeling the front wheel touch down. *Gentle braking. Gentle braking.*

"Fuck," she heard Jay say.

They were heading too fast—much too fast—into the side of a hill, where the river bent to the right. Isabel, out of instructions, hit the brakes as hard as she could, which caused the plane to skid and veer sharply to the right before coming to a stop and flipping onto its right wing, cracking it in half, spilling her against her window and piling the inert Jake Decker on top of her. Shoving the door open, she fell out, first landing on the broken wing, and then tumbling to the ground with Decker still on top of her. Shoving him away, she got to her feet and saw Jay, blood running down his face, jump to the ground, holding his knapsack and her bag in one hand and both pistols in the other.

Isabel took the bags and guns from Jay and led him as quickly as she could along the riverbed to a small pool of water about a hundred feet away.

"Can you wash yourself?" she asked. "You're bleeding badly."

"I'm fine," Jay answered. Then he knelt at the pool and splashed water on his face and head. Isabel knelt next to him. When he turned toward her, she saw that the laceration on his scalp was superficial. She pulled one of her blouses out of her bag and pressed it against the wound.

"Hold it there," she said. "We need to get on a bus. You can't be bleeding."

"What bus?"

"I saw a couple go by on the highway. It is market day somewhere nearby. We will join the locals."

"Isabel," Jay said. "You're Superman."

"No," she replied. "The plane is a Cessna 150, the only plane I could possibly have landed."

"Do you think the prayer helped?"

"Yes. The brake is also the rudder. When I slammed it down it forced the plane to turn sharply. I forgot the brake pedal was the rudder as well. You're supposed to apply pressure just to the top. I panicked. It wasn't me who turned the plane."

Isabel watched Jay absorb this. They were both still kneeling. Both now had head wounds, and Jay's hands, she could see, were still raw from moving boulders last night, which seemed like a distant memory now.

"What now?" Jay asked.

"I know only one person who would consider helping us."

"Who?"

"Sister Josefina. She lives in Santiago, in the Mountains."

"How far is that?"

"Not far, I don't think. A few hours by bus or car."

"What about him?" Jay gestured toward Decker, lying where Isabel had pushed him away.

"We will tie him to the plane, and leave him water."

"He might be dead."

"That was not my intention."

"Yes, but even if he is, I think we're in a just war here. Don't you agree?"

Jay smiled as he said this, and Isabel smiled back.

"I agree," she said.

Decker was still unconscious when they got to him. Jay tied him to the landing gear with electrical cable he found in the tool locker in the plane's belly. While he was doing this, Isabel took Jay's two thousand dollars from the pilot's flight bag along with a bottle of Jameson. When she was searching the rear compartment for the flight bag, she saw bullet holes on both sides of the cabin, lower on the right, higher on the left. Jay's scalp wound was arrow-straight and long, and now she understood why. It's a good thing he was asleep. Another miracle.

"How's your head," Isabel asked Jay as he finished up with Decker and stepped back. Jay had tied the blood-soaked blouse around his head in order to work on Decker. He removed it and bent forward so that Isabel could see the wound.

"It's better," she said, "the bleeding has almost stopped."

Jay found a clean spot on the blouse and pressed it to his head. As he did this, the sound of a large vehicle—a bus or a truck—could be heard on the highway, which was, Isabel realized, very close by, just over the hill to her left.

"I will look," she said, taking one of the Glocks, which she had placed on the ground next to the bags. "If it is a bus, I will hail it. If it is troops, we will die here."

55.
6:00 PM, December 26, 2004, Santiago Ixtayutla, Mexico

Except for special occasions, of which there had been a dozen or so in the last five years, evenly divided between weddings and funerals, Sister Josefina de los Angeles wore street clothes in Santiago. A simple skirt and blouse from the Sears catalogue and a pair of Nikes had become her new habit. In church, where she sat now, she covered her short salt-and-pepper hair with the white headpiece with black piping that was part of her old uniform. She missed her flowing white robe and coif, but they were not practical in Santiago, where she taught school, ran a crude clinic, tended a community garden, and helped maintain the few working motor vehicles, including her own VW Beetle, in the small, impoverished town of eleven hundred souls.

Early on she formed the habit of putting on her headdress and walking across the village's tiny square to the primitive and starkly simple Church of the Precious Blood of Christ to say a rosary at fixed hours. She knew she looked a sight with her skinny legs, bulky sneakers, and thick glasses, but it was this public display of religion, of loyalty to Mary, that eventually won her the trust of the villagers, mostly women whose husbands and sons were *al otro lado*—on the other side—in the US, living and working illegally, sending the dollars back that kept the town, literally, alive.

Having accomplished little in five years to alleviate Santiago's misery—only a handful of houses had electricity or indoor plumbing, most had dirt floors and mud roofs, the school stopped at grade six, the weekly market in the square had died a sad death— Sister Josefina had taken recently to saying a special prayer to the Virgin. If anything, however, things had gotten worse. When the boys turned sixteen, they left. Their fathers and brothers and uncles were not coming back because there was no indigenous economy except for one family that made chocolate and another three or four who weaved or made simple furniture. The rest scratched at the earth with mule-drawn ploughs for their living. She had been reading lately about microbanks and their role in Third World economies, but of course the seed money required—several hundred thousand dollars—was beyond even the imaginations of the people of Santiago. Several *hundred* dollars would have been difficult to raise.

Sister was, this evening, contemplating this state of affairs, having just finished her rosary and made her special petition, when Juanito, the boy who had become her *de facto* assistant, tapped her on the shoulder.

"Sister," he said.

Turning, Josefina saw something in Juanito's face she had never seen before, but that she could not place. Had he seen a ghost, or a space creature?

"Yes, Juanito," she replied.

"You have visitors."

"Visitors? Is it *padre*?"

Though there was a church in Santiago Ixtayutla, there was no priest. On Sundays, a priest from one of the "rich" towns in the valley came to say mass. Hence all priests were *padre* because they never knew who would appear on any given Sunday.

"They are injured, Sister," was Juanito's reply.

Josefina rose without a word and strode out of the church, taking her headpiece off as she entered the patch of dirt that passed for the village's zocalo. Halfway across she stopped in mid-stride and stared at the two people, a man and a woman, sitting on the whitewashed concrete steps of her tiny house. Starting again, going slowly, she approached them and, for reasons completely unknown to her, a dam in her heart burst when she confirmed that it was Isabel Perez sitting there, a large, ugly bruise on her forehead and a grim look on her still beautiful, still angelic face.

"Isabel?"

"Yes, Sister, it's me."

"What happened to your face?"

"Sister, this is my friend, Jay."

Josefina could see swelling on the man's head as well, and a long scab starting above the hairline running to the top of his scalp. She turned to Juanito, who was standing in his customary position—slightly behind her and to her right—whenever they were together in public, and said, "Juanito, go, please, to the clinic and bring me bandages and antiseptic, and get your father's razor."

Josefina watched the boy run off, then, turning to Isabel, said, in Spanish, "Is your friend ill?"

"Yes, Sister," Isabel replied in English, "he has had dengue fever, and has had no sleep for two days. We need your help."

"What has happened?"

"If I tell you, you will be in danger."

"Have you committed a crime?"

Isabel's eyes turned inward as she pondered this question.

In them Josefina saw great sorrow. The word *haunted* came to her mind, a mind still very sharp at fifty-two. What has she done? What has been done to her?

"Crimes, no," Isabel answered, finally. "But sins, yes."

"What about your family?" Sister asked. "*Tio Hermano?*"

As quickly as it had appeared, the haunted look vanished from Isabel's eyes, replaced now by something very dark. Not sadness, Josefina thought, darkness. What could that be? "Never mind," she said out loud, seeing Juanito jogging toward them. "Let's get you cleaned up. We will talk later."

"Sister," Jay said; his first word.

"Yes, senor."

"You don't have to help us. We can get cleaned up and go."

"Are you Isabel's friend?" Josefina asked.

She watched carefully as Jay and Isabel looked at each other. They were exhausted, that was obvious, but something very strong was holding them up, and together. Perhaps love, perhaps a glimpse of hell, perhaps both.

"Yes," Jay answered.

"You are blessed, then. She is very special."

"There are people looking for us," Jay said. "Trying to kill us."

"Do they know you're here?"

"No."

"Here is Juanito," Sister said. "Let's go inside."

• • •

At nine o'clock Isabel and Sister Josefina were sitting at the wooden table in the nun's small kitchen. Through the beaded curtain behind them, they could see Jay asleep in Josefina's bed, an army cot, in the house's only other room, a sitting room/bedroom/office onto which the villagers had tacked a skeletal bathroom which contained Josefina's one luxury, a shower. Jay had consumed a huge amount of rice and beans and a large glass of Jake Decker's Irish whiskey. Showered, fed, his head shaved and sutured, he was snoring lightly, but had not changed position for two hours.

"He will sleep all night," said Josefina.

Isabel nodded. She was not tired. She should have been, but she wasn't. The cup of hot chocolate she had been sipping from, laced with the same whiskey, sat on the table in front of her, half full. A hurricane lantern, fueled by a pale yellow oil, rested between them, shedding light on the women's hands and partially exposing their faces to each other.

"I am not used to seeing you without your habit," Isabel said.

"Yes, it hid all my faults."

"What faults?"

"I am not beautiful, as you can see, and I am old now."

"Shall I tell you something, Sister?"

"Yes."

"Your face—the memory of your face—kept me many times from committing suicide."

"What happened, Isabelita? Please tell me," Josefina said. There was no shock in her eyes, or even surprise, as if, Isabel thought, she already knew or sensed that something was deeply wrong. "I will suffer more," Sister said, "if you keep this barrier between us."

The evening had been busy. Juanito's mother, Esperanza, had appeared with her husband's razor, a sewing kit, and the food. Isabel had listened while Sister Josefina had blandly lied to Esperanza, telling her in Spanish that her visitors were an old student from Mexico City and her friend whose bus had run into a large pothole while taking them from Oaxaca City to the coast. They would be staying a few days while their wounds healed. A small canyon—*un pequeño cañón*—she had called the pothole, and Esperanza, apparently familiar with the state of the roads in their rural and forgotten part of Mexico, had nodded knowingly. Esperanza had left with Jay and Isabel's dirty clothes to launder, and Juanito had returned with the thick slab of bittersweet chocolate for their after-dinner drinks.

In the moments they were alone Isabel had avoided Sister's searching looks, but there was no sense putting off the inevitable.

• • •

At ten o'clock, Josefina took another lantern from a kitchen shelf, lit it, and stood silently before Isabel.

"Are you going to bed?" Isabel asked. "Where will you sleep?"

"I will sleep in the church," the nun said, "but first I will pray."

"Pray for an answer?"

"No. I will be thanking Our Lady."

"Thanking her?"

"Yes, for sending you to me."

"So you will do it?"

"Yes, I will make the call. But only on one condition—that I will be the one to kill Herman Santaria."

Staring at Sister Josefina's homely face, Isabel now realized why she had remained so beautiful in her memory. The kindness of her heart shone brightly on it, a brightness now dimmed, no doubt by the horror of Isabel's story, leaving in its place the drawn and haggard face of a woman who had seen too much suffering and was old before her time.

"I am responsible for what happened to you, Isabel," Josefina continued when Isabel remained silent. "I was blinded by Herman's money, by the good it could do for the other children. I was proud of my role in bringing in that money. I should have asked many questions. If I had, I might have saved you. It is a bitter lesson."

"Sister . . ."

"Yes, Isabel."

"I am no longer *Isabelita*?"

"Not tonight, no . . ."

Isabel could see the tears welling in Sister's eyes. "Go," she said, "and pray for me as well, and for Jay. Tomorrow we will make our plans." But I will pull the trigger, she said to herself, not you, nor anyone else. *Me.* I will do it.

56.
2:00 PM, December 27, 2004
Oaxaca City, Mexico

"Hermano? Tio Hermano?"

"Who's calling?"

"It is Sister Josefina from the Santa Maria Orphanage in Polanco. Do you remember me? I am calling about Isabel Perez."

Josefina was sitting facing the large baroque fountain in the center of Oaxaca City's beautiful zocalo. She was in her street clothes but had her headpiece on so that she would be recognized as a nun and obtain the minor but often helpful advantages that this status conferred almost everywhere in Mexico. In the pause that followed her last statement, she watched as two schoolgirls, sitting on the fountain's low perimeter wall, bent to cup water in their hands and splash it onto their faces. The weather was hot for the winter, ninety degrees or more, and she made a note to herself to do the same thing when she was finished with Herman Santaria.

"Yes, Sister, it is me, Herman. How is Isabel?"

"She is not good, that's why I'm calling. I need your help." *Bueno*, Josefina thought, so far so good.

"I will help, of course, Sister. Where is she?" So sincere. Be careful, Josefina.

"She is in hiding," the nun answered.

"In hiding? Has she done something?"

"I don't know," Sister replied. "She seems almost out of her mind. She is talking about murder and drugs and documents and tapes, and . . ."

"Yes, Sister?"

"And incest."

"Incest, my God"

"She is raving, senor. I am very worried."

"Sister," Herman said, "I must tell you, Isabel was not well in her mind. We often had to send her for treatment. She hallucinated and had what the doctors called multiple personalities."

"I did not know this."

"I did not want to burden you. She was my responsibility."

"She needs treatment now, senor."

"I will take care of her. Where is she?"

"I think it best if I brought you to her, senor. She told me not to call you. I think she is ashamed. If you and I went to her together, it would be best, I think."

"*Bueno.* I understand. Where shall I meet you?"

"I am stationed in Santiago Ixtayutla."

"Where is that?"

"About sixty miles south of Oaxaca City."

"*Bueno*, I will come now."

"No, senor, come on Wednesday morning. Our priest will be there for a funeral. He will help us persuade Isabel to go with you."

"Is she staying with you, Sister?"

"No, senor. She is in the mountains. She has promised to call me tomorrow. I will persuade her to come down. The funeral is for Sister Adelina, who Isabel loved. It is the only way."

Herman did not reply immediately. As Josefina waited for him to speak, she glanced over at the schoolgirls. They had dunked their whole heads into the fountain, sunglasses and all, and, laughing, were wiping the water from their faces and their black, Mexican hair, which was shimmering in the bright sunlight.

"Yes, Sister, that is a good plan," said Santaria finally. "I will meet you there at nine on Wednesday. Is there only one church in the town?"

"Yes, the Church of the Precious Blood of Christ, on the plaza."

"*Bueno.* Sister?"

"Yes?"

"I will bring you a check for your troubles. For the parish."

"Oh, no, senor . . ."

"I insist. One more thing, Sister."

"Yes?"

"Have you seen these so-called documents?"

"No, senor. They are locked in a suitcase which she guards with her life."

"*Bueno*, Sister. I will see you on Wednesday."

57.
6:00 PM, December 27, 2004, Santiago Ixtayutla, Mexico

"Who did you speak to?"

"Your friend, Angelo."

"Was he at Victor's?"

"No, they went next door to get him."

"Did he believe you?"

"Yes, I told him the things you said."

"And?"

"He said he would contact Frank. He said to tell you they're on their way."

Jay and Sister Josefina were sitting in Sister's kitchen, drinking lemonade as yellow shafts of late-day sunlight crossed between them over the top of her scarred but sturdy little table. In the morning he had given her Bryce Powers's satchel-full of documents and tapes to bring to the nearest FedEx office in Oaxaca City to send to Linda Marshall. He had taped the business card Linda gave him at the Spanish Tavern to the top document, Powers's meticulous twenty-page list of money laundering transactions going back to 1982. He had given Josefina the money for this plus additional cash to buy a prepaid cell phone to use to make her two calls.

"Did you throw the phone away?"

"Yes."

"Did you use a phony name?"

"Of course, as you told me. But they did not ask me for identification."

"When will the package arrive?"

"Tomorrow morning, as you requested."

Josefina rose. Her refrigerator, a Frigidaire from the fifties, had started clanking and rattling from somewhere deep in its dying innards. She kicked it swiftly and hard on its left flank and the noise stopped. Opening it, she pulled out the half full plastic pitcher of lemonade and brought it to the table.

"And the other call?" Jay asked.

"Yes, I made that, too."

"Yes, and?"

"It went well. He is meeting me here at the church on Wednesday morning at nine."

Jay looked at his watch. Could Dunn and Angelo get here in thirty-six hours? Would it matter?

"Tell me what you said and what he said."

"As we discussed, I told him Isabel had contacted me with a crazy story about murder and drugs and documents. And incest. That she seemed out of her head. That I didn't know who to call except him. I begged him for his help. He asked several times for her exact location, as we suspected he would. I told him I thought it would be best if he met me here and I brought him to her. That she was in a very fragile state. He agreed finally."

"Did he believe you?"

"I have made a discovery: I am a good liar."

"When you have to be."

"Yes."

"Thank you, Sister."

"*De nada* . . . Jay?"

"Yes."

"How is your head?"

"Getting better."

"And your heart?"

"My heart?"

"Do you love Isabel?"

"Yes."

"Tell me about your parents."

"My parents?"

"Yes."

"They're both dead."

"Yes, Isabel told me. But tell me about them. Do you miss them?"

Jay did not answer. He looked straight at Sister Josefina, through her black-rimmed soda-bottle glasses into her dark brown eyes. *Do I miss them?*

"Sister . . ." he said, shaking his head almost imperceptibly.

"You must honor them by thinking about them and talking about them. They are waiting for you to do that. Their death has brought you here, to Isabel, to me. I will pray for them for the rest of my life."

Before Jay could answer, the small house's front door swung open and Isabel entered. She was carrying garments—one black, one white—which she laid over the back of an empty chair. In her free hand she had a manila folder, which she placed on the table before sitting down herself.

"How did it go?" she said, looking first at Sister and then at Jay.

"Well," Josefina said. "He will be here on Wednesday morning at nine."

"Did he believe you?"

"I lied well, Isabelita," Sister said.

"*Bueno,*" said Isabel. Then, nudging the folder on the table toward Josefina, she said, "My will is in there."

"Your will?" Jay asked.

"Yes, I wrote it while Esperanza was sewing."

"You are not going to die," Josefina said.

"I will if Herman brings federal troops."

"I will pray that he comes alone."

"Or a small bodyguard," said Jay. "We can handle that."

"*Bueno*, I will pray for a small bodyguard only."

Josefina was in deadly earnest as she said this, as if she were already formulating the prayer in her mind—how best to approach the Lord with a request that Herman Santaria's entourage be small enough to be easily killed when the shooting started on Wednesday? But Jay could not help smiling, and neither, he saw, could Isabel. What else was there to do? The dice had been thrown. No more running.

58.
9:00 AM, December 29, 2004, Santiago Ixtayutla

Herman Santaria did not think that Sister Josefina was setting a trap for him. The idiot Jake Decker's plane had been found some eighty miles away from Santiago Ixtayutla. It would make sense that Isabel would make her way to Sister Josefina. Perhaps Cassio was still with her, perhaps not. He had called the Dominican Provincialate in Mexico City and learned that Sister Josefina de los Angeles had indeed been posted to Santiago Ixtayutla for the last five years and that Sister Adelina de la Croce had retired, at the age of eighty-one, two years ago, and had been given dispensation to live in the State of Oaxaca with her family. An online search of the obituaries in Oaxacan newspapers yielded nothing concerning Sister Adelina's death, but in those dirt-floor valley and mountain villages there were no such things as newspapers, let alone printed obituaries.

The Feria brothers had gone missing. This was perplexing, but he had two new panthers with him, Paulo and Diego, picked out of the same Mexico City garbage dump as the Ferias, as well as his driver and personal bodyguard, the giant-sized but extremely mobile and lethal Stefan. If Cassio was nearby, they could easily deal with him. Chances were both he and Isabel had been injured in the plane crash and were licking their wounds somewhere they thought was safe.

They had arrived early and driven slowly through Santiago Ixtayutla as the sun was rising and saw nothing suspicious. Indeed, gazing intently through the tinted windows of Herman's Cadillac Escalade, they saw nothing at all in the fifteen seconds it took them to pass in and out of the village, which consisted of a small square with no fountain or adornment of any kind, a decrepit church, and a group of a few hundred mud or wooden huts creeping up the hillside behind the square.

Now, at eight fifty, the square was still empty, as was the small, dusty, hardpan courtyard in front of the Precious Blood church. Stefan parked crosswise to the gate in the stucco wall, blocking access and egress with the big black American car. No one bothered to look up or they might have seen Juanito's head pop up for a second above the old church's crumbling stucco parapet and then quickly disappear.

"Stay here," Herman said to Stefan. "We won't be long."

The two panthers, dressed in black, their hands in their jackets, pushed the heavy wooden doors open and stood adjusting their eyes to an interior lit only by the morning sunlight filtering weakly through the wooden shutters that covered the small church's four open-air windows. Herman looked intently as well. Kneeling in a front pew, in a white habit and headdress, was Sister. In the aisle next to her was a raw wooden casket on a draped dolly. At the altar, a young priest with thick, dark hair, his back to them, was laying out a chipped chalice and water bowl and lighting candles at either end of a small table covered in white cloth.

Herman nudged his panthers to the side—"Stay close," he said to them, "but not too close, we are not here to frighten anyone,"—and made his way up the short, narrow aisle. As he got to within a few feet of the nun, the church's bells began ringing, their clanging booms abruptly filling the small space and causing Herman to stop for a second. Continuing, he reached the first pew and tapped Sister on the shoulder. She rose and turned toward him, a pistol in her right hand aimed at his chest. "Good-bye, Herman," Isabel said, and then he was flat on his back, a searing pain where he knew his heart was.

• • •

The panthers had been looking up, annoyed by the booming bells, when Isabel shot Herman. The sound of the bells was so loud that the first they knew of a problem was when Herman stumbled backward into Paulo before falling to the stone floor. As Paulo and Diego were drawing their guns, Jay—the priest—and Angelo and Dunn—emerging swiftly from nearby confessionals—were upon them, shooting each in the chest several times at point-blank range. The bells stopped—Juanito's arms must have gotten tired—and at the same moment the church's doors swung open again and Chris Markey and Ted Stevens burst in and strode toward them. Juanito also appeared, and was tugging at Isabel's habit.

"What the fuck?" Markey said, looking at the carnage on the floor.

"*Hay un gigante afuera!*" Juanito was saying. "*Hay un gigante afuera!*"

"What's he saying?" said Markey.

"He says there is a giant outside," said Isabel.

"Tell him the giant's in handcuffs," said Markey.

Isabel translated this for Juanito, holding his shoulder and pushing him gently toward Sister Josefina, who had emerged from the sacristy when the shooting stopped and was approaching the group. "Come with me, Juanito," Sister said when she arrived, taking the boy's hand and leading him away from the three dead men on the floor.

"Fancy meeting you here," Frank Dunn said to Markey, when Josefina was gone.

"Yes, just in time to charge you with murder," Markey replied.

"They drew on us," said Dunn, looking down at the automatic pistols lying next to Diego and Paulo on the floor. "Besides, you don't have any jurisdiction here."

"Put these people under arrest," Markey said to Stevens, but before Stevens could move, Angelo had his gun out and was pointing it at Stevens. Dunn did the same, training his on Markey.

"Listen, Markey," Angelo said, "I've had enough of you threatening people. If you or your puppy here makes a move I'll shoot your kneecaps off. This is between us and the Mexican authorities. I don't know how you found us but I'm glad you did. I'm putting *you* under arrest, you little prick, and then we're calling the local police and we'll see whose story holds up."

"I'm with him," said Dunn, gesturing toward Angelo and smiling. "By the way, I made some calls recently to old friends. They say the rumor is you're tapping phones illegally all over the place, and setting up innocent people to die for some jihad you're supposed to be on. That's another thing we'll have to sort out when we get back to the States."

Before Markey could answer, the front doors swung open a third time, and Jack Voynik strode quickly into the church.

"Chris," he said when he reached the group in the aisle, "you won't believe this. Lazaro Santaria's committed suicide. Rafael de Leon's under arrest."

"What?"

"A story broke late last night over the Internet. Lazaro and Herman and de Leon have been running drugs and laundering money for the cartels for twenty years. It's all over the wires. The *Star-Ledger* printed photographs, Swiss bank accounts, transcripts of tapes, a shitload. The president of Mexico is on television and radio right now, giving a news conference."

"And Herman Santaria's dead," said Jay, nudging Herman's corpse with his foot.

"Yes, and may he burn in hell," said Isabel, who had taken off her headpiece and was standing straight and tall, her blue eyes shining clear and unburdened for the first time in thirteen years.

Epilogue
3:00 PM, February 5, 2005, Miami

The brass band that Angelo had hired was on a break. Their instruments lay gleaming on wooden chairs in a semicircle at the back of the large terra-cotta–tiled patio that Sam had added to the rear of El Pulpo. The band members were mingling with the thirty or so guests at and around the tables under the latticed arbor that covered the patio, above which spread South Florida's bright blue winter sky. Via new sliding glass doors, people were going into and coming out of the dining room where the buffet table and bar were set up, drinks and plates of food in hand. When the band stopped playing, Sam had put on a loop that he had told Jay he made for the occasion. Sinatra, Édith Piaf, Aaron Neville, Patsy Cline.

"He's got great taste in music, your brother," Jay said to Angelo.

"You wouldn't know it with that crooked nose and cauliflower ear of his."

"How many fights did he have?"

"Twenty-one in the ring."

"And out?"

"A couple. He's calmed down now."

They were standing near the band instruments, next to

one of the sturdy white-painted wooden posts holding up the arbor.

"How did it go up north?" Angelo asked.

"Good. I made a deal with the young guy who was running my practice. Don Jacobs."

"Are you taking the bar down here?"

"Maybe. I'm keeping my options open."

"You're married now," said Frank Dunn. "You *have* no options." Dunn had gone inside for a fresh drink and had just rejoined them.

Dunn and Angelo followed Jay's gaze across the patio to the small lawn that bordered it, where Isabel was having her picture taken with Maria. Jay had been following her movements for the last few minutes, taken by her beauty as if he had never seen her before today. She was wearing Maria's mother's wedding dress. Maria had cried throughout the ceremony at nearby St. Philomena's Church, but was smiling broadly now, hugging Isabel and then stepping back to admire the dress, while Victor Ponce snapped away with his bulky Nikon. Watching them, waiting to get their picture taken, were Linda Marshall and Cheryl Stone, Jay's secretary.

"What's Cheryl going to do," Dunn asked.

"She's working for Jacobs."

"Perfect."

"And Linda will get her Pulitzer," said Dunn.

"She deserves it," said Jay.

"I talked to Sid Ironson," Dunn said. "He says it's a lock."

"She's running a story tomorrow," Jay said, "about the confiscation of the Powers assets under the federal forfeiture act."

"The daughters will have to find jobs," said Dunn.

Jay and Dunn both smiled, thinking of Marcy and

Melissa facing the loss of all those millions and wondering where their next Hermes bag would come from.

"I noticed you didn't invite Agent Markey," said Angelo.

Jay smiled, thinking of Angelo calling Markey a little prick and threatening to shoot off his kneecaps—and of the events that had since transpired, including the lawsuit that Victor Ponce had filed after a repairman discovered the illegal tap on his phone and traced it to Markey. This lawsuit, coupled with the revelations of the agent's illegal and embarrassing law enforcement activities in Mexico, had forced Markey to retire in disgrace. Then Jay thought of Markey's daughter going down in a plane and he stopped smiling.

"Maybe I should have," he said. "We're all off the hook."

"Yeah," said Angelo, "thanks to Bryce Powers."

The day after returning from Mexico, they had all "lawyered up" as Frank Dunn put it. Their lawyers had immediately teamed up with the *Star-Ledger*'s lawyers to negotiate a deal with the US Attorneys in New Jersey and Florida; the paper would give up Bryce Powers's treasure trove in return for immunity for Linda, Jay, Isabel, Frank, Angelo, and Maria. And most important, for a guarantee that Isabel would not be extradited to Mexico.

On the lawn, Linda and Cheryl were now standing on either side of Isabel, their arms around her, while Victor did his thing. Waiting their turn were Sister Josefina, Juanito, and Esperanza, all eating wedding cake from plastic plates. All smiling big smiles.

"Actually," said Jay, "Isabel's lawyer called this morning. "The new Mexican AG wants her to testify down there. They want to put de Leon away for a long time. If she does, she'll get complete immunity from them."

"What did she say?" Frank asked.

"She said she'd do it. And while she's there she'll help

Sister Josefina start her bank." Isabel had not hesitated, Jay remembered, even though it meant looking Rafael de Leon in the eye. *I want to be able to go to Mexico when I please,* she had said. *There are things I want to do there.*

Lorrie Cohen had now joined the group taking pictures with Isabel. She was smoking a cigarette and drinking a Corona, doing some kind of a dance—the twist, perhaps—with Juanito, a salsa tune now playing on Sam's tape.

"What about you?" Jay asked Dunn.

"Haven't you heard?"

"Heard what?"

"Lorrie and I are moving down here. I'm going into the private eye business with Angelo and Gary Shaw."

"When did this happen?"

"Today. We made the deal right after you got married."

"Right in the church?"

"We thought it would be lucky."

Jay smiled. Shaw had framed the sling he had worn on his right arm for two months, on which he had signed his name inside a big heart, and given it to Jay and Isabel as a wedding present. He and his wife, Michele, were watching the picture-taking antics, drinks in hand. Next to them were Isabel's childhood friend Hector and his wife.

Hearing a slight buzz, Jay, Dunn, and Angelo turned to see Sam Perna coming onto the patio from the dining room carrying two buckets of ice, with a bottle of champagne in each. Four waiters followed with more champagne on ice and trays of fluted glasses. They cleared a table and set the buckets and glasses down. Then Sam popped a bottle and began pouring. The waiters followed suit until thirty or so glasses were fizzing on the white-clad table. Isabel walked over to stand beside Jay, murmuring "*mi amado*" as she took his hand.

"A toast," said Sam. "Who wants to make a toast?"

"You," someone yelled.

"Not me," Sam said, "I got marbles in my mouth."

"*I* will," said Sister Josefina.

The guests, who had been gathering around the champagne table reaching for glasses, turned to see who had volunteered, and then began to make way for the nun, who was wearing her headpiece and a pale blue dress and white shoes that she and Isabel had shopped for the day before. She lifted a glass and looked for Jay and Isabel. Finding them, she raised it.

"May the good Lord bless you," she said. "May Our Lady of Guadalupe watch over you. And—orphans no more—may you be surrounded by your family always, as you are today."

Thank you for reading *Blood of My Brother*, a novel that allowed me as I wrote it (and re-wrote it numerous times) to explore many things: the child shaping the man, the loss of loved ones, human cruelty, and the forces that compel us to either live or die in the face of despair. When we don't have to choose, life is easy, or seems to be; when we do, it can become very difficult. Danny, Jay and Isabel made choices: Danny's led to his death, Jay and Isabel's to love.

The characters in my next novel, *Sons and Princes*, also face difficult choices. The brothers Chris and Joseph Massi, and the beautiful heroin addict, Michele Mathias, are each haunted by a past that refuses to loosen its terrible grip, until the moment arrives for each of them to choose.

Sons and Princes is the third novel in my Tristate Trilogy, three stand-alone novels whose central characters are from the New York—New Jersey—Connecticut area, novels whose connection is thematic: the forces that shape our lives, the consequences of our decisions, and the crucibles that forge our destinies.

— James LePore
Venice, Florida
April, 2010

Sons and Princes goes on sale in November 2010 wherever books are sold.

Made in the USA
Lexington, KY
22 May 2011